the immortal game

the
immortal
game

mark coggins

poltroon press
mcmxcix

AUTHOR AND PHOTOGRAPHER'S NOTE

THE AUTHOR wishes to thank his fellow writers George DeWitt, Terry Gamble, Donna Levin, Monica Mapa, Mike Padilla and Susan Pinkwater for helping him make *The Immortal Game* the best he can make it. Thanks are also due to Linda Allen, Penny Campbell, Preston Carter, Lisa Franck and Cynthia Marchi for their important contributions to the book.

All the characters in the novel are fictional, but while most of the places in this volume are real, some of them — such as the old brewery in San Francisco's North Beach neighborhood — have been put to uses that are complete figments of the author's imagination.

Likewise, the majority of the photographs in this special edition are true portrayals of San Francisco Bay Area locales, but some have been included not because they are literal illustrations of a particular place where action in the book takes place, but because they suggest an atmosphere or a mood that is *en rapport* with the text.

Finally, both the author and photographer (although they are the same person) would like to give special thanks to Larry Berger: the author for Mr. Berger's incomparable expertise on jazz music and antique hi-fi equipment, and the photographer for Mr. Berger's willingness to "ride shotgun" in some particularly perilous shooting locations — such as the Tenderloin and East Palo Alto.

ISBN: 0-918395-17-8

Printed in the USA

Poltroon Press
P. O. Box 5476
Berkeley, CA 94705-0476

Distributed by Small Press Distribution (www.spdboooks.org)

For M.R. Ballou

"Chess is the most violent existing sport."
— Gary Kasparov

"There just isn't enough televised chess."
— David Letterman

the immortal game

Chapter 1

opening moves

tHE LEFT FRONT TIRE of my battered Ford Galaxy jolted into a pothole, and the last of my factory original hubcaps popped off and went rolling down the slope behind me. I slowed the car to a stop and watched in the rear view mirror as the hubcap hit the shoulder of the road and bounced into the brush below. I had planned to use the hubcap with my silver tea service as a crumpet tray, but I could see now that those plans were kaput.

Another car appeared in the rear view mirror, so I eased off on the brake and continued my journey up King's Mountain Road. I was driving from my office in San Francisco to the Woodside residence of a potential client, Edwin J. Bishop. Woodside is an exclusive, semi-rural community nestled in the coastal hills of the San Francisco Peninsula. All I knew about Bishop was that he had founded and taken public three very successful computer game companies and he needed a discreet private detective with a strong sense of professional ethics. It was his tough luck he happened to pick me.

I zigged and zagged along King's Mountain for another half mile until I came to a narrow driveway guarded by a tall wrought iron gate. The gate had the name Bishop written in iron script along the top and stood between flagstone columns. I pulled into the drive and got out to fiddle with the speaker gizmo on the right column. I punched the call button a few times and eventually a high-pitched voice issued from the speaker:

"Who is it, please?"

"Riordan," I said. "August Riordan. I have an appointment to see Mr. Bishop."

Something buzzed inside the gate column, and an electric motor kicked in. I watched as the gate swung open and then got back into my car and entered the grounds.

The drive wound its way through a stand of aging oak and then abruptly the trees ended and the road climbed lazily up a grassy knoll. At the crest of the knoll stood the house, a tall, solid-looking structure with flagstone walls, a peaked slate roof and plenty of latticework windows. The windows on the second floor had wooden flower boxes beneath them with a full crop of brilliant red tulips. Four stone chimneys sprouted from the rooftop and two ornate weather vanes in the shape of fighting cocks kept them company. A detached garage big enough to hold the Hughes Spruce Goose stood on the left. I parked next to the garage by a gleaming Jaguar convertible and legged it up to the front porch.

There I found a wide green door with the wrought iron silhouette of a bishop chess piece tacked in the middle. The bell played somebody's famous waltz when I pressed it, but we weren't on a first name basis. Shuffling steps sounded inside, and the door was opened by a lanky young man with frizzy brown hair and a long frizzy beard. Gold wire rim glasses were balanced on his thin nose, and he wore cutoff jeans and a tie-dyed shirt that looked like the cross section of a sick man's colon. He was shod in heavy leather sandals that only partially obscured feet that were black with dirt. His toenails were long enough to slice bread.

"Mr. Bishop?" I asked reluctantly.

"Yes, I'm Bishop. You're the detective then?"

I admitted I was.

"Good," he said, and thrust the door open wide. "We need to take quick action on this. Please come with me."

Bishop executed a sharp pirouette and marched out of sight. I stepped inside and closed the door behind me. Five yards ahead, Bishop was making good progress down a wide hallway that ran the length of the house. Maroon tapestries hung at regular intervals on the interior wall, and two knights in armor were placed in strategic locations by the front windows. Even more impressive was the floor. It was covered by slabs of highly polished gray marble with gold metal inlaid along the edges. Linoleum was just a funny word to this guy.

I quickened my stride and caught up with Bishop as he

stopped by a door in the hallway. He made a big show of holding it open for me and I walked past him into a large room with dark mahogany paneling and carpet so thick you needed hip waders to get around. In the center of the room was a grand piano splattered with piles of haphazardly stacked sheet music. Over the piano hung a massive chandelier that was better at looking regal than giving off light. The remainder of the room's furnishings were clustered in the far corner: a long desk with various pieces of computer equipment strewn across it, a high-backed chair to go with the desk, a coffee table, a small chess table with chessmen set out across the top, and a brown leather couch.

There were also two blondes in string bikinis lying on the floor playing a game of Monopoly.

"Jodie and Lisa," said Bishop behind me, "I'd like you to meet Mr. Riordan."

The two women stood up to face me. Both were tall with hair cropped closely in the same ultra modern style. Their lips and nails were painted dark crimson, and their microscopic swimsuits revealed a lot of well-shaped and deeply tanned California girl flesh. The one named Jodie had a more generous figure and smiled a brighter smile. Lisa was a shade thinner and seemed more reserved. I shook hands with both of them, feeling about as silly as you can feel when you're introduced to near-naked women while wearing a business suit.

Bishop came up behind them and patted them each on the butt. "You'll have to excuse us, girls," he said. "Mr. Riordan and I need to talk over the theft of my software." The women gathered up the Monopoly equipment and walked out of the room. I turned to stare at their backsides and was caught in the act by Jodie. She giggled a bit and flashed me a smile that you could take to bed with you.

Bishop gestured for me to sit down on the couch and settled himself in the high-backed chair behind the desk. He looked me over slowly without saying anything, and then tilted up his chin and began stroking the underside of his beard with the back of his hand. I stood about a half minute of the performance, then said, "Nice friends you got there."

"Jodie and Lisa are my paid companions, of course," said Bishop. "I don't have the time or disposition to interface with women in the traditional manner. I find this arrangement satisfies my needs with the greatest expediency."

"Yeah," I said, "I've been to a few Tijuana hookers myself."

Bishop took his glasses off slowly and laid them carefully on the desktop. "If you were a physician, you would not get high marks for your bedside manner."

"Then I guess it's a good thing you're not hiring me to remove your adenoids."

"Hardly, Mr. Riordan. In point of fact, I haven't hired you to do anything. I think now I'm inclined to find out a little more about you before I do."

Bishop had contacted me through his lawyer, Mark Richie, so I said, "I assumed Richie gave you the dope on my background."

"He did — to a certain extent. In any case, I'd like to hear about it again and I'd also like to ask a few questions."

I shifted a bit in my chair. I'd been through this sort of thing before with clients and it usually had less to do with my qualifications than with the client's reluctance to spill the beans about the assignment. "All right," I said. "Why don't we start with the bare essentials and then you can dig in where you like.

"I've been in the biz now for fifteen years, working mostly down south and here in the Bay Area. Before that I covered the metro beat for the *L. A. Times*, and before that I attended UCLA. I've handled most kinds of jobs people hire investigators for, and I've typically given good service for the dollar. I've got a reference list made up of former clients and law enforcement officers that you can check out, but maybe Richie already covered that angle for you. Anyway, that's the top line."

"I'm curious why you moved from journalism to private investigations."

"There's no great mystery. I come from a long line of drunken Irish cops — on my mother's side anyway. My mom's dad, for instance, was chief of police in Santa Monica. When I made the switch to PI work it was just a matter of joining the family business."

"I take it then your father was not in the 'family business?'"

"We don't talk about my father," I said bluntly. "And I'm not interviewing for camp counselor here. Do you think maybe we could stick to relevant questions, or even better, get to the part where you tell me what the hell it is you want done?"

Any hope I had of bulldozing the slight man in front of me was short lived. He bulldozed about as well as Egyptian pyramids. "I will not be rushed, Mr. Riordan," he said, and treated me to another in the series of great beard stroking performances. Then:

"My lawyer recommended you as someone who has had experience investigating so-called 'high-tech' crimes. Is that correct?"

"I've worked on a number of cases which involved the theft of computer chips, if that's what you mean. I wouldn't classify myself as an expert, though."

"I heard from other sources that you retired from private investigations for a time after a run-in with the police in Phoenix, Arizona. It's my understanding that you only recently returned to the business."

"That's correct as far as it goes. I was held for questioning in connection with an incident that occurred during an insurance investigation I was handling. But no charges were ever brought against me."

"What was the exact nature of this incident?"

I grinned at him. "I think you know very well what the nature of the incident was. If you want me to say it to your face, I'll oblige you: I shot and killed three people with a Colt Army .45."

"And that was why you quit?"

"No, I quit because I ran out of bullets."

Bishop stiffened. "I have a right to know something of the background of the men I hire. You are correct in assuming I already knew some of the details surrounding the incident. I wanted to hear your version of the story and assure myself that your decision to return to private investigations was the correct one. I wanted to be sure you still had the resolve for the job."

"Resolve, Mr. Bishop, is something I've got in spades."

Bishop made a strained, wheezing noise like a cat choking on a fur ball. I wasn't entirely sure what to make of it, but I guessed he was laughing. "Yes, I believe you do," he said after the fur had subsided. "Very well, I'll take a chance on you. As I'm sure you're aware, I develop software for computers. I'm quite good at it, and I've made a lot of money as a result. My chief interest is computer games — computer chess being my specialty."

"So that's the tie-in with the chess piece on your front door?"

"Yes, that's right. Having Bishop for my surname makes the tie-in complete." He laughed again, then stopped abruptly. "Listen to me now. I've spent eleven months of my life cooped up in this room writing the best chess program that's ever been developed for a small computer. It's faster, more intelligent and simpler to play than anything else on the market. I invited Stephen Flamberg — a local GM — to play against an early version of the program and the best he could manage was a draw in two of the three games he played. The third game ended in his defeat."

"I don't want to flaunt my ignorance," I said. "But apart from a large American car company, what's a GM?"

Annoyance flickered across Bishop's face. "A GM, or grandmaster, is a tournament chess player of the very highest caliber. To be classified as a GM, a player must achieve a grading level 2601 in two or more tournaments in which at least 24 games in all are played."

"How many bowls of cereal does your average GM have to eat before he gets the 2601 box tops?"

"Quite humorous Mr. Riordan. The important point here is that no chess program written for personal computers has been sophisticated enough to routinely play a qualified grandmaster to a draw. Mine is the first in history." He paused for effect. "And now it has been stolen."

I furrowed my brow to show my deep concern. "I take it you want me to try and recover the program?"

"Yes, that's the general idea, but there's more to it than simply recovering the software."

"Meaning what?"

Bishop shifted in his chair and stared down at his lap. "I have good reason to believe that one of my female companions stole the program."

"You mean Jodie or Lisa?"

"No. This girl's name is Terri McCulloch. She was employed in the same capacity as the other two girls until recently. We had a disagreement about her duties and I was forced to dismiss her." Bishop looked up from his lap. "I believe she stole the program at the time of her departure to get back at me."

"Then you noticed the program was missing immediately after she left?"

"Not precisely. I put the finishing touches on the program a month ago and then set it aside with the intention of seeking a publisher for the game after a short respite. Terri left my employ the following week, and it didn't even occur to me to check if the program was missing at the time. The first indication I received that the program had been stolen was at a computer trade show I attended last Friday. I was walking around the exhibition stalls and I encountered a computer vendor who was demonstrating a chess program exactly like mine. It was mine in fact."

"You're sure of that?"

"Yes. Absolutely. They hadn't even bothered to make the cosmetic changes necessary to camouflage the software's origin."

"So your idea is that Terri McCulloch stole the program when she was fired and then sold or gave it to the guy at the computer show, who then exhibited the game as his own?"

"Don't strain too hard to keep the skepticism out of your voice Mr. Riordan. That's exactly the way it must have happened."

"Did you ask the exhibitor how he got hold of the game?"

"Yes, yes, of course. He claimed that his company had developed it in-house. But I am well acquainted with the staff at Mephisto Software, and none of their developers are talented enough to produce a chess program of this caliber. That is a moot point in any case: as I told you, I'm quite sure the program was mine."

If I had a beard and was inclined to stroke it, I would have started up right about then. Instead, I rubbed the back of my neck and plowed on:

"I assume you checked to see if your program was missing when you returned home from the trade show?"

Bishop smiled ruefully. "I did indeed. All my copies of the program — including the master — were missing. In fact, they had all been erased from the computer disks where they were stored. That is a key point, too, Mr. Riordan. As you may know, it is relatively easy to make copies of computer software. To steal the program, Terri needed only to copy it off the master disk. She did that, but in addition, she methodically searched out and destroyed every last trace of it from my computer files."

"Leaving you no way to prove that you developed the program originally?"

"Exactly."

"How can you be so sure that Terri McCulloch is the one who took the program?"

Bishop pursed his lips and shook his head wearily like I was a slow learner. "It's obvious. No other valuables were taken and there were no signs of a burglary. That means someone with unrestricted access to the house must have taken it. Jodie and Lisa lack any in-depth knowledge of computers, so they are eliminated. The same reasoning applies to my housekeeper. Terri, on the other hand, has a good understanding of computers. I know because I taught her myself. She also had the motive of revenge from her dismissal."

"Yeah, you were pretty vague on that before. Why did you fire her? Had she developed a chronic headache?"

Bishop didn't catch on immediately, but when he did he reddened and tugged hard on the end of his beard. "That is a personal matter between Terri and myself. I will not tell you anything further about it. If you should speak with Terri in the course of your investigation — and it seems likely you will — I absolutely forbid you to discuss the topic with her."

I could tell by the subtle vibrations in the room that this wasn't a popular topic with Bishop. "Okay," I said, trying to sound properly chastened. "Assuming Terri McCulloch did steal the software, exactly what do you want done?"

"My first priority is the return of my chess program. My second is to secure its return without involving Terri or myself with the authorities. That is my primary purpose in hiring you. If I wasn't still concerned with Terri's welfare, I would have simply phoned the police and reported the chess game missing."

I didn't bother to remind him that he no longer had any proof that he'd actually developed the program. "All right. I'll need addresses for Terri McCulloch and the software firm that exhibited your program at the trade show. Mephisto, you called them?"

"Yes, Mephisto is correct." Bishop opened a drawer in the desk and pulled out a long white envelope that he passed over to me. "You'll find both addresses inside, plus a photograph of Terri and a check for $2500. I hope that amount is enough to get you started."

I tucked the envelope into my breast pocket. "Yes, that should get me started and keep me going for a good while. One last question. Have you spoken with Ms. McCulloch or the Mephisto people since you discovered the game at the trade show?"

"No, I was too upset about the whole thing to deal with it rationally. I'm leaving the matter in your hands."

I should have said something like, "I'm sure you won't regret it," but neither Bishop nor I was ready to swallow a line like that so late in the conversation. Bishop didn't offer to see me out. I stood up and shook hands with him over the desk and walked out of the room, down the long hallway to the front door and out onto the porch. I was sort of hoping to find Jodie and Lisa playing volleyball on the front lawn in their bikinis, but evidently they were still occupied by the Monopoly game.

Sighing audibly, I climbed into my car and started down the winding highway towards the Peninsula town of Redwood City. When I passed the point on the road where I had lost my hubcap, I craned my neck out of the car and scanned the underbrush. Nothing doing: I could definitely kiss the crumpets good-bye.

Chapter 2

teller talks tough

bEFORE DRIVING ON TO Mephisto Software I stopped at a taco joint in Redwood City that advertised authentic Mexican cuisine. I ordered two tacos and watched in silent awe as the Chinese woman behind the counter stirred a gigantic vat of ground beef with a boat oar, then plopped two scoops of the greasy meat into a pair of brittle tortilla shells.

"You like sour cream?" she asked cheerfully.

I nodded dumbly and the woman picked up a caulking gun and squirted ribbons of white paste down the middle of the tacos. She finished by mummifying them in orange wax paper and rang up the sale for $2.89.

I sat down on one of the plastic bench seats they had out front and broke off pieces of taco shell to munch on while I examined the photograph of Terri McCulloch that Bishop had given me. The picture showed an attractive young woman with dark hair sitting at the wheel of a convertible sports car. She was smiling broadly and had her hand held up in a rodeo queen wave, but you could tell her heart wasn't in it. Something about her eyes gave her away — there was too much depth in them for you to be fooled into thinking she was just another one of Bishop's "companions."

Then again, maybe that was just a lot of sentimental hooey and she was busy riding a $75 john in a San Francisco tenderloin hotel just at that moment.

After I'd eaten all the pieces of taco shell I cared to salvage, I got back into my car and headed a short ways north on Highway 101 to the offices of Mephisto Software. They were off the Redwood Shores Parkway across from a set of round glass buildings of varying heights that looked like a loser's dwindling stake of poker chips. The buildings comprised the campus of Oracle Software, the second largest software corporation in the world, and a company about as far away from losing as you can get in Silicon Valley. Mephisto itself was housed in a modest, prefab building that had been tarted up by the architect with an acid washed copper roof and some futuristic-looking designs etched into the otherwise stark concrete exterior walls.

Mephisto's lobby was decorated in brave new colors that

didn't quite match. A number of *objets d'art* graced the walls, including two mosaics made of leftover computer chips and a tapestry woven from bits of colored wire and coaxial cable. I found a picture of the company's thirty-two year old founder and president — a Mr. Roland Teller — under a small spotlight near the drinking fountain. The caption beneath the picture explained that Teller had started the company in 1989 with a $10,000 investment, and by selling innovative computer games with brilliant marketing techniques, had parlayed the seed money into the $36 million company that Mephisto Software was today. This was the guy I wanted to talk to.

A male receptionist wearing a crisp blue suit and a telephone headset sat behind a horseshoe-shaped counter near the back of the lobby. I placed one of my business cards in reach and asked to speak with Mr. Teller.

The receptionist gave me a steely look, then picked up the card and stared down his nose at it for moment. When the info on the card sunk in, he dropped the stiff-neck attitude and said amiably, "Private investigator, huh? We don't get many of those around here. Still, you don't stand much chance of getting an audience with his nibs. Not unless you've got photos of him with a naked woman at the mountain cabin or something."

"Nope — I left the lens cap on. Could you give him a try anyway? I've a hunch he'll agree to see me."

"My pleasure. What may I say is your business?"

"I'd like to discuss charges my client is planning to bring against him for piracy of the new chess game Mephisto is exhibiting."

The receptionist whistled softly. "Not bad, not bad. Okay, we here go." He reached down and pressed a button on the telephone console in front of him. "Hello, Ms.

Hansen? Yes, this is Chris at reception. I have a private investigator named August Riordan who would like to speak with Mr. Teller. Yes, yes, I know. But Mr. Riordan claims that Mephisto is going to be charged with theft of the chess program we're about to release and wants to talk with Mr. Teller before the charges are actually filed." There was a pause. "Okay, I'll hold."

He pushed down the microphone on the telephone head set. "Hope you don't mind my little embellishments," he chirped.

"No, you're doing great."

The receptionist listened for a second, then re-adjusted the microphone. "Yes, Mr. Teller I will ask him." He looked up. "Mr. Teller would like to know who you are representing."

"Edwin Bishop," I said.

"Mr. Teller, he says Edwin Bishop is his client...Yes sir. I will direct him." The receptionist gave me the thumbs up sign. "You're in. Put this on and go through the door behind me and down the aisle. The throne room is in the middle of the building on the right. You can't miss it. He's got the only private office in the whole place."

I thanked him, and clipped the plastic visitor's badge to the outside of my suit pocket. He twisted around to watch me as I walked past the counter to the double glass door he had indicated. "By the way," he said with a sappy grin, "tell him for me that somebody with a wax pencil keeps drawing a mustache on his picture in the lobby." I grinned back at him and stepped through the door.

The room I walked into looked more like an overgrown psychology experiment than a place to work. Tall gray metal partitions divided a half acre or so of bare floor space into a maze of tiny work cells. The maze was populated by software developers instead of rats, and computer equipment — monitors, printers, and disk drives — was used as bait in place of cheese. A bleary-eyed female with glasses as thick and square as dominoes and a complexion like a cave-dwelling newt stuck her head over a partition as I walked by. I gave her a sly wink, which she acknowledged by darting back behind the partition with lightning speed. That old Riordan magic with the ladies was still casting its spell.

I continued up the aisle until I came to a carpeted area with a large number of potted plants. Standing beside a baby palm was a heavyset man with dark curly hair, thick features, and powerful arms that didn't need any help from Wheaties. The pinstriped suit he wore was well made, but wasn't cut with an eye toward expansion. My guess was that Roland Teller would do at least as good a job in professional wrestling as he did in computer software.

"I expected Bishop would try something," he said in a low purr, "but I didn't think he'd go out and hire himself a private eye."

"Some people get crazy ideas when you steal their property."

"That's nice. Hit me right between the eyes with it first thing. Into my office with you. I don't want the whole floor watching while I screw your head on straight."

Teller's office had been decorated by the same group of Martians who had done the lobby. The carpet was a bright shade of purple, the walls forest green, and the office furniture a blend of chrome and white enamel. The art collection consisted of several framed enlargements of computer chips and a number of wooden plaques commemorating industry awards Mephisto had received. Teller's desk was situated under a triangular sky light, the inventory on top included a leather-bound cigar box, a matching chrome pen and pencil set and a combination telephone and fax machine.

Teller pointed at the visitor's chair and then dropped into the astronaut's couch behind the desk. "I don't know what Bishop's angle is, Riordan," he said in a tight voice, "but let's get one thing clear from the start: we did not steal any software from that little twerp. We agreed to pay him $300,000 plus twenty percent royalties for rights to produce and distribute the game. I have the signed contract in my desk. If he thinks he can weasel out of the deal by raising a stink at the computer trade show or by sending bozos like you around to intimidate me, he's got another thing coming."

"Were you at the trade show when Bishop came by your exhibit?"

"No, but I heard about it soon enough. Evidently Bishop started squawking the moment he saw the game and didn't shut up until they threatened to call in the security guards."

"If you bought the rights to the software, then why did your man at the trade show tell Bishop that Mephisto had developed the game internally?"

Teller snorted. "That act is getting a little stale, chum. Don't expect me to believe Bishop sent you down here without giving you any details of our agreement."

"Humor me and answer the question."

Teller blew out air through his lips and massaged a meaty biceps. "Bishop agreed to keep his involvement a secret. The contract says that Mephisto will take credit for developing the game, and the guy at the trade show didn't know any different."

"You didn't think it was strange that Bishop was willing to pass up credit for developing the game?"

"Sure, I was a little surprised, but we more than compensated him for keeping his trap shut." Teller narrowed his eyes at me. "Just what are you driving at?"

I ignored the question. "Did you ever meet Bishop face to face during the negotiations?"

"He doesn't deal directly. We always worked through his agent."

I pulled Terri McCulloch's picture out of my breast pocket and handed it over to Teller. "Is this the woman who claimed to represent Bishop?"

"A real cutie, isn't she? But what do you mean 'claimed' to represent Bishop?"

"You've been had, Teller. Terri McCulloch left Bishop's employ three weeks ago. She had no authority to represent him in any negotiations, then or now. Bishop believes McCulloch stole the chess game at the time of her departure to revenge herself on Bishop for firing her. If you bought the chess game from her, then you purchased stolen property."

Teller stared at me like I told him my goldfish played the glockenspiel. "So that's your dodge," he said abruptly. "Well, it's not going to work. We have Bishop's signature on that contract and we'll damn well make it stick."

"Don't go simple on me," I said, thinking he didn't have far to go. "That signature is almost certainly a forgery. You'll be laughed out of court if you try to enter it as evidence. The smart way to handle it is to return the game to Bishop and let us deal with Terri McCulloch."

"What a horse laugh. You tell Bishop I'll wring his neck personal if he keeps up with this business. Now get your butt out of my office and take your girlie photo with you."

Teller flung Terri McCulloch's picture across the desk and stood up with his fists clenched. He looked eager to split the seams of his elegant pinstripe while landing a few hard ones on my jaw.

I figured I could take Teller if it came to that, but it would likely be a Pyrrhic victory. I slipped the photo back into my pocket, got up and walked over to the door. "Just for your information," I said with my hand on the knob, "someone with a wax pencil has been touching up your picture in the lobby."

Teller blinked dumbly. "I don't get it. I told facilities to clean that up last week."

When I returned to the lobby I found the receptionist reading a thick volume with the title *Great Games in Chess History*. Tucked behind his ear was a stubby wax pencil with a blunt point. I glanced over to Teller's picture and noted the addition of a Hitler mustache and a crudely drawn dueling scar. Gesturing at the pencil, I said:

"You must value free expression in art a great deal more than regular employment."

"Oh," he responded in a fluttery voice, "you've opened a window onto my soul and perceived my true being."

I rolled my eyes. "Skip the dramatics: you're stampeding my lunch. What's with the chess book?"

"It's a hobby. As much as I hate this crummy job, being at Mephisto does give me a chance to stay current with chess and chess software. And I have to say this new release is really hot."

The receptionist's bright manner was beginning to grate a little, but I decided I'd better take the opportunity to learn something. "That's what I've heard. But if you're an expert, then maybe you can tell me just what makes this program so swell. Bishop gave me a patter about

GM's and grading level 2601's but it didn't make much of an impression."

The receptionist looked at me for a long moment, and then flashed an ingenuous smile. "You live around here?" he asked.

I told him San Francisco.

"Me too. Look, my name is Chris Duckworth," he said and held out his hand. I shook it. "Why don't you meet me at a bar this evening and I'll tell you all you want to know about the game. I really can't take the time now because they don't like me gabbing with friends at the desk. Besides, it's hardly in Mephisto's best interest for us to talk."

He was right about Mephisto, but I wasn't sure there was that much to gain from talking to him. On the other hand, I didn't have any plans for the evening, so I said, "Okay, I'd appreciate that. Where and when?"

"Let's say 6:30 at The Stigmata."

"The Stigmata? What the hell kind of bar is that?"

The receptionist chortled. "The name says it all. It's south of Market, corner of 9th and Harrison. See you then."

I thanked him and went out the lobby door. Something told me The Stigmata wasn't exactly cut in the mold of a California fern bar.

Chapter 3

down EPA way

*t*ERRI McCULLOCH'S current residence was quite a step down from Bishop's Woodside mansion. She now lived in a run-down apartment complex on Woodland Avenue in the impoverished little Peninsula community of East Palo Alto. The building was a three story architectural mutation from the early sixties — liberal use of filmy glass panels giving it the appearance of a dirty fish tank. I parked in the street next to a Chevy Impala teetering on jack stands and walked up a weedy sidewalk to the front door.

The door was propped open by a busted steam iron. After checking the apartment directory, I entered the building and started up the formed concrete staircase in the middle of the lobby to reach Terri McCulloch's second floor apartment. I was about halfway up the stairs when a nasally whine from below stopped me in my tracks:

"Just where do you think you're going?"

I looked over the railing to find a middle-aged woman shaped like a bowling pin advancing in my wake. She was wearing a billowy green smock and wide, square-toed pilgrim shoes that clunked loudly as she climbed. The wispy brown hair on her head was lashed to bright orange curlers the way a prisoner is lashed to the rack. Her face was deeply furrowed, and it had enough makeup on it to protect it from re-entry into the earth's atmosphere. It probably hadn't made the trip more than a half dozen times.

"I'm visiting Ms. McCulloch," I said.

"Looks to me like you're sneaking in to steal something. Anyway, the McCulloch girl ain't home."

"When do you expect her?"

"I expect her when I see her. I don't keep tabs on my tenants." She waved a hand at me in disgust, then turned to go back down the stairs. "This is getting to be a real frazzle. We've had more odd characters running around here since that girl moved in than I have the patience to deal with."

"What kind of odd characters?"

"Characters like you, buster." She stopped at the bottom and glowered up at me. "Now get your little fanny out of my apartment house or I'm calling the cops."

I love it when women give me compliments, but there didn't seem to be much percentage in arguing with her. I suspected this was a time when burglary tools were going to be more persuasive than impassioned rhetoric. I walked past the landlady, who was still expending a great deal of effort looking tough, and on out the door. When I hit the sidewalk I made a short detour to a liquor store about a block up the street and bought a can of beer and some beef jerky.

I chewed jerky and swilled beer on the curb in front of the store and then snuck back to my car and pulled around to a spot that was a little less conspicuous. Taking the set of tools I referred to as "mother's little helpers" from the glove box, I walked back to the apartment building and then climbed the gate at the entrance of the sunken carport that ran the length of the complex. You would have needed a barrel of Bond-o to patch all the dents in the autos parked there, but there was plenty of other junk in the stalls besides cars: rusting barbecue grills, exercise equipment, a baby's crib, stained mattresses, and even a pink toilet commode. I went the length of the carport to the back of the building, where I found an exposed metal stairway leading to fire exits for the second and third floors.

The lock on the second floor fire escape was a cheap number with a spring bolt, but there was a metal plate covering the place where the bolt met the jamb to prevent anyone from snicking the bolt back with a credit card. I took a short pry bar from my kit and worked one flattened end well under the brass piece that fitted around the doorknob. I gave the bar a sharp jab and the door knob popped off like the cork from a bottle of Cold Duck, bounced once on the rusted metal flooring, and then clattered all the way down the steps to the concrete below. I crammed one end of the pry bar into the exposed latch mechanism and twisted the bar until the bolt pulled back and I could open the door.

The hallway I stepped into was as dim and empty as a spinster's mailbox. Ancient wallpaper sloughed from its sides in long, yellowed strips. The carpet — grease-stained and torn — was thinner than the felt from a ghetto pool table. I found Terri McCulloch's apartment at the far end of the hall on the left, number 221. I knocked softly at the door, and when I got no answer, slipped out a pair of lock picks and bent to the task of tricking open the lock. After a few anxious minutes, the tumblers fell in line. I pulled open the door, stepped inside.

I was standing in a small studio apartment with a sliding glass door at the back. The door opened out to a terrace with what I imagined was an excellent view of the junky carport area. On my right was a kitchenette, separated from the main room by an island of free standing cabinets. The gray linoleum on the kitchenette floor was buckled in several places, and it curled up entirely where it came to the base of a gas water heater that had been installed freestanding next to the refrigerator in violation of innumerable codes. The kitchen counter tops were a pale green Formica and sported a dense pattern of cigarette burns and deep gouges that exposed the dark, greasy wood underneath.

The main room had brown carpet and cheap, hard-looking furnishings, none of which would suffer in the least from being shot out of a circus cannon. On the left was a wall bed that folded into a unit made of unfinished particle board with shelves and nightstands on either side. Across from that were a vinyl sofa and a green metal trunk with a hook rug spread over the top. A 1950's dinette set made of rolled metal tubing stood between the sofa and the kitchenette. The only thing in the whole place that would have cost more than 25 bucks at a thrift store was a flossy, new TV/VCR combo sitting on the table.

There were no pictures, flowers, bric-a-brac or stacks of *Cosmopolitan* magazines to give you the least little hint that a woman lived here.

My idea in coming was to frisk the joint while Terri McCulloch was away, so I went into the kitchenette and searched through all the cabinets, stove and refrigerator. I found food, pots and pans, and dishes in a variety of patterns—no two of which matched. In the closet in the main room there were dresses, shirts and slacks on hangers, underwear, stockings, scarves and socks in stacked wire baskets, and a good two dozen pairs of shoes. There was also an unlabeled videotape concealed in a hatbox on the top shelf.

I didn't think Bishop's chess program could be stored on videotape, but the fact the tape had been so carefully hidden intrigued me. I put it on the table next to the VCR for later.

I went to the bathroom and searched it carefully. I took the lid off the toilet tank and peered inside. Water and rusting plumbing peered back at me. I pawed through the stuff in the cabinets and drawers under the sink and in the medicine cabinet above. There seemed to be nothing unusual or important, except that Terri McCulloch had prescriptions for both Valium and Prozac. I looked into the shower stall and searched through the hamper of dirty clothes. Nothing.

Back in the main room, I pulled down the wall bed and looked under the mattress. Same story. I sat on the edge of the bed and went through the drawers in the nightstands. I found a checkbook, a bank statement and some bills, but none of them had any transactions for large amounts, either going in or coming out. I also found a loaded .22 automatic wrapped in a cotton cloth — not such a bad idea given the neighborhood, but not exactly standard issue for your happy-go-lucky brunette bimbette. I let the bed up and pulled one of the dinette chairs under the ceiling fixture and stood on the chair to unscrew the piece holding the glass bowl. There were three dead flies and a lot of dust.

I moved to the sofa and pulled it apart, searching in all the cracks and unzipping the vinyl covers on the cushions to run my hand all the way round inside. This netted me two dimes, an emery board and an empty foil condom package. I straightened up and looked around the room. The only thing left was the trunk. It was locked, but when I pushed it back from the sofa in preparation to using the pry bar, I found the key lying on the carpet underneath.

I had hoped that I would find Bishop's missing software in the apartment, but what I found in the trunk would be better classified as hardware. The first thing I saw was a black leather corset that was designed to come over the hips and tie in the back with a criss-cross of leather straps. Below that was a folded pair of thigh-high leather boots with zippers up the sides, pointy toes and three-inch stiletto heels. Next came a long, rather stiff riding crop with a thick handle and a broader than typical flap of leather at the end. That covered the dominatrix portion of the collection.

In the dominee portion, we had leather cuffs for restraining wrists and ankles, complete with D-rings to attach to the set of chains and "spreader bars" piled up at the bottom of the trunk. There were also blind-folds, gags, nipple clamps, a variety of buckling straps and harnesses that I could only guess at the purpose of — and even more puzzling — an item that looked for all the world like a horse's tail. It was fashioned out of long lengths of horse-hair attached to a plastic handle with a bulbous tip.

I picked it up to examine it more closely. It seemed an unlikely scourge with the soft horsehair and the too awk-ward handle. Then I remembered Jesse Helms's outrage at an infamous Robert Mapplethorpe self-portrait. As it dawned on me that the picture featured Mapplethorpe with something very similar sticking out of his backside, I dropped the so-called handle like a live grenade and wiped my hand on the nap of the carpet.

I dumped the rest of the gear back in the trunk, locked it and put the key and the hook rug back where they had been. I had been in the apartment for a good half-hour and was starting to worry about Terri McCulloch return-ing, but I had yet to review the videotape. I could take it with me or I could fast forward through it here. Go or stay? I picked up the tape and hefted it in my hand as if its weight would tell me something, and then made the decision to stay. I was reluctant to remove anything from the apartment, and I didn't figure Terri McCulloch could get me into much trouble if she barged in on me.

I put the tape into the VCR and punched the play but-ton. A grainy picture came on that showed a darkened concrete room with plywood on the floor. Hanging on the walls were a variety of switches, paddles, riding crops and nasty looking whips. These were just window dressing for the main attraction. In the center of the room, suspended from the ceiling by four heavy chains, was a solid disk of polished wood about eight feet in diameter and about three inches thick. Lying naked, spread-eagle on the disk

— hands and feet fastened to the suspending chains and pale butt facing the camera — was a lanky young man with frizzy hair. Although his face was out of view, I guessed it was Bishop even before I recognized his voice from the cries he made.

He had plenty of reason to make noise, too. Sitting next to Bishop, with her legs dangling casually off to one side, was a woman in a black leather corset wielding a birch rod. While she held Bishop with a firm hand to the small of the back, she applied sharp, stinging blows up and down his buttocks. Terry McCulloch looked just like her picture — except the picture I had didn't feature the tattoo above her left breast and the metal rings that pierced each of her nipples.

I was leaning into the television monitor, trying to make out exactly what the tattoo was when the sound of someone putting key to lock at the apartment door registered over Bishop's little aria. With no time to think of anything better, I powered off the TV, bounded over to the sliding glass door and let myself out onto the terrace. Crouching off to one side, I peered through the glass and watched as the apartment door swung open to reveal the dumpy landlady. She made a ponderous tour of the room, stopping once to rifle the night stand drawers I had searched earlier, and again to examine the TV/VCR combo. She put her hand to the back of it like she was checking to see if it had been running, and then stood for a long moment with her arms akimbo, head swiveling side to side on her thick neck like a tank rotating its turret. My pulse rocketed when her gaze settled on the terrace door.

I watched just long enough to see her waddling my way, and pressed myself into the near corner where the terrace railing met the side of the building. The glass door slid open and the landlady's roller-encrusted head emerged over the threshold. I held my breath, willing myself invisible. But instead of looking around the terrace, the landlady hawked loudly, chewed thoughtfully on the results and then launched a prodigious loogie clear over the back railing into the carport. Accompanied by another throat-clearing growl, her head retracted into the apartment. The glass door slid closed.

I released my breath and squinted through the glass. The landlady trundled across the room and straight out the door without stopping. I reached for the handle of the door and tugged at it, afraid she had locked me out. It opened easily enough, so I ducked back inside and powered on the VCR long enough to eject the videotape. I put the tape under my arm and went out the door and down the fire escape as I had come. My visit had given me plenty to think about, but it was already five-thirty and time to get back to the city for my appointment with the Mephisto receptionist.

the stigmata

THERE ARE A LOT of Victorian houses in San Francisco with bay windows, steep-gabled dormers, cornices and ornate plasterwork. Restored in the late 1960's and early 1970's, many of the houses were given super-colorful paint jobs, inspiring the term "painted ladies" and the publication of innumerable coffee-table books. Although it had all the right architectural features, I could tell immediately that the Victorian on the corner of 9th and Harrison that housed The Stigmata had not made the grade for the coffee-table books. It was painted jet black, from the tip of its highest cupola to the steps of the portico that covered the entrance—windows included.

I went up the black steps and through the swinging door at the top. There was a tall, sallow-looking character sitting just inside on a stool, reading a paperback book and smoking a cigarette made with harsh, Turkish tobacco. I loitered a moment, expecting a greeting or a request to pay a cover charge, until he glanced up at me and said with asperity, "What are you waiting for — a royal summons? Loosen your tie and go on in. There's no cover until the first show at eight."

Ahead was a curtained doorway. I stepped through into a large room that probably began life as the house's front parlor. Now there was a long oak bar along the back wall, with the requisite mirror behind. Across from the bar, nestled in the space in front of a large bay window, was a tiny stage with a pair of microphones on stands. Spread out between the bar and the stage were a dozen or so cocktail tables. The floor was a dull and grimy oak parquet, and the walls had oak wainscoting with old-timey damask rose wallpaper above that. Owing to the blacked-out windows, light in the place was scarce: most of it came from a heavy crystal chandelier in the center of the room and a couple of brass fixtures behind the bar. I counted eight people at the bar and the cocktail tables — all of them men. But then, I had long since figured it was that kind of place.

The men were dressed in everything from business suits to jeans to bicycle shorts. All of them had short hair, a few had closely trimmed beards or goatees, and most of them looked better "put together" than the typical straight guy you'd find in a sports bar after work. The exception to that was the fellow in the far corner table who was wearing some sort of goofy space goggles and a single metallic glove. Michael Jackson he was not.

I didn't see Chris Duckworth among the patrons so I went up to the bar and sat down to order a drink. I thought the bartender owed a lot to "Mr. Clean" of liquid detergent fame, but I opted not to mention it to him. He had a muscular build, a closely shaved balding head, and he was wearing a tight tee shirt with the sleeves partially rolled up. There was a gold hoop earring in his right ear. I ordered a draft beer and was congratulating myself on what a great job I was doing of not acting ill-at-ease when the bartender came back with the beer and a cardboard drink coaster, and said, "Top or bottom?"

"What?" I sputtered.

"Guess you haven't been here before, have you?" said the bartender. "I'm talking about the beer mat. See, one side says 'top' and the other says 'bottom.' It's just a little game we play. So, which side do you want up?"

"Ah, top. Definitely top."

"Yeah, I figured." said the bartender, and went away smiling. I drank some of my beer and lit one of the half dozen cigarettes I permitted myself a day. Fifteen minutes went by. An old Broadway show tune started playing over the speaker system in soft tones. More men came in — none of them Chris Duckworth — and the bartender got a lot more busy. I was trying to decide between calling it quits and ordering another beer when I felt a warm hand touch my shoulder and squeeze it gently. I looked across to the bar mirror and saw myself flanked by two of the wildest looking drag queens I'd ever set eyes on.

The one with his hand on my shoulder was tall, thin and black with a flowing platinum wig, pink lipstick and nails, and a sequined pink mini-skirt with enough padding in the chest region to pass the federal bumper crash test. On the other side was a Latin bombshell with a tower of henna-colored hair piled high, a backless green chiffon gown, false eyelashes so long they affected weather patterns when he batted them, and an outrageous make-up job — complete with beauty mark — that Earl Scheib would've been hard pressed to match for $29.95.

The blonde reached around me and tapped my drink coaster with an inch-long pink fingernail. "Well Mr. Top Man, how about buying a working girl a little drink?"

I looked from one to the other and said, "You boys are

as cute as a couple of flocked Christmas trees. I'll spring for all the tap water you can drink — at the other end of the bar."

The redhead wriggled his hips. "Oh," he said breathlessly. "We'd just love it if your spring was sprung. Is there a lot of tension?"

"Let me be real clear. I take mine with two X-chromosomes. Now buzz off."

The blonde threw his head back and laughed. Turning to the back of the room, he yelled, "Hey Chris, teasing your friend isn't half as much fun as you said it would be."

I looked back to see the guy with the space goggles slip them off and walk up to the bar. It was Chris Duckworth.

"Hope you enjoyed yourself," I said when he came up.

"To tell the truth, we wanted you to run screaming from the place, or at least have a spasm of some sort."

"Sorry to disappoint."

"That's okay. Meet Solome & Giselle. They're putting on a show later this evening." Solome & Giselle both proffered a hand like the Pope holding out his ring to be kissed, and I shook each in turn. After ordering another round of drinks, Chris Duckworth and I went back to his table and sat down. The goggles and glove he had been wearing were sitting on top of the table, as well as an odd looking metal board with two wires coming out of the side.

"So what's with the Flash Gordon get-up?" I asked.

"Since you've seen fit to accuse Mephisto of software piracy, I decided to take a look at the product in question."

"I'm not following. We're talking about a chess game that you play on a personal computer. Not this goofy stuff."

Duckworth laughed. "It's best when you accuse someone of theft to get a good description of the stolen property. Take a closer look. This is a virtual reality chess computer. When you put on the goggles you see animated chess pieces on a board that looks like a miniature battlefield. You can 'pick up' and move a piece while wearing the glove, and the computer uses the sensors in the glove to figure out what you are trying to do and updates the image you see through the goggles accordingly. Put on the glove and goggles and see for yourself."

I slipped on the glove, which was made from a synthetic fabric with wires stitched along the fingers and palm, and then put on the wide plastic goggles. Both were attached to the board by an insulated wire. I had to admit the view through the goggles was pretty astounding. Looking down at the board I saw a full set of chess pieces in three dimensions. All the pieces were modeled after medieval soldiers, the tallest appearing about six inches high. The pawns were foot soldiers armed with pikes, the knights were knights in armor on horseback, the rooks were dismounted knights armed with broadswords, and so on up to the king and queen which were decked out in robes, wearing magnificent crowns and holding royal scepters. If that were not enough, each piece moved in place, making menacing gestures at the enemy across the board.

"Wait until you see what happens when you capture a piece," said Duckworth. "Use your gloved hand and take the black pawn in the center of the board with the white one that is next to it."

I reached down to the board and moved the white pawn Duckworth suggested across the diagonal into the square occupied by the black pawn. As I released it, the white pawn thrust forward with its pike, impaling the black one, causing it to dissolve slowly into the board like a sandcastle melting in the tide.

I took off the goggles and glove. "That is very impressive," I said. "But Bishop didn't say anything about this stuff to me. I had the distinct impression that the game had been developed for personal computers and was something you could buy in a software store on floppy disk or CD ROM."

"Yes, Mephisto is releasing a version of the game for personal computers, and it will be sold on floppy disk or CD ROM. The original author of the game — be he an employee of Mephisto or not — would have developed the software in that format as well. But we're also releasing a version of the game that runs on a virtual reality computer like this. It's more expensive of course, but it's also a lot more entertaining."

"All right, then. Let me get back to the question I asked earlier today. Just what is it that makes this program so swell?"

Duckworth sipped some of his white wine and grinned at me over the glass. "Well, I'm not really an expert, but the game is head and shoulders above any I've ever seen and it's easy to say why: it thinks and plays like a person, not a computer. Did you notice the way the board was set up when you looked through the goggles? The chessmen were arranged as they were immediately before the eleventh move in a game between two old farts from the nineteenth century, Anderssen and Kieseritzky. Chess historians have dubbed this particular match 'The Immortal Game' because of the exceptional play of Anderssen.

"Anyway, Anderssen has begun the game with a gambit — an opening in which a player places a piece in jeopardy in hopes of gaining a positional advantage over his opponent. Kind of like a Trojan horse. It's Anderssen's turn to play but the piece he has placed in jeopardy is about to be taken. If he's had a change of heart and wants to save the chess piece, this is his last opportunity to do it. What do you think he does?"

"If his original plan was to let the piece be captured, I imagine he tells it good-bye and sends a letter to the widow."

"Yes, of course. But if you set the pieces up like this for any other chess program and let the computer make Anderssen's next move, the other programs will invariably move the piece out of harm's way. But not this one. This program makes the exact same move that Anderssen made — king's rook to king's knight one — thereby permitting capture of the gambit piece."

"So what does that prove? This program plays more aggressively than other programs?"

"Sort of. Other programs make their moves on the basis of rather short-term cost-benefit analysis. They aren't capable of following a strategy that requires some sacrifice up front to achieve the desired long-term goal. If a piece is in danger, move it. That's all they think to do. This program, like a human player, is more flexible. It can balance the long term priorities with the short term and take a few lumps along the way if that's what's required to get the job done."

I wasn't sure I understood the explanation completely, but being a private investigator I could relate very well to the part about taking a few lumps to get your job done. "Okay," I said. "I think I get the main points. But there's still something I'm not clear on. It goes back to what you said about getting a description of the stolen property: just exactly what is it that I'm looking for? If Bishop's program can take so many forms, how will I know which is the right one? Do I have to recover them all?"

Duckworth laughed out loud. "You really are a babe in the woods, aren't you? You're not looking for a compiled version of the game. That's what the end consumer buys in the store. What you're looking for is the source code."

"Right. The source code. I'm glad we cleared that up."

Duckworth grinned and shook his head. "I ought to be charging you by the hour. All computer software starts out as source code. The source code, in turn, is 'compiled' into a program that runs on your computer. Think of sheet music for a song: that's like source code. The process of playing the song from the sheet music is analogous to compiling the source code, and a recording made from that performance would be similar to a finished program."

"So the source code is the valuable thing because it gives you the 'notes' for a computer program."

"Right. Without the source, you can't change a computer program — just like you can't alter a song unless you have the notes for it. What's more, you can't compile the program for other kinds of computers — just like you couldn't play the song on other instruments."

"Enough already. If I get within a mile of anything that smells even remotely like source code, I'll consult an expert. But I have to say, listening to you talk about this you sure don't sound like someone who hates his job."

"You bet I do. When I told you that today I meant it. There's a heck of a difference between having an interest in chess and computer software and suffering through eight hours a day of sheer boredom working for people you don't respect."

"There's the obvious question."

"Why don't I quit? Precisely because it is so boring and easy. As a struggling entertainer who works nights, I need a day job that isn't too taxing."

I thought I could tell which way the drag queen was sashaying. "Don't tell me..."

Duckworth smiled, cocked his head and made a gesture like he was fluffing his 'do.' "You guessed it. Just call me Cassandra — that's a Greek name that means 'helper of men.' I'm doing the late show after Solome and Giselle. In fact, I should probably be getting back to the dressing room soon."

"I play a little jazz bass myself. I wouldn't want to stand in the way of show biz. But, do you mind if I call you later if I think of anything else?"

"Not at all. I'll give you my card."

Duckworth pulled a card from his shirt pocket and handed it to me. One side was sturdy gray card stock with his name and office number engraved in plain black type. The other side was lavender with the name Cassandra written in script, along with a home phone number.

"Thanks," I said. "I have to say I feel better now that I know you work here. I was pretty sure the only reason you had me come here was to shock me."

Duckworth laughed. "*Non, mon cherie!* There are much better ways to shock." In a sudden movement, he lurched across the table and planted a wet one on my cheek.

I yelped like I was snakebit and jumped out of my chair.

"Now there's shocking for you," said Duckworth impishly.

I touched my cheek where he kissed me and waggled my finger at him. As I made for the exit, an emcee walked up to one of the microphones on the stage and announced:

"And now, what you've all been waiting for — the most dangerous entertainment in San Francisco for $10!"

Chapter 5

threatener's anonymous

PARKING LEGALLY in San Francisco is like trying to wedge that last coffee cup into an already over-crowded dishwasher: it seems possible, but it often can't be done. I don't even try anymore. It was close to nine when I drove back from The Stigmata and pulled my car into the back half of a bus stop near my apartment. That's normally good for a $250 ticket, but I plopped a laminated placard reading, "San Francisco Chronicle, Official Press Business" onto the dash before I got out. No doubt the meter maid finds it surprising how many newsworthy events happen near me.

I lived on the top floor of a four story building on the corner of Post and Hyde. It was close enough to the sleazy Tenderloin district that I didn't pay much in rent, but far enough away to avoid doing the hootchie-cootchie with drug dealers and winos every time I came or left. I stopped at the entryway to pick up my mail — two questionnaires, one titled, "Are You Curious About Yourself?" from the Church of Scientology and another from a dating service that blared, "Want to Meet Quality People?"— and went upstairs to my apartment.

While the water molecules in the chicken potpie I took from the freezer were being energized in the microwave, I filled out both questionnaires and sealed them up in the postage paid envelopes that accompanied them. I told the Church of Scientology that I was indeed curious about myself, but gave my name as Don Giovanni with the address and telephone number of the dating service. I gave the address and phone number of the church to the dating service, and said my name was L. Ron Hubbard and I wanted to meet someone who liked science fiction.

I garnished the pie with rosettes made from that cheese you squirt from a can, then poured myself a glass of Maker's Mark bourbon and took the whole movable feast into the living room and set it down on the card table where I eat my meals. I can't fit a bigger table in the room because it is almost entirely filled with stereo equipment, phonograph records and tapes. I have an extensive collection of jazz recordings — mostly from the 30's, 40's and 50's — but it's my hi fi system that I really pride myself on. It's made up almost entirely of components manufactured and sold before 1980, before the introduction of digital recordings on CD ROM, and before stereo manufacturers started caring more about glitzy consoles with small footprints than they did about the quality of the sound. The heart of the system is a pair of Altec Lansing "Voice of the Theater" speakers. These babies are about five feet tall and they consist of a large subwoofer unit with a set of four tweeter horns stacked on top. They were made primarily for use in movie theaters, and the truth is I can rarely play them at even a quarter of full volume — and there's also the little problem of them taking up about 18 square feet of my living room floor.

I picked out the 1957 Benny Carter LP *Jazz Giants* and got it started on my Empire Troubadour turntable. While I munched on the pie accompanied by Carter's ornate filigrees on alto sax, I reviewed the day's events. The assignment Bishop had given me seemed to be basically on the level. Certainly everything Teller said and did when I talked to him at Mephisto was consistent with the set-up I got from Bishop. Still, even without seeing Terri McCulloch's video tape, it was clear the relationship between Bishop and McCulloch was a complex one and Bishop wasn't eager to have me prying into it. Having watched the tape, one had to wonder whether the theft of the software didn't fit into some broader power exchange or struggle between the two of them. I wasn't sure I really wanted to find out. Why a man would enjoy being humiliated in that way — particularly a smug, sanctimonious bastard like Bishop — was beyond me.

But what about the woman who did the humiliating? I had already decided there was more to Terri McCulloch than Bishop's other girl friends, Jodie and Lisa. Now with her tattoo, pierced nipples and s&m accessories, it seemed even with that assessment I'd sold Terri shorter than flea market patio furniture. All I knew was, when I finally did run into her, I was keeping my trousers tightly buckled and my butt cheeks pressed firmly against the wall.

I finished up with the chicken potpie and went back to the kitchen to pour myself another glass of bourbon. I was heading to the bedroom to grab my electric bass when the phone rang. Perching on the edge of the bed, I picked up the extension on my nightstand and listened as a faint sound of street traffic came over the wire. A male voice, low and muffled, said:

"You could find better ways to spend your time, Riordan."

The voice was not familiar. I said, "You mean stamp collecting, crochet, things like that?"

"Can it," said the voice, louder and less muffled. "You know what I'm talking about."

"Yes," I said airily. "I believe I do. You are referring to home composting, aren't you?"

"Look, shit head, what I'm telling you is leave Terri McCulloch alone. That's the only warning we'll give you."

"So now there's more than one of you. Part of the Junior League, maybe? I hear they travel in packs." He started to say something, but I cut him off. "Say, have you heard about the new service from the phone company? It's called caller ID. It lets you know —"

There was a sharp click. I pressed the plunger down to get a tone and dialed the number on my display. It rang a long time, but eventually a different male voice answered with, "You know this is a pay phone, don't you?"

I said I assumed so and asked the location of the phone and whether anyone was just using it. I was told the corner of Chestnut and Columbus, and, no, nobody had been near the phone.

Chestnut and Columbus is smack dab in the middle of North Beach, the Italian district. That corner in particular was home to Bimbo's 365 Club, an old nightclub famous for its "girl in the fish tank" gimmick, now better known as an intimate venue for medium-sized rock and jazz acts. In any case, the call was puzzling because I'd hardly been on the job long enough for anyone to know about it unless Bishop had blabbed. I made a mental note to ask him the next time we spoke.

I picked up my electric bass again and headed back to the living room. There I plugged into the auxiliary input of my Crown amplifier (a classic powerhouse from the late 1960's), and spun up Billy Cobham's 1973 LP *Spectrum* to play the bass tracks along with Billy's bassist, Lee Sklar. I stayed with it until about 11:30 when I knocked off for bed.

Chapter 6

threats of a feather

i GOT UP the next morning at eight, showered, dressed and walked over to a cafe near Post and Leavenworth called Postworth. I ordered eggs and bacon with hash browns and washed it all down with a pot or so of coffee. In between bites, I read the paper and argued with the waitress about borrowing your partner's tooth-brush on sleepovers. She said it was perfectly okay, but I said it was a disgusting practice, and besides, why did all women's toothbrushes look like they'd been used to scour Nelson's column at Trafalgar square.

After breakfast, I continued down Post until I came to Powell, and then turned right and walked towards Market. This took me past Union Square and into the heart of a six square block area that vied with Fisherman's Wharf for the highest concentration of tourists in the city. The main draw was the cable car turn-around where Powell dead-ended into Market. This was the start of the cable car line that ran back up Powell over Nob Hill and down into North Beach.

Everything and everybody near the turn-around was set up to separate tourists from their money. First there was the cable car itself — three bucks for a two mile ride on a rickety, exposed carriage that crept along at 10 miles an hour, was filled with cold, overweight tourists and their preteen progeny, and on occasion slipped the cable and went zinging down Nob Hill towards a violent encounter with a bus or garbage truck. The last such encounter cost a tourist his leg, and caused the manufacturer of a well-known prepackaged rice dish to remove their billboards from the back of the cars.

Next there were the glitzy camera and consumer electronics stores that lined the street near the turn-around. Here you could buy the latest miniature video camera for 120% of the price you'd pay back home in a good department store, often without the knowledge that you were getting a factory refurbished unit, and always with the very minimum in customer service and the prohibition "No Refunds or Exchanges" printed at the bottom of your receipt.

Moving down the food chain were the street vendors. They specialized in knock-off sunglasses, silk ties sealed in plastic wrap like smoked salmon from the deli, hand-made jewelry and leather goods, and a complete assortment of New Age trinkets and fetishes, including magic crystals, soapstone carvings, cassette tapes of whale mating calls, and chips of red rock supposedly harvested from psychic "vortices" in Sedona, Arizona, but more likely obtained by taking hammer and chisel to Uncle Ed's flagstone patio.

At bottom, and employing the most direct approach to raising cash, were the panhandlers. Among this group there was considerable variance in technique. Some merely sat on the sidewalk, heads bowed, with a cardboard sign stating their plight and a cup or a hat nearby to collect change. Others stood and barked a pitch at passersby. This might be a straightforward request for money or could involve humor, such as, "Please contribute to the United Negro Pizza Fund." Often, the most successful panhandlers brought props with them to garner sympathy and interest. These included cats, dogs and children that looked cute or needed to be fed.

My personal favorite was the woman who held an infant swaddled in blankets close to her chest and looked up at you with mournful eyes as you approached. The last time I had dug into my pocket to give her some change, I realized the "baby" she held was really a plastic doll and rapped it sharply on the head with the quarter I'd retrieved. "Sounds a little hollow in there," I said. This prompted a string of invective, followed by a quick series of blows to *my* head as the woman swung the baby doll by the foot like a club.

I waded through the sea of tourists and panhandlers near the cable car turn-around without incident, and went east down Market toward the Ferry Building. Only a little ways on, I paused to indulge in a superstitious ritual of mine by tapping the Samuel's Jewelers street clock, then headed into the lobby of the Flood Building at 870 Market where I had my office. I rented a couple of rooms on the 12th floor near the back. The front room I subleased to an insurance agent, and he and the part-time secretary we shared occupied it. The back room I kept for myself.

The insurance agent was named Ben Bonacker, and he was without question the biggest horse's ass on the planet. The secretary was named Gretchen Sabatini — and we had once been engaged.

I came through the door and dropped the two questionnaires I filled out the day before on the out-going mail stack. Bonacker was standing by the coffee machine pouring sugar into his coffee cup at the rate a cement mixer pours concrete. He was about 50 years old, about five feet eight inches tall, and had a belly like a Hefty bag filled with Jell-O. He had white hair, a white beard and a ruddy complexion from too much drinking. His teeth were large and obviously capped, yet through nature or lack of skill on the dentist's part, his uppers protruded in a significant overbite. He was wearing one of the two business suits in his closet — a powder blue number from JC Penney — with suspenders, a threadbare dress shirt and a tie that looked like it had been used to wipe out a soiled petri dish.

"Riordan, you little pecker head!" he said affably. "How the hell are you?"

"Swell, Ben, just swell. Remember how I promised to feed your face into the document shredder the next time you called me a pecker head?"

Bonacker blanched and stepped back involuntarily, causing the flow of sugar to shift from his coffee cup to the top of his stomach, and from there to the floor. "Shit," he said, and thrust his cup and the sugar container down to brush himself off. "Lighten up, buddy. I'm just trying to make with the friendly here." He gave me a smile that was about as genuine as the capped teeth it exposed. "Say, I heard a joke that I know you'll like."

Every time you saw Bonacker he had at least one new joke, usually involving a recent disaster, minorities or a bodily function. I knew from experience there was no way to duck this one.

"What's the gift that keeps on giving?" he asked with a broad grin.

"You got me."

"A fart cut in a revolving door."

I rolled my eyes and walked past him to Gretchen's desk, which was a few feet from my office. She looked up at me with a amused expression, and said, "Good morning, Auggie. You should count yourself lucky. I've already heard it three times."

I generally liked people shortening my first name to Auggie about as well as I like them calling me pecker head, and I had fought innumerable battles in grade school to make the point stick. But I didn't mind it when Gretchen did it because she was, well, Gretchen. The product of a second generation German mother, and a first generation Italian father, she never got the joke when I called her my "Axis Powers girl" during the time we were going out. Her eyes were a devastating cornflower blue, and seen without make-up, they looked touchingly like those of a young child. She had a lithe figure with an extremely narrow waist and beautiful, shoulder-length auburn hair that women were forever asking her where she had cut — as if the same hairstyle would somehow equate to the same luxuriant locks. While her nose was small, she had inherited the shape of her father's heavy

Italian schnozz, and that and the freckles that dusted her chest were her least favorite features. I loved them both — along with the rest of her.

We had been engaged for about six months when I broke it off because I felt hemmed in and burdened by the need to support her financially. She took it in stride and within two weeks was going out with a rich urologist she met while sailing on the bay with friends. I was intensely jealous and on the verge of asking her back when she came into the office one day with two skinned knees and a couple of skinned elbows. "What in the world happened to you?" I asked.

"Rug burn," she said with a mischievous smile.

Hearing that cut my heart out and cauterized the wound in a single step. I never thought of us together again.

I said good morning to Gretchen and walked past her into my office. Nobody was beating down my door to feature pictures of it in *Architectural Digest*: it looked like the office of a vice-principal in a poor school district. I knew because I'd bought everything at an auction when the school burned down. There was a large gray metal desk with a Formica top and touch of smoke damage, two gray metal chairs with no arms and very little upholstery for clients, and a hard, wooden swivel chair behind the desk on which I could play the *William Tell Overture* in squeaks. The only things that made the office mine were a couple of framed black and white pictures of my favorite bass players. Those, and the half dozen or so paper cups of rancid coffee with spots of mold floating on top I was too lazy to clean up.

I plopped down in the swivel chair and began sorting through the mail and phone messages Gretchen had left on the desk blotter for me. There were two messages from Bishop so I dragged the phone over & dialed his number.

I could tell right away that he was cranky. "Riordan," he almost shouted. "Just what have you been up to in the last 24 hours?"

"Oh, let's see. I've been to a drag bar, done a spot of breaking and entering, and watched a very interesting porno tape. All in all, it's been a *spanking* good time. Why, what's it to you?"

"Whatever you've been doing, you've stirred up trouble — trouble for me. Last night I got a threatening phone call. I was told to stop hounding Terri McCulloch and to call off my private investigator."

I sat up a little straighter. "Did you recognize the caller?"

"No, it was a man and he was obviously trying to disguise his voice. However, I don't think he reckoned on my having 'Caller ID,' and I recorded the phone number from which he called."

Bishop read the number off to me and then I explained to him about my own call and told him I thought the numbers were the same but would double-check. I ended with, "What I don't get is how Terri's friend — if that's who he is — knew so quickly that I was involved. Have you told anyone you were hiring me?"

"No one apart from my lawyer. I assumed the call was triggered by an over-zealous pursuit of the software on your part, perhaps in conversations with Terri herself."

"I never got that far. She hasn't been home. If neither of us has told her about my involvement, that leaves only Roland Teller at Mephisto software. He wasn't any too happy yesterday to hear that Terri McCulloch had ripped him off. It's conceivable he got hold of her and give her an ear full."

Bishop produced one of his wheezing fur ball laughs, which over the phone sounded like the cat was in an iron lung. "That's certainly possible, given Mr. Teller's pugnacious reputation in the industry. However, it does beg the question of why Teller seems able to locate Terri McCulloch more easily than you. I've already given you her address and phone number. Would you like me to prepare a map as well?"

"Let me dish the sarcasm, Mr. Bishop. I'm a trained professional. I'll locate Terri all right, but in the meantime I suggest you have your lawyer contact Mephisto and encourage them to put on hold any plans they have for your software. My sources tell me Mephisto is very close to releasing a variety of products based on the program, and I don't think we want that happening before we can prove ownership."

"Yes, that point had occurred to me. I'll take care of it today."

I said good-bye after promising to get to the bottom of the phone calls, and then put in a couple of hours working on a report for another client. I was trying to decide whether to hide a whopping bar tab under "fees paid for information" (i.e., bribes) or "mileage, parking and tolls" when Gretchen sauntered into the office, closed the door and leaned against it negligently. I noticed for the first time that she was wearing a black linen jacket with a pleated black skirt. But then, she always wore black.

"You have a visitor, Mr. Riordan," she said in a tone that sounded more like I had a social disease.

"Oh, yeah? What's its name?"

"Jodie something-or-other. But I suspect most people know her by her title: 'Ms. D Cup of Northern California.'"

"That's right," I said. "It slipped my mind. The pageant committee asked me to do a credentials certification. Send her right in."

Gretchen mumbled, "Little boys," pulled open the door, exited. A moment later, Jodie something-or-other of bikini and Monopoly fame stepped in.

Chapter 7

jodie's tip

SHE WORE A short white dress made of neo-prene rubber. It fit like a milk bath. A silver-colored zipper with a large pull ring ran down the middle. Zipped as far as the tensile strength of the rubber would permit, it still exposed enough to certify her member in good standing, D Cup Delegation. Two more zippers for pockets were installed above her hips, in the off chance she wanted to tote around a dime or a postage stamp.

She wore matching white pumps, dangling silver earrings and a silver Egyptian *ankh* on a chain around her neck. If she were wearing anything else, I'd have needed a CAT scan or a strip search to find it.

"I feel like I've been sent to the principal's office," she said, taking in the room and its meager contents.

"Vice-principal, actually. But I've been empowered to act on his authority. Have a seat and I'll adjudicate your case."

I struggled to keep my eyes above her waist as she sat down in one of the hard metal chairs and crossed her legs. "Adjudicate?" she said. "Is that something we can do sitting down?"

"You're probably thinking of something else. I just meant I would decide what punishment to give you."

She grinned at me. "I know what adjudicate means, Mr. Riordan. My dad happens to be a judge of the District Appellate Court. I was just pushing your buttons."

"I'll say. So, can I get you something? A cup of coffee? A diamond mine in South Africa? My heart on a platter?"

"You're sweet. I don't need anything right now, especially coffee." She gestured at the many half-filled cups around the room. "It looks like you've got too many cups already."

"Doctor's orders. Keeps the humidity up."

She nodded at me like I'd said something important. I felt the pressure of a growing silence. When I couldn't take it any longer, I tilted my chair back with a loud squeak and said, "I forget. Did I call this meeting or did you?"

"I'm sorry. It's just that I'm not sure what to say. I hate going behind Edwin's back."

"I take it you have something to tell me about the chess software."

"More or less." She picked up the Egyptian *ankh* and began moving it back and forth on the chain in front of her chest. It was very distracting. "Look," she said abruptly, "it's like this. I'm pretty sure that Terri did take the software. There's been a lot of bad blood between her and Edwin, and I wouldn't put it past her to take it from him when he kicked her out. But she's a good friend of mine, and I don't want to see her get into any more trouble. She's already screwed up enough as it is."

"You don't want Terri to get into trouble," I said. "Check. But what specifically did you want me to know?"

Jodie sighed and let the *ankh* fall back to her chest. "I suppose it's nothing that you wouldn't have found out eventually, but before I tell you I want you to promise that you'll protect Terri. Once you convince her to give the software back, you've got to keep Edwin from filing charges against her with the police."

"I can't guarantee that. There are too many variables outside my control. Terri might not have held onto the software, or she might refuse to give it back. If she does have it and agrees to return it, Bishop might still want his pound of flesh. And if the cops aren't brought in by Bishop, they could get in some other way, like through Mephisto."

Jodie thought for a moment, then said, "Okay, just promise you'll do your best for her. However things turn out."

"All right, I promise. Now what's the deal — have you got her waiting downstairs in the car?"

"No, but I know where's she's working."

"Where then?"

"At a place called The Power Station."

"I gather we're not talking about generation of electricity here."

"No, it's an S&M club."

I picked a paper clip off my desk and began bending it into a miniature version of Rodin's *The Gates of Hell.* Either that or a badly formed letter "C"— I wasn't sure which. "That's just swell," I said. "This isn't under the same management as The Stigmata by any chance?"

"I've never heard of that," she said.

"Never mind, not your kind of place. So what's Terri doing at The Power Station? Handing out towels in the locker room. That sort of thing?"

Jodie giggled. "The dungeon would be more like it. And she's probably handing out a lot more than towels."

"I suppose I asked for that. Where is this place and how do I get into it? I mean do I have to flash my piercings at the door?"

"It's in North Beach, in the old brewery on Chestnut near Powell. You can walk right in. There's a public section that's open to everyone. There's also a private section for club members that you need a referral to get into. I can set you up with that if you want."

I flung the paper clip into the waste can and leaned forward over the desk. "Jodie, what's the story with you girls? Are you all into this stuff? And for that matter, what in the heck are you doing with Bishop at all?"

Jodie made an impatient gesture. "Next you're going to ask what my parents would think. We're not living in Saudi Arabia here, Mr. Riordan. Women don't have to wear veils and kowtow to men. I don't happen to be into the S&M scene, but I'd never judge Terri for participating — there's something to be said for kicking a little male behind and getting paid while you're at it. As for Edwin, I'm very happy to be with him. He's intelligent, he treats me well, and he really asks very little in return."

That was more dignity and strength of will than I expected from her side of the table. It didn't make her right, though. "You win that round on points," I said. "Let's get back to Terri. What I want to know is why Bishop kicked her out in the first place."

"She was doing drugs."

"What sort of drugs?"

"Several kinds I guess. I know she did Special K and Edwin told me she also shot heroin."

"Better and better," I said. "By 'Special K' you mean that stuff they invented to knock out rogue elephants?"

"Yes, Ketamine. It's some kind of animal tranquilizer. That and Ecstasy are the drugs of choice for the rave set."

"What happened exactly? Did Bishop catch her shooting up one day and kick her out, or did he work his way up to it."

Jodie pushed the heels of her hands into the seat cushion, lifted herself up and recrossed her legs. I nearly had an out of body experience. "Edwin knew she'd been taking drugs for some time," she said. "He kept trying to get her to stop, but one day she OD'ed on Special K and he had to rush her to the hospital. After she came home, they had a big fight and he told her she couldn't stay."

"Did she leave immediately after the fight? Or did he give her time to find a new place and so on?"

"No, she didn't leave immediately. She would have had enough time at the house before she left to take the software."

"When's the last time you spoke with her?"

"She called the day she got the job at The Power Station to tell me about it. That was about a week ago. I haven't talked to her since."

That seemed a tad unlikely. "You mean you didn't get

hold of her once Bishop discovered the software was missing?"

"I tried. I called and left messages and I even drove over to her apartment one evening. She doesn't seem to have been there much."

"And there was no talk about taking the software or getting even with Bishop in any of your prior conversations?"

Jodie hugged herself and shifted uncomfortably in her chair. "Look," she said with some asperity. "I told you that I think she took the software. She never said word one about it to me, but she was extremely upset with Edwin, and she can do some pretty crazy and irresponsible things at times. Her relationship with him has always been very — well, very charged. It's different than Lisa's and mine. Anyway, the way things were between them, what happened doesn't surprise me."

"You mean when you have someone literally licking your boots, it's pretty easy to graduate to ripping them off?"

"That's not very nice, Mr. Riordan."

"I suppose not," I said. "I haven't been keeping up with my blue green algae, so it's probably the result of a selenium deficiency — whatever that is."

Jodie's lips curled provocatively. She said, "Maybe it's because you're not getting laid."

Now this was a girl who had deep insight into the human condition. Suffering from a sudden inability to focus on the topic at hand, I wrapped up the discussion of Terri McCulloch by asking Jodie for the address of The Power Station and a pass to the back room. She pulled an engraved card from her purse that had nothing but the name of the place written in gothic script and a Chestnut Street address and phone number in small print on the bottom. She asked for a pen and wrote, "I nominate August Riordan" with her signature on the back of the card before passing it over.

After that the conversation drifted to other things, including sex and jazz and the framed pictures of Jimmy Blanton and Paul Chambers on the wall. I explained that I played jazz bass on a semi-professional basis, and that I especially admired Blanton and Chambers because, although they had relatively short careers, they both were innovators who moved the state of the art forward.

I invited her to come to a gig I had that evening and we ended by going to lunch at John's Grill on Ellis Street, where Jodie impressed the hell out of Rupert, the *maître d'*, who had never seen a rubber dress before.

Chapter 8

the power station

*I*F THE DRIVER of the cab I flagged to take me
to The Power Station thought there was anything funny
about the address I gave him, he didn't show it. We pulled
up across the street, and whether for nerves or curiosity, I
decided to walk the perimeter of the old brewery before
making my assault on the club inside.

Now that I saw it, I thought I remembered reading an article about the planned demolition of the building. It was a buff-colored, concrete monstrosity from the 1930's that took up the whole block between Chestnut and Francisco Streets. The Chestnut Street side was a storefront built to house the brewery offices and was only three stories tall. As the building went back to Francisco Street, however, it grew to a peaked facade about seven stories in height. The facade housed a grain elevator and screened the five rows of rusting brewing tanks that sat on the roof. Scaffolding was bolted to the facade to support a boom for scooping grain out of railroad cars, but the time when tracks ran up from the bay was long since gone.

Walking along the Francisco Street side, I could peer down through an iron grating into the basement. In the gloom I saw squat brick ovens for roasting hops and a jumbled lattice of rollers, chutes and conveyors to fuel the ovens and move the grain. The fact the basement would also make a nifty dungeon was not lost on me.

I went back around to Chestnut Street, and up to what had formally been the brewery office door. There were signs of remodeling here, including patched stucco, new paint, a new door with polished brass fixtures and a discreet plaque reading, "The Power Station" in the same script as the card Jodie had given me. I used the knocker — which was shaped like a lion's head — and waited.

The door swung back, and I was looking at a tall woman in a pantsuit made of a flowing, diaphanous material. It was chartreuse. So was the turban wrapped around her head, but her sash and open-toed sandals were gold. She was middle-aged, stout, and no piker when it came to the costume jewelry counter. She had hoop earrings trained hamsters could jump through, bracelets aplenty, rings on every finger and enough gold chains around her neck to weigh down a dead body.

She looked me up and down. "Yes?" she said in an imperious tone.

"Guess you left the house without your anklets," I said with a smile. That bought me nothing but a puzzled stare — she probably *had* forgotten them. "Pass that," I said quickly. "I was hoping I could come in and get a look at the club. You know, see what there is to see. Find out what you have to offer. That kind of thing."

"The club is not open to the public during the day. Only members and their guests are permitted. You may come back after eight PM, if you wish. After eight, we have demonstrations in the public area, and docents available to give tours and explain membership benefits."

I proffered the card Jodie had given me. "I was told this would get me an in on the private stuff."

The woman took the card and squinted at it from arm's length. "If you have been nominated by a member, Mr., ah, Riordan, then of course you are welcome. Please come inside."

She held open the door and I walked past her into the club. Going by, I inhaled a lot of perfume of the sort a woman in a chartreuse turban wears. That, or a flea bomb had just gone off. The entrance was on a raised platform with rails. It looked down on a cavernous room with a concrete floor and rough, concrete walls. There was a lighted podium at the foot of the entryway, and an area for lounging off to the right with black leather sofas, heavy, iron-bound coffee tables, ornate floor lamps and potted plants, all arranged on top of an elaborately patterned Persian rug. Further back were a series of tall concrete partitions that came out about twenty feet from each side of the room, leaving a corridor about ten feet wide down the middle and effectively dividing the remaining space into six open-ended cubicles. It reminded me of nothing so much as a series of handball courts, but I suspected they were intended for a different kind of sport.

The woman with the turban went down the stairs ahead of me, paused to take a glossy folder from behind the podium and then led me over to the lounge area. "My name is Amanda," she said. "Please sit down." She sat on the sofa across from me and placed the folder on the coffee table between us. "This is some information about The Power Station you may read at your leisure. If you have specific questions about the club, I'd be happy to answer them now. Or perhaps you would just like to hear an overview and then take a tour?"

Her tone was so matter-of-fact you'd have thought she was selling time-share condos. I said, "Let's get things rolling with the overview and see where that takes us."

"Certainly," she said with a thin smile. "The Power Station is a private club established to provide its members a discreet, safe and well-equipped environment for practicing bondage and discipline. Members may reserve any one of ten private dungeons for sessions with other members, guests or personal trainers from our staff. Each dungeon is equipped with a differing selection of restraints, cages, etc., allowing you to experiment with a variety of styles of play. Members may also make use of the public dungeons you see behind us, if exhibitionism or public humiliation are to be emphasized. In addition, the public dungeons are used by our staff to demonstrate new equipment — which is available for purchase in our 'Pro Shop'— or to hold seminars in bondage and discipline technique for neophytes."

"What kind of money are we talking about here?"

"Club dues are $200 a month with separate hourly fees for the private dungeons and sessions with personal trainers. In addition, there is a one-time initiation fee of $1000. Guests may use the facilities if they are with a member or are sponsored by one. Of course, the hourly fees we charge non-members are necessarily higher. This portion of the club is open to the public most evenings — for a $25 cover charge — to encourage new membership and promote interest in bondage and discipline."

This was like the Beverly Hills Country Club meets the Marquis de Sade with a touch of the Rotary Club's good works for the community thrown in. "Do I get handcuffs with the club emblem if I join?"

The woman in the turban didn't miss a beat. "No, we've discussed that in the past, but not everyone likes that sort of restraint. Members receive an unadorned iron ring, such as the one I'm wearing here." She gestured to a plain black ring on the middle finger of her left hand. "This allows members identify each other outside the club. That can be useful because we do not use last names here or publish membership rolls."

"Why make it easy on the Vice Squad, eh?"

That one scored a hit. Her face spasmed like she swallowed her retainer. "There's nothing illegal about what we do here. All members and their guests are 18 years or older. All play is consensual and refereed to prevent injury."

"What about the 'personal trainers?' Isn't there a niggling little law about sex for pay on the books?"

She pursed her lips and shook her head slightly. "I'm beginning to think you don't know much about bondage and discipline," she said. "For the submissive personality, most of the excitement in the experience comes from the feeling of giving up control or being humiliated. It is strict club policy that our trainers may not touch or fondle their client's genitals during a session. That would be illegal. If climax is desired, then the trainer can order the client to touch him or herself. Often this is more exciting for the submissive personality anyway."

"At least that's what my old pappy used to say. On a different topic, how did you end up in this brewery? I thought I read it was going to be torn down to build condominiums."

"It is a nice space, isn't it? It was going to be torn down, but the city designated it a historic site and restricted the type and extent of alterations that could be made to the building. Since the owner couldn't sell it for development, he leased it to us. We have renovated about a third of the interior for our purposes and left the rest as it was — which meets the city restrictions."

S&M and historic preservation working hand in hand. I said, "I was wondering if it would be possible to schedule a session with one of your trainers today."

"Y-e-s," she said with some hesitance. "Aren't you interested in a tour first?" Then after a pause, "And you do realize that our trainers always assume the dominant role?"

"I think I will pass on the tour. You've already given me a very clear picture of the club. As far as the trainers go, I have in mind a particular individual who I've worked with before. I believe she's now an employee of The Power Station. Her name is —"

"Excuse me please," the woman with the turban interrupted. "As I mentioned, we really don't like to use full names at the club. The trainers, in particular, like to keep their role at the club well segregated from the rest of their personal lives. In fact, many of them find it advantageous to assume an entirely different name and identity while they are here." She reached down to the folder on the table between us and flipped it open. "Here are the biographies of the trainers we have on staff. Perhaps you will recognize the individual you've worked with before." She paused a moment, then tittered.

That surprised me. It hardly fit with her stiff demeanor. "What's funny?" I said.

"Well, you might recognize your old trainer, assuming you weren't blind-folded the whole time!" She struggled a moment to keep her composure, then produced a good old-fashioned guffaw.

I yanked the pages with the trainer bios out of the folder and thumbed through them. "That's hardly the sort of comment I'd expect from someone in your position," I said in a huff.

"You're right — I'm sorry. Still, one mustn't take oneself too seriously. After all, bondage and discipline is all about having a good time, isn't it?"

I grunted. I found Terri McCulloch's bio about half way down the second page. The picture was a head shot that didn't show off any leather garb she might or might not been wearing. The text said she had been in the biz for ten years, specialized in sensory deprivation, humiliation and flogging, and gave her moniker as "Mistress Tamara." I put the sheet with Terri's write-up down on the table and pointed to her picture. "That's the girl for me."

The turban lady nodded. "Mistress Tamara. She joined us recently. You must be fairly well advanced if you've worked with her before. I believe she is available this afternoon, but there are a couple of preliminaries. First, I need you to read and sign this form from the folder. Essentially, it states that you are aware that your session with the trainer will not involve sexual contact, and that you participate at your own risk and will not hold the club or the trainer liable in case of injury."

I scanned the form quickly and signed it. There wasn't going to be any "play" between Terri McCulloch and myself, just talk. I didn't care what the form said.

"Second," said the turban lady. "We have the matter of payment. Hourly rates with a trainer in a dungeon for non-members are $150. I would recommend a two-hour session, so that would come to $300. A credit card or cash are best."

I handed over my credit card and the woman left the table, taking the card and the signed form with it. "I'll be right back with your receipt," she said.

Bishop was going to love this entry on the expense report. I watched as she walked down the corridor between the public dungeons, losing sight of her as she turned down a hallway screened from view. She was gone for maybe ten minutes, and when she returned, she had a strained look on her face. "I couldn't get the transaction to go through," she said. "Nothing wrong with your card. The phone lines just seem to be busy." She passed back the card. "We can try again after your session. Why don't you come with me now."

We retraced her route between the public dungeons. When we came to the hallway at the end we turned right and went down a staircase that led to a concrete walkway about five feet wide. Spaced at even intervals along the back wall were tall doors of rough-hewn lumber bound with iron. We walked up to the first one and the turban lady grasped the iron handle and pushed it open. "Please go in," she said. "You may exchange your clothes for the robe you see on the table, or wait for instructions from Mistress Tamara."

"I think I'll wait," I said.

"Make yourself comfortable, then. Mistress Tamara will join you shortly."

The door closed with a loud clank and I felt a creepy chill go up my spine. It was hard to see why people would pay money for this. I walked around the room. It had great ambiance: rough concrete walls, sloping concrete floor with a drain in the middle, dim overhead fixtures and the overall salubrious feel of a concentration camp shower room. All the requisite S&M gear was present, including a square metal cage just large enough for a man to crawl into and an upholstered table in the shape of an "X" with posts at each corner for binding hands and feet. On closer inspection, I found a crank under the table that caused the posts of the table to extend or retract — a sort of a modern day rack. I was squatting by the side of the table moving the crank back and forth to observe the mechanism when I heard the door open behind me. I straightened up and turned, looking forward to finally meeting Terri McCulloch.

What I met instead was a fist full of knuckles.

The punch hit me square on the side of the jaw and knocked me back onto the table. Lights danced in my head, then someone reached over and pulled me upright by the lapels. That would be good for another punch in the face, so I brought my leg up sharply and planted a shoe my assailant's stomach. I kicked for all I was worth. I heard a loud grunt as something heavy hit the floor. I rolled off the table and stepped back to see what was what.

Kneeling on one knee in front of me was a thickset man

in a black silk tee shirt and tailored slacks. His thinning hair was slicked back and he had a nice gold watch and a dark, even tan that came from a booth, not the beach. His arms were heavily muscled and his neck gargantuan, but his tailor was fighting a losing battle to hide his gut. All in all, he looked like a retired ball player gone soft from the good life. "Is that the kind of punishment you came for?" he said.

"Ask me when you're not on the floor," I said.

He lurched up and charged. As he came in, I found his stomach again with a solid left uppercut. He bent over the punch and I matched it with one from my right. I managed two more in quick succession before he snaked his arm around the back of my neck and began to pull me down. I resisted for as long as I could, then I pancaked my legs out and fell on top of him. It was a short ride to the concrete floor. His forehead hit first with a sickening thud and his body went limp beneath me. Wrenching his arm off my back, I rolled him over to see if he was still breathing. He was. But he was also going to have a one hell of a headache.

The take from his pockets was meager. A money clip with a little under 200 bucks, a pocket comb and a small ring of keys were all that I found. He was probably one of those guys who carried his wallet in his briefcase so it didn't ruin the line of his clothes. I put all the stuff back where I found it and stood up.

The turban lady must have decided there was something funny about my interest in Terri McCulloch and alerted this guy. Or Terri recognized my name when the turban lady went to fetch her. It didn't matter. What mattered is I was standing in an S&M dungeon, my jacket was torn, my jaw felt like someone had bounced a Chrysler off it and I still hadn't gotten hold of Terri McCulloch. I left sleeping beauty on the floor and went out into the corridor.

I marched down the walkway, pulling open doors to dungeons as I went. At number eight I found a white-haired guy with a leather collar making a snack out of the boot heel of a beefy broad with a crew cut and little round glasses. "Hey," she said as I slammed the dungeon door closed. I retraced my steps, went up the stairs and across and down to the walkway for dungeons one through five. I opened the door on two more tableaus, neither of which involved Terri McCulloch.

At the back of the building I found a door to a suite of offices and yanked it open. The turban lady was trying to hide under one of the desks, but there were about three yards of chartreuse material visible below the bottom edge. "Go away," she bleated. "I called the police. They'll be here any minute."

"I'll bet you called them. Police in this place would be like a fresh breeze in the malaria ward. Where's Terri McCulloch?"

"There's no one here by that name."

"Drop the veil, lady. You know who I mean."

"She left with the rest of the staff when you started tearing through the dungeons."

I was having trouble hearing her. "This isn't an earthquake drill," I said. "Stand up and talk to me like a normal person." She got up off the floor and stood behind the desk, red-faced and trembling.

"Who's the no-neck you sent into the dungeon in place of Mistress Tamara?"

"His name is Chuck," she said. "He works here, in security. You didn't hurt him, did you?" She glanced behind me and her eyes got wide.

"Naw," said a voice. "He didn't hurt me. He just beat my fucking head into cement and twisted off my goddamned arm."

I turned to find the bruiser from the dungeon leaning against the office doorway. He was very wobbly. In one hand he held his head, fingers partially covering one eye, elbow crooked against his side. In the other, a chrome plated revolver.

I watched with disbelief as his finger tightened on the trigger. The gun went off with a terrific roar in the enclosed space and a slug kissed into the wall about three feet to my left. The turban lady screamed. My heart missed more beats than a grade school band.

"There," he said. "I feel better. Now why don't you kind of get the hell out of here. And quick."

"Are you telling me I won't be enjoying the benefits of club membership?"

"Go!" he shouted.

He moved out of the doorway and I edged past him. I turned my back to the revolver and went out of there, the nerves between my shoulder blades — where I imagined the bullets would hit — twanging the whole way.

Chapter 9

wharf tour

i NEEDED A DRINK — badly. I met up with one in the bar of the Hotel San Remo on Mason Street. It was a quaint Victorian building with no more than 30 rooms. Outside they were setting up for a shot from the new TV cop show that was being filmed in San Francisco with lights, reflectors, heavy cables and prop and make-up people crowding the sidewalk in front. Inside, I had the place to myself.

I ordered a bourbon and soda. The bartender was a tall Indian with a high forehead, receding silver and iron colored hair, a thick black mustache and wire rim glasses. He wanted to talk, and women were what he wanted to talk about.

"They take your energy," he said in a singsong voice. "They take your life energy by tempting you with sex. A man derives his strength from the seed in his loins. And a woman steals it when she copulates with him."

I wanted to hear this bit of eastern mumbo-jumbo about as much as I wanted to hear *Ode to a Nightingale* read by the Elk's Lodge Women's Auxiliary. "Interesting theory," I said. "I feel the same way about mucus. Never blow my nose."

The bartender gave me a queer look and walked down to the other end of the bar: a sudden crisis involving dirty beer glasses apparently.

I nursed my bourbon and fired up a cigarette and looked forward to the time my pulse would come down to the low 90's. I never get used to being shot at, no matter how many times it happens. Minutes crept by like ice floes on the Volga, and presently a rangy-looking guy in jeans and an Oakland Raider's sweatshirt came in. He was wearing the ubiquitous baseball cap turned backwards with a pair of mirrored sunglasses. He gave me a brief glance and then took a seat at the other end of the bar. I figured him for a member of the TV crew.

After my cigarette was long gone and I had chewed all the ice in the bottom of my glass, I flagged the bartender and settled my tab. I had decided to go back to The Power Station and pull a little stakeout duty. When you stir up an anthill with a stick, the ants eventually come back to put things right. I was hoping Terri McCulloch would be in their number. I threaded my way through the TV para-phernalia in front of the hotel and went up Mason Street. As I turned on Chestnut, I looked back and caught sight of the guy in the Raider's sweatshirt from the bar. Appearing to take notice of my glance, he bent down in front of a newspaper machine and went through the motions of buying a paper. That didn't mean he had to be following me, but if he was, he surely did stink.

I continued east on Chestnut, past The Power Station, without looking behind me. Three blocks up at Grant I went into the neighborhood branch of the public library, strolled past the front desk and found a place to lurk in the stacks where I could see the front door. Five minutes later the guy in the sweatshirt came breezing in without his paper. He stopped at the front desk to ask something, had the librarian shake her head no in response, and then cautiously glanced around the room. Not seeing me, he sat down in a chair along the back wall near the magazine racks. He made a show of reading one, but kept looking out from behind it like a squirrel afraid of losing its nut.

I crept along behind the stacks, then stepped out and walked briskly across the room to where he was sitting. Snagging the pole that held *The New York Times* as I went, I slammed it across the arms of his chair when I reached him. "What the hell" was his response.

"You should give up on *Highlights* and get something you can really sink your teeth into," I said.

He was still wearing his mirrored glasses. Up close, his skin had a greasy pallor and his breath smelled like the fumes from a rendering plant. "Go ahead," he said. "Be funny. Just do it somewheres I'm not."

"That would be easier if you weren't stuck to me like so much discarded chewing gum."

He grabbed the newspaper pole and jerked it out of my hands. "No need to talk sense on my account."

"You followed me here from the hotel bar."

"No I didn't. I found it on my own. I go all around the city every day without any help from you. You'd be amazed."

I felt the slightest twinge of doubt. "You're telling me you just happened to go into the bar for a drink at the same time I did, and then you just happened to go to the library right afterward."

"I wasn't telling you anything, strictly speaking. But if you have to be told, I came here to get last week's ball scores since the paper didn't have them." He pointed at the football magazine he had been reading.

We were beginning to attract attention. The old guy in the chair next to us was giving us dirty looks and the librarian had come out from behind the desk. The sweatshirt guy noticed me looking around and gave me an oily grin. "Maybe you should ask the nice librarian lady to help you find a book. You could look under D — for delusional. Now, buzz off. Take the air. Go burp your Tupperware, Riordan."

His face dropped as he said my name. We stared at one another for a long moment and suddenly he lunged forward with the newspaper pole, impaling me in the stomach. The sharp thrust knocked the wind out of me and he pressed his advantage by charging out of the chair, one arm wrapped around the pole like a jousting knight, the other bending to elbow me in the jaw. I flew ass over teakettle onto the floor.

He was already sprinting out the door by the time I rolled upright. "Good Lord! What was that about?" said the librarian, who had come up beside me.

I got to my feet and rubbed my jaw. Two solid shots in one day: if this kept up I would have to send it back to the factory. I said, "He was upset because I was reading over his shoulder," and started after him. I pushed through the double doors of the library and then stopped short to look around. I spotted him a half block down Chestnut going back towards The Power Station. He had slowed to a brisk walk, but when he looked back and saw me he started running again. I went after him at full speed. I'm no marathoner, but when it comes to a sprint I can cover the ground pretty quickly.

By the time he reached Stockton, I was only 50 yards away. In the next block to Powell I closed the gap further and I could easily make out the Raider's slogan on his sweatshirt. He twisted around to look at me, and his glasses flew off as he snapped his head to the front, frightened by my proximity. I stomped the lenses into the sidewalk. Approaching Mason he was just out of my grasp, but I was starting to wheeze like a busted accordion.

A clump of cars and TV people from the shoot at the Hotel San Remo were crowding the intersection, a large black limo in the middle of it. The guy in the sweatshirt ran through the crowd, jostling and shoving people as he went. I did the same. Right as we came to the limo, the back door opened and out stepped a guy in an expensive suit and meticulously coifed hair. It was Dan Hanson, star of the TV cop show. I watched as the sweatshirt guy grabbed hold of Hanson and flung him directly into my path. I hit Hanson square in the shoulders, taking him down for a ten-yard loss. As we bounced off the side of the limo and rolled into the street, one part of my brain was thinking that it was ridiculous to dress a guy playing a cop in a suit like that, and the other was hoping that I didn't slam my jaw into something new.

We rolled to a stop in the gutter, and while Hanson was too dazed to say anything, his handlers were hopping mad. With a woman in a black beret and short blonde hair screaming obscenities in my face, I stepped up from the wreckage and helped pull the actor to his feet and dust him off. His stiffly moussed hair was standing up on end like a rooster's comb, and his cheek was abraded from the asphalt. I mumbled something about being sorry, gave Hanson a little shot in the arm, and said, "Now you're looking like a real cop."

The guy in the sweatshirt was nowhere to be found along Mason. However, two blocks up on Chestnut I saw someone who looked like him turn right at the intersection and walk out of view. I double-timed it up Chestnut, past rows of colorfully painted condominiums, past a construction site with a tall crane where more were being built, until I came to the three-way intersection. Here Chestnut and Taylor lay perpendicular to one another and Columbus cut through on a slant. Across the street on Columbus, I could see Bimbo's 365 Club. I didn't think it was a coincidence that The Power Station was in walking distance from the place where threatening phone calls to Bishop and me were made.

There was nothing doing on Columbus so I looked down Taylor in the direction the sweatshirt guy had turned. The Powell and Mason cable car line terminated a short ways up at Bay, and there was a crowd of people in a semi-circle behind a rail at the turn-around. I caught sight of the back of my man's head, the bill of his baseball cap bobbing up and down as he walked briskly through the waiting tourists. Holding tight to the near side of the street, I went after him as fast as I could without drawing attention to myself. My chest was still heaving and I was soaked with sweat, and I didn't want to spook him into another foot race.

As I approached the turn-around I went past a series of graffiti'ed, bunker-like buildings that comprised the Bay Street public housing complex. It is one of the ironies of city planning in San Francisco that tourists fresh off the cable car get dumped right into the middle of the projects. I threaded my way around the back of the crowd and popped out by the stop light at the intersection of Bay and Taylor. I could see the guy in the sweatshirt across the street, going down Taylor into the heart of Fisherman's Wharf. I was just concluding he thought I was out of the picture when he looked back and spotted me standing at the intersection. He broke into a run.

I dove across the intersection against the light, dodging cars and pedicabs carrying tourists. I pounded down Taylor across North Point, then Beach, then Jefferson and finally came panting to a stop underneath a gigantic ship's wheel with a picture of a crab in the middle. It had been donated by the big restaurant owners in the area, was tacky as hell, and had become the unofficial symbol of the Wharf thanks to prominent display on the opening credits of yet another TV cop show from the 1970's.

I leaned against the crab wheel, completely out of breath with no sign of the sweatshirt guy anywhere.

I had lost sight of him about a block back, and was now surrounded by large schools of tourists moving up and down the wharf like so many migrating tuna. Some were heading west towards the twin temptations of The Cannery and Ghiradelli Square, some were going east towards Pier 39 — the citadel of crass commercialism in the area — and still others were feeding among the row of restau-

rants ahead of me. Included among these were the famous Fishermen's Grotto and Alioto's, where you could
get crab cocktail and sour dough bread for $9.95 from the
take-away stands out front. This entitled you to brag to
your friends back home you'd eaten the quintessential
San Francisco meal, but you probably didn't mention that
the bread was baked in Oakland, and the crab flown in
from Alaska.

A musical group from Chile dressed in native costume
and packing pipes and drums was making noise in a
paved area in front of the restaurants. I drifted over to
join the crush of people watching them, burrowing between a fat lady in a pink running suit and a tall kid holding a skateboard. I stood two songs worth of their reper-
toire, hunkering low, looking up and down the wharf, before I spotted the guy in the sweatshirt. He was directly
across from me in the audience, trying his damnedest to
blend in too.

I broke off from the crowd and looped around behind
him, screening myself from view with the aid of several
strategically placed hot dog and pretzel stands. When I
was directly in back of him, I reached across a pair of nuns
in habit and grabbed him by the neck of his sweatshirt.
He jumped like a hooked marlin. I gave a sharp yank,
causing him to topple backward and land in a sprawl on
the asphalt. The nuns gasped. While he thrashed and
twitched and clutched at his throat where the sweatshirt
was cutting into him, I dragged him along the ground to
a concrete bench near the food stands. I leaned down to
take two handfuls of his sweatshirt and jerked him onto
the bench beside me. His baseball cap was twisted side-
ways, his face was flushed and he was breathing like an
asthmatic at the cherry blossom festival. I said:

"First off, unless you're playing catcher for the Giants this year — and I haven't seen your ugly pan on my bubble gum cards — wear your freaking cap the right way round." I pulled the bill of his cap roughly around to the front. "Second, I'll have an answer now to the question of why you were following me and exactly how you know my name."

The sweatshirt guy licked his lips and swallowed. "You haven't got a thing on me. You aren't the cops and you can't do anything here to make me talk."

He was right. I wasn't the sort to break fingers and I didn't have a gun I could wave in his face. He watched me thinking these things and that oily grin from the library crept onto his face. "Give it up Riordan, you're whipped. As much as I've enjoyed rubbing your nose in it, it's time we went our separate ways."

Desperate times call for desperate measures. I wasn't going to chase him all over North Beach with nothing to show. I reached across his torso and took hold of a belt loop on the far side of his body. In one movement I stood up and yanked him like I was starting a lawn mower. It was the last thing he expected. He spun over on the bench, landed on his stomach and tried to bite the near armrest. He seemed to lose consciousness. I reached down to extract his wallet and moved a few steps away to examine my prize.

His name was Todd Nagel and he was a member of a construction union. He was 32 years old and he lived in Daly City, a suburb just south of San Francisco. He had a Sears charge card, a BART ticket, not much cash, and a whole bunch of nudie pictures. I started flipping through them looking for familiar faces — or other body parts — but I let myself get too absorbed in my task. When I glanced up to see how Mr. Nagel was doing on the bench, I found he wasn't there: he was standing right next to me with a squeeze bottle of mustard from the hot dog cart.

He fired a stream of it directly into my eyes. I suddenly had a very good idea where the Germans got the name for mustard gas in World War I. My eyes teared over immediately, and I felt the wallet slapped from my hands. I pulled out my shirttail and hunched over it, trying to wipe the mustard out of my eyes. My left eye was out of commission, but I could just squint out of my right. Through it I saw Nagel ahead of me, running in the direction of the bay. I stumbled after him, but kept bumping into people or pulling up short to wipe my tears. At the edge of the wharf I paused to scan the area through a mustardy haze. There was a pier for the submarine Pampanito — guided tours for five dollars — a set of coin-operated telescopes for looking at Alcatraz and Angel Islands, and a pier for the Red & White Fleet, which ran ferries to Tiburon and Sausalito. Nagel was charging up the walkway to one of the ferries.

"Final boarding at gate number two for the Sausalito Ferry," came an announcement.

I lurched toward the walkway, but without a ticket was stopped at the gate by the attendant. I was in no condition to crash through. I turned and fought my way up the line at the ticket window, but by the time I purchased one, the boat had left the pier.

I stood at the edge of the wharf next to the telescopes — elbowed by little boys climbing the railing and swiveling the scopes without any quarters to spend, mustard all up and down my shirt, tears still streaming from my eyes — and watched as the boat powered out into the bay. Nagel stood at the stern of the ferry and waved good-bye.

Although I didn't know exactly what it meant, the only thing that made me feel the slightest bit better was the naked picture of Jodie I had seen in his wallet.

Chapter 10

in the key of g

i MANAGED THE TRIP home without re-enacting any more highlights from Three Stooges films. It was 6:20. I dumped a can of spaghetti into a pot, mixed in a can of pinto beans, threw in a dash of hot sauce, heated the mixture until it burped like molten lava, and then ladled the whole mess onto three slices of sourdough toast. I accompanied the meal with two cans of beer and a classic 1937 Roy Eldridge Vocalion reissue. I showered, changed and killed the rest of the time before leaving for my 9:30 gig by pressing ice packs to the side of my face. It had swollen up like I was packing a three-plug chaw.

I was subbing that night for the bass player of a jazz quintet called Distant Opposition. Their regular bassist, Leo Rand, was down in LA doing some studio work on a breakfast cereal jingle. Most of the gigs I got were like that: one-night stands where I subbed for a bassist in a regular group or played in a pick-up ensemble put together to support a big name who was in town for one show.

Distant Opposition played classic jazz without a lot of electric amplification. That meant I was taking my "wife" to the show — wife being the slang term among jazz musicians for a string bass. I lugged the bass down to the street and loaded it into the Galaxy 500 in a specially designed rack I had installed in place of the back seat. I had to crank the starter four or five times before the car turned over. When it did, I pointed it down Hyde in the direction of a South of Market dive called In the Key of G.

You can count on two hands the number of clubs in San Francisco that regularly feature jazz. In the Key of G was among the hardiest. What it lacked in atmosphere, acoustics, seating capacity and interior illumination, it made up in a dedicated cadre of patrons, a commitment to quality acts and a peerless bartender named Slim. I parked my car on 8th, next to the converted brick warehouse that was home to the club, and navigated my bass down the dingy concrete steps of the entrance on Minna. A stifling amalgamation of cigarette smoke, rowdy bar talk, clinking glasses and the smell of beer assailed me as I stepped through the doors of the basement room.

The space was long and narrow with the stage wedged in the back against a bare brick wall. Along the right was a chromium metal bar that looked like an examining table at the morgue. A set of bar stools with more duct tape than upholstery went with it, and a random collection of cocktail tables — some round, some square, some wood, some metal, all of them wobbly — was arranged in front of the stage.

The crowd was just as eclectic. There were the cool "South of Market" types: the young women in black, synthetic clothing with clunky shoes and ridiculous purses like miniature backpacks and the guys in jeans with heavy leather boots, wide leather belts and tight short-sleeve shirts. Hair dyed improbable shades of red, blonde or purple was common among both sexes, as were tattoos and piercings of all kinds in every conceivable place. One woman seated at the bar had enough loops in her ear to hang a shower curtain.

Standing shoulder to shoulder with these were the well-heeled yuppies who worked in the financial district downtown. Men dressed in Italian suits with the latest designer ties selected by their wives talked about IPO's, NASDAQ, venture capital and the Internet — all while making double-arm gestures that could be used to wave in a jet. Leavening the crowd were a handful of inner-city blacks who showed up to support Cornelius Crawford, Distant Opposition's outstanding alto sax player, a hometown hero who was on a trajectory for greater glory.

There were even a few ordinary schmo's who came to get out of the house, have a drink and hear some live jazz.

Using my bass as shield, I waded through the crowd until I came abreast of the bar. Slim was standing behind it, straining a bright pink concoction from a shaker into a glass. He was wearing his usual white shirt and red bow tie. He was balding, bony and had an Adam's apple so prominent it waggled his tie when he swallowed. "Got your Pink Lady right here, August," he boomed. "Straight up, just like you like it."

"Sorry, I only drink those when I play my concertina and yodel. I don't think the guys would go for it tonight."

"Suit yourself."

I hauled the bass the rest of the way up to the stage and set it down carefully on its side. The other musicians were already there getting set up. I shook hands all around and thanked Sol Hodges, the bandleader and drummer, for giving me the gig. I pulled out the square of carpet I carry to anchor the bass on slick surfaces and plopped it down in back, between the piano and the drum kit. Then I took the bass out of its zipper bag and wiped off the strings with a rag. As I began tuning up, I heard all the usual grousing that goes with musicians on club dates. Cornelius Crawford wasn't happy with the reed on his mouthpiece. At first it was too dry, then too wet. Tristan Sinclair, the pianist, didn't like the house piano for the same reason that all pianists hate house pianos: it was out of tune. Hodges was having trouble squeezing his ride cymbal in next to me, and the tendonitis in his elbow was acting up. Nick Dundee, the trumpeter, said the valve action on his horn wasn't smooth enough and was busily dousing the valves with oil.

Hodges passed around a rumpled cocktail napkin where he'd written the set list. I didn't pay much attention to anything but the first tune because I knew he would call each one before we started and he never stuck to the list anyway. The first tune was a bouncy, up-tempo standard by Charlie Shavers called *Undecided*. When we were ready to roll, Hodges gave Slim the high sign, and Slim flicked on a mic he kept behind the bar.

"Ladies and gentlemen, welcome to In the Key of G. Tonight we are featuring the best in classic jazz from a group of young lions who know how to shake it up and pour it. Please give a big round of applause to Sol Hodges' quintet, Distant Opposition, featuring Cornelius Crawford on alto sax."

The applause started in the middle of Slim's intro and crested when he got to Crawford's name. A number of people in the audience shouted, "Crawdad, Crawdad." The house lights went down and spots came on. Looking back into a smoky tunnel of light with my heart pounding and my fingers slick and slippery on the strings, I felt a rush of excitement like I was standing at the top of a high dive. Hodges counted off a tempo and cued Sinclair, who played an introduction on the piano. At the end of four bars the rest of us dove in. Crawford and Dundee led us through a chorus of the melody in unison — four sections of eight bars, the third being the bridge. Things were a little ragged at the start, and Dundee blew one outright clam. Crawford came in smoothly after the melody and played two choruses of jubilant solo. He got a big round of applause when he stepped back, and Sinclair followed him with two more choruses on the piano.

Dundee came next and more than made up for the clam, straining his back like a limbo dancer, horn jabbing at the ceiling as he hit the high hard ones. He also earned a solid round of applause. The bass and the drum don't always solo, but when I looked over to Hodges near the end of Dundee's he yelled, "trade fours," which meant that he and I were to alternate with four bars each. I kicked it off and resisted the temptation to play upstairs since I knew Hodges was a traditionalist and liked the bass to sound like one with deep, fundamental notes. When I passed to Hodges, he showed off some of the excellent brushwork he'd made his name with and then it was right back to me. We went back and forth like that until it was

time to go back to the melody — or so I thought. I'd forgotten that Shavers' arrangement had a shout chorus at
the end. I fluffed several notes until I dropped the melody
and picked up with the shout. Fortunately the horns were
going great guns by then and the only one who noticed
was Hodges, who gave me a dirty look. We closed with a
rousing turnout and got a nice ovation from the crowd.

More cries of "Crawdad" rose above the applause, but
surprisingly, someone also called my name. I looked down
into the audience and found Jodie sitting by herself at a
table in the third row. She had traded her neoprene skirt
for a simple black leotard and jeans, but she still had
enough sex appeal to make a speech therapist talk in
tongues. She waved enthusiastically when she caught my
eye, and I waved back. Dundee saw the exchange and
twisted round to give me a good look of him simulating
fellatio with his trumpet.

"That's some nice skank there, Riordan," he said, grin-
ning like a baboon. "Why don't you fix me up with that at
the break."

"Sorry Dundee — she doesn't like guys who blow their
own horn."

"Ha!"

"Can it," Hodges said harshly, then called out: "Blue
Monk." *Blue Monk* was a 12-bar blues number by Thelon-
ious Monk. Hodges didn't care for most of Monk's com-
position because he regarded them as self-indulgent and
too dissonant-sounding. In fact, he had once said that the
sheet music for Monk's tunes looked like flies had walked
across the paper. *Blue Monk* was different, though. It was
an approachable, straight-ahead blues number.

Dundee scrambled to get the mute on his horn, and
then Hodges called out the slower blues tempo. Piano,
bass and drums came in together and laid down the

theme immediately. For me, the melody to *Blue Monk* had always evoked the image of a drunk stumbling home late at night. The front line joined us after the bridge, Dundee's muted horn dominating and giving a real blue mood to the piece. At the end of the chorus, Hodges went into a soft drum press and yelled for me to "walk it." I played a fluid, constant progression that provided a sort of rhythmic propulsion for the music. Dundee took the first solo and blew directly at Jodie. I had to admit that he sounded great and I didn't get any argument from the audience. Dundee looked back at me when he was finished and stroked his goatee with a wise ass expression as if to say: beat that.

Crawford took the next chorus, and if anything, played better than Dundee. Sinclair followed with a credible solo on the piano, but probably could have used more left hand, which was a complaint I'd heard about him before. Hodges called for me next, and whether because I felt I was competing with Dundee for Jodie's attention, or was inspired by the image of the drunk, I gave one of my better solos: a moody, resonant, shambling kind of thing. It provoked table pounding and shouts of "oh yeah" from the audience. Dundee looked back to stick his tongue out, and I responded by moving the bass up a few inches.

We stepped cleanly back into the head of the melody then, with all the players on board. Crawford came to the front and we followed his lead on an improvised ending that sounded rehearsed. It was nicely done.

We played five more tunes in the set, closing with Sonny Stitt's *Loose Walk*. The house lights went up, and after I wiped down the bass and laid it carefully on the stage, I went over to join Jodie. Dundee was already at the table leering over her, but I said, "Amscray chumperoo," and elbowed him off to the side.

"He's cute," said Jodie after I sat down. "What's his name?"

"Josef Mengele. We call him 'the doc.'"

"Nice try, August. I know about Auschwitz and it's not something you should be joking about."

"I'm sorry — you're right. His name is Nick Dundee, but pay him no mind because there's a strong tradition in jazz that says the bass player gets all the women."

"Well, I'm not exactly what you call a traditional girl. What happened to your face?"

"Funny you should ask," I said and signaled the waitress for a round of drinks. "A couple of friends of yours entertained themselves today by taking swipes at it." I told her about my encounter at The Power Station and the chase with the guy in the sweatshirt, without mentioning the photo in his wallet. "So what's the story with this Chuck character?"

Jodie sipped from her drink and then shrugged. "There's not much to tell. He works in security, just as you were told. His last name is Hastrup and he played pro ball in Pittsburgh for several years. That's all I know about him, except that he's a real hard ass. He's not somebody you want to tangle with, August."

"I've already ascertained that through independent research. But what's his connection to Terri McCullogh? Why did he stick his beak into it?"

"I don't know that he has any special connection to Terri — except that he works at The Power Station. Frankly, it doesn't surprise me that he was alerted when you went there. From what you told me, it doesn't sound like you came across as a very credible client. You would have done better to present the card I gave you and simply ask to talk with Terri."

"Yeah, maybe. What about this other joker, Nagel? What do you know about him?"

"Nothing. Why would I?"

"No particular reason," I said. "Except maybe the picture he had of you sitting on the beach playing the ukulele in your birthday suit."

Jodie reddened slightly. "Oh, that one. That's from a spread in *Pussyfoot* I did a couple of years ago. Anybody with $5.95 can get a copy."

"So you're saying it's just a coincidence that Nagel had one too?"

"Yep, an embarrassing coincidence, but still a coincidence."

"Okay, one last question."

"Shoot."

"What's it going to take to get you to come on stage and join us for a tune in the same getup?"

Jodie reached across the table to tweak my nose. "A lot more than $5.95. A lot more."

"Well, thanks for coming. It's great to have the support— and make Nick Dundee jealous as hell."

Jodie left before the second set. The band was smoother and looser, both because we were warmed up and because we'd all had a drink or two or three during the break. We did a half dozen more tunes, and closed with *Perdido* from the Ellington songbook. I hung around for a time to shoot the breeze, but got bored with it after Slim closed the bar and Sol Hodges started to tell the hoary old story about the time that Buddy Rich cursed out his band at the top of his lungs in the middle of a gig. I said my good-byes and carried my bass up the stairs to the street. Outside there was a dense fog, and the air felt cold and damp on my face after the close atmosphere of the club.

Chapter 11

exit wifey & hello my fair lady

i WENT ALONG Minna to 8th Street. My Galaxy was parked across the way, under a diffuse cone of orange light projecting from a sodium vapor lamp. No cars moved on the street, and as I looked north towards the intersection at Mission, I could see the traffic light flashing red through the fog like a distant ship signaling at sea. The only sign of life was a dark shape swathed in grimy blankets lying in a doorway.

I went across the street to the Ford. I propped the bass against the rear bumper and bent down to open the door. As I straightened up, I looked over the roof and saw two men get out of a white van parked further up on Minna. Both were tall with heavy builds and both were dressed in white. One I recognized as the bouncer from The Power Station; the other was a black man with a shaved head that glistened eerily as he stepped into the light. I cursed under my breath. It seemed that there had been more than enough today without this. I said:

"I didn't think the diaper service ran this late."

Hastrup, the bouncer, walked around the front of the car, pulled a gun from the small of his back, pointed it at me.

"Tell me you're happy to see me," he sneered.

I turned to face him, noticing the square bandage taped to his forehead. "I'm happy to see you."

"The words are right, but the conviction is lacking. We'll have to work on that. But first things first. Jimmy, here, is kinda curious about your big violin. How much do they go for?"

"It's called a string bass. They cost anywhere from four grand on up."

Hastrup nodded to the black man. "That's quite an investment. I expect it'll take a lot of keyhole peeping to replace it." Jimmy went around to the back of the car and took hold of the bass by the neck. He levered it onto his back and swung it over his shoulders like a gigantic club. It hit the asphalt with a brittle, dry-sounding crunch. Jimmy let go of the neck and jumped in the air and came down on the bass with his big size 12's. There was more dry crunching, and Jimmy repeated the process until the zipper bag lost all definition and was nothing more than a sack full of kindling. That bass had been made in Italy by the famous craftsman, Alberto Begliomini, and was virtually irreplaceable.

"You're getting gladder to see me by the minute," said Hastrup. "I can see it in your eyes." He pushed the revolver forward until the cold, oily muzzle butted against my forehead. "How's about I treat you to a headache like the one you gave me this afternoon, huh big boy?" He crowded in close, aching for me to react.

"Let's dispense with the tired theatrics," I said in a tight voice. "It's only a half hour show."

Hastrup snorted. "Okay, we'll cut to the chase. Put your fucking arms behind you." Then to the black man: "Come on, Jimmy."

Jimmy came up behind me and snapped a pair of handcuffs roughly around my wrists. He grabbed each of my arms above the elbow and bent me back like a trussed pheasant. "Try not to bleed too much," he said, his hot breath tickling my ear. "It's hell getting blood out of whites — white clothes that is." He laughed sourly.

Hastrup shoved the revolver back under his waistband. "I might have caused some confusion about the purpose of our visit this evening. This isn't about you and me and our run-in at The Power Station. This is about Terri McCulloch. This is about Terri McCulloch and you staying the fuck away from her like you were told. Tonight we busted up the big viola and now we are gonna bust you up. But later, we'll be watching. We know what your game is. If this warning doesn't take, there won't be another. You go anywhere near Terri again and the Coast Guard will be fishing you out of the water beneath the Golden Gate Bridge. Assisted suicide — that's what it will be."

He stopped short and drew in his breath. He leaned forward, face glistening with sweat. "Now give us the witty comeback, Riordan. The bright repartee. We wouldn't expect anything less of you."

I had barely formed a word in my mouth when Hastrup took a mincing step forward and landed a sharp jab to my cheek. My head snapped back and butted into Jimmy's forehead. "Shit," he yelped. "Watch it Chuck."

Hastrup stepped in close and began to work over my mid-section. He knew what he was doing. I tensed my muscles to protect my gut, but Hastrup hit me square under the breastbone with a punishing shot and I lost all control. The blows came fast and hard then—relentlessly, inexorably. Soon I couldn't distinguish between them and all I knew was a haze of pain and nausea and the feeling of not being able to breathe.

Gradually I became aware that Hastrup had stopped, and I slumped against Jimmy's arms, head lolling, mouth gaping for air. I heard Hastrup's voice from far away, like I was at the end of a tunnel. "How much would you pay for a busted fiddle and a beat up private eye? Two cents? A nickel? But w-a-i-t: there's more." I sensed, rather than saw, a blur of motion and an explosion of pain radiated out from my groin. Jimmy released my arms and I poured onto the ground, too weak and battered even to curl up.

"A busted fiddle, a beat up private eye and a bruised pair of gonads," said the far away voice. "But wait, there's *still* more." Something cold and hard hit me on the back of the head. I released my clutch on consciousness and went swirling down into the blackness.

✻

The first thing I saw was a gold lamé pump. Then its mate. Then the shapely anklcs that went with them, sheathed in fishnet stockings. I thought maybe I'd died and gone to heaven.

Then I heard, "August, wake up!" in a distinctly male voice and I knew I'd gone to hell.

As near as I could figure, I was lying on my side in a dank alley under a street lamp. My mouth tasted like a used dress shield, my head felt like it had been mined for rocks, and the way my groin felt, I was riding for a spot on the Vienna Boys Choir. I rolled over on my back and looked up at the owner of the pumps.

She, or more accurately he, was a shapely blonde wearing a long sleeve, gold lamé gown that was form-fitting from the waist up, but puffed out in a fantastic, crinkly bell from the waist down. "August," he said. "It's me, Chris Duckworth. What are you doing here?"

"Damn you," I croaked. "I've paid my dues to get hcre — wherever this is. Don't go questioning me about my business. What in the hell are *you* doing here?"

Duckworth squatted beside me on his high heels, the material from his gown crumpling around him in a big circle. "Yeesh, you're grumpy when you wake up. And will you look at what this is doing to my dress." He yanked the fabric of the skirt over his knees and folded it in a wad on his lap. "You're just going to have to be a gentlemen and refrain from looking up my crotch."

"It's gonna take every ounce of will power," I said and squeezed my eyes shut, fighting the pain. "Look, I'm not in too good a shape right now, so let's keep it simple: where are we, what time is it, and how did you get here?"

"We're in an alleyway off 9th, about a block from Mission. My Lady Timex is in the shop, but my guess is around 3:30. I did the late show at The Stigmata tonight. I couldn't catch a cab at Harrison and I figured I'd have better luck if I walked up to Mission or Market."

"All right. I'm with you so far. Everything clear and sensible. Next question: how'd you spot me?"

"It was hard not to August. The sidewalk is littered with pieces of a broken cello—"

"String bass," I interrupted.

"Whatever. The trail led up the alley a short way and you were at the end of it. Now can I ask what you're doing here?"

"In a minute. Did you see anyone else nearby? Two big guys dressed in white, for instance."

"No, a girl could hardly have missed something like that."

I opened my eyes and Duckworth gave me a broad wink.

"Believe me, Chris," I said. "Those guys are definitely not your type." I briefly recounted what had happened.

"My God," said Duckworth. "That's horrible. You should go to the police. Or the hospital. In fact, we should go to the hospital right now."

I rolled over on one arm and struggled to sit upright. My head whirled like a carnival ride and my dinner threatened to return to its homeland. "No," I said. "No hospitals and no cops. Just help me get to my car. I'll deal with Mr. Hastrup when the time comes."

"August," said Duckworth in a strained voice, glancing behind me.

"What?"

"There's a note on your back."

"What's it say?"

"August, it's *stapled* to your back."

Now that I thought about it, there was a place between

my shoulder blades that felt stiff and sore, but comparing that pain to the pain from my other injuries was like comparing a chirping parakeet to a screaming eagle. I said, "Pull out the staple."

"I can't," said Duckworth. "I can't do that."

"We're not talking about a Comanche arrow here. It's just a staple. Now, pull it out."

"I'll break my nail."

Exasperated, I flung my hand over my shoulder and strained to reach the note. I grasped the top of the paper and gave a sharp yank. The staple pulled out — smarting like hell. The note was written in ballpoint pen in block letters on a piece of lined notebook paper. There was a bloodstain at the top where the staple had been. It said:

Riordan,
I wonder how you'll look on the deck of a Coast
Guard cutter with your mouth full of sand? Next
time this note will say, "Good-bye cruel world."

I crumpled the paper into a ball and threw it away from me. "Come on," I said. "Help me to my car."

Duckworth straightened and put his hands under my arms to pull me up. I got to my feet, but fell back against him and nearly toppled us both.

"Whoa," said Duckworth. "You weigh a ton. You're never going to make it to your car, much less drive it."

"Yes I will," I said stubbornly, but black spots swam in front of my eyes as I said the words. I hunched over to keep from passing out.

"Yeah, and I was Judy Garland in my prior life," said Duckworth. He steered me over to the alley wall. "Lean against this and I'll get us a cab."

Duckworth went away and I occupied the time by alternatively sweating, tingling all over and counting the holes in the wing tip pattern on my shoes. I did some lip biting too. Carbon atoms on a distant planet rearranged themselves into DNA, microorganisms formed, grew backbones, swam around the ocean, mutated into amphibians and crawled onto dry land — and finally a cab appeared at the mouth of the alley. I straightened up and stumbled over to the car with all the casual insouciance of the Frankenstein monster taking his first steps. Duckworth jumped out, tugged nervously at his preposterous gown and held open the door while I fell into the back seat like I was flopping into a rowboat in stormy seas.

The driver looked back at us after Duckworth sat down and said, "You people make me sick. I'm only taking this fare because there's no other calls."

Duckworth cursed and looked down at the driver's photo ID. "You're taking this fare, Mr. Lester P. Knoll, hydrocephloid homophobe Esquire, because it's the goddamn law. Now shut up or I'm reporting you to the taxi commission."

"Right on, honey," I said weakly, then gave the driver my address. As we pulled away from the curb, I caught a glimpse of a sign across the street that asked, "Are you an organ and tissue donor?" Given my present state of health, it seemed an extraordinarily apt question.

We drove in silence to my building. Duckworth paid the fare with bills he took from a tiny clutch purse and helped me to the entrance. I fumbled with the keys until he got impatient and grabbed them from my hands and opened the door. We climbed the stairs to the fourth floor the way overweight tourists from the Bronx would hike out of the Grand Canyon: sweating, breathing hard, resting at every opportunity and arguing the whole way. Duckworth used the keys again to open my apartment, and I went straight to the liquor cabinet. I downed three shots of bourbon rapid fire and dropped into bed. I went under almost immediately, but I have a vague memory of Duckworth pulling off my shoes and covering me with a blanket.

Chapter 12

a detective or a punching bag

i DREAMED I was standing with my back to a wall in front of a firing squad. Beside me was my string bass. The captain of the firing squad was Hastrup. He grinned malevolently, shouted, "Take aim, F—"

"No!" I yelled, and sat bolt upright in my bed. Chris Duckworth came running in from the other room. He was dressed in a pair of my sweat pants and one of my tee shirts, and given the differences in our sizes, he looked like a little kid who had been playing in his father's wardrobe. He held a frying pan that sizzled and steamed. The smell of scrambled eggs wafted over.

"I like mine with hot sauce mixed in," I said.

"Judging from the accretions I scrubbed out of the bottom of this pan, you pretty much like anything in the catsup or steak sauce family. Today you'll make do with rosemary and dill weed."

"Hmm," I said. "I don't know about any accretions, but I'll bet there were lots of layers of stuff built up in that pan."

"Very funny. I refuse to let your challenged vocabulary make simpleminded word choice a sine quo non."

"Oh, now you're talking Dago."

"Drop it, will you? How're you doing?"

That was a topic I was trying not to dwell on. "I've felt worse. Everything is stiff and sore, but I don't think anything's broken or missing. The results from all precincts won't be in, though, until I see if there's blood in my pee."

"That's disgusting, August. I don't need to know things like that."

"Don't ask, don't tell."

"Yeah, right," said Duckworth, and walked out of the room. "Breakfast in 15 minutes," he called back.

I rolled out of bed and hobbled over to the bathroom. The results of the urine test were negative. However, my cheek was puffy, there were several large bruises on my stomach, and there was a bump on the back of my head big enough to convince me it was reproducing by fission. I showered, shaved and dressed in slow motion, like I was doing a space walk. It was well over 15 minutes by the time I sat down at the kitchen table, but Duckworth had kept the food warm. He poured me a cup of hot coffee and sat down across from me.

"Say, this is good," I said after sampling the scrambled eggs. "You sleep on the couch?"

"No, why would I? I crawled into bed with you."

I paused with my fork in mid-air. The eggs fell off and bounced back onto the plate. "You better be joking. Otherwise, I'll have to kill you."

"Whoa, big fella. Yes, I slept on the couch. I would have gone home, but I didn't want you to croak in your sleep. You should have gone to the hospital like I said."

"Well, I didn't. But thanks for everything."

Duckworth glanced down into his coffee, almost shyly. "You're welcome. It was kind of exciting. That sort of thing happen to you a lot?"

"What sort of thing? Getting beat up, or getting picked up on the street by drag queens?"

Duckworth laughed. "Either."

"The former is something I try to avoid, but not with complete success. The latter is an entirely new experience."

Duckworth scraped his fork aimlessly across the plate. "Say," he said, looking up intently. "You wouldn't need an assistant, would you? Someone to do your office work, pitch in on investigations — be your right hand man...so to speak."

"Sorry, Chris, that would never fly. I already have a secretary, and she only works part time. As for the investigations, I don't have the temperament for a partner — or the volume of business to justify it."

"I didn't think you'd go for it."

"You got canned from Mephisto, didn't you?"

He grinned sheepishly. "Busted," he said. "After my last photo touch-up, Teller finally put two and two together and fired my ass. You should have seen his big red face when he told me. I thought his head would explode for sure. But it's no big thing. I've got a good lead on at job at a multimedia firm in the City. Better company, better boss and no commute. It's perfect."

"Well, I'm glad to hear it. The way this case is going, *I* may not be employed in private investigations much longer."

Duckworth sat up in his chair. "So who were the men from last night?"

I hesitated a moment before responding, not wanting to encourage him. "One is a bouncer from an S&M club where Terri McCulloch works," I said. "McCulloch is the girl that peddled Bishop's chess game to Mephisto, and she's evidently asked the bouncer — Hastrup — to protect her. In addition to beating the stuffing out of me, I think he's also responsible for some threatening phone calls. What I don't get is how Hastrup knew where I would be yesterday evening."

"Could they have followed you to your gig?"

I reached over to a kitchen drawer and took out a pack of cigarettes, shook one out, lit it. I blew a stream of smoke up to the ceiling. "It's possible. There was a ghoul-ish-looking beanpole following me around yesterday named Todd Nagel. He might be working with them, keeping tabs on me. Nagel is a bit of an enigma in his own right, though."

Duckworth waved ineffectually at the smoke. "You might have at least asked if I minded. Why is Nagel an enigma?"

"Sorry," I said. "Nagel doesn't have any obvious connec-tions to the other players, except I found a photo of Jodie — another girl employed by Bishop — in his wallet. I asked Jodie about that last night at the jazz club, and she had a fairly plausible explanation. Still, I wonder. Nagel knew my name and was following me around for a reason. Does he have Jodie's photo because he's hot for her and she's conned him into tailing me? And if that's true, what is Jodie's angle? She claims to be a friend of Terri's, but she gave me the tip on where Terri works. Might be she has an ax of her own to grind and is just trying to speed Terri's fall."

"That really doesn't explain why she'd have this guy Nagel follow you around. Just to see how you're making out with her information?"

"I guess."

Duckworth leaned forward on the table, his face flushed. "No, that's not it. I know what's going on, August. They are all working together to protect McCulloch. Jodie set you up by sending you over to the S&M club. You would have found out eventually where McCulloch was working, so that was no great tip. The important thing was to get you there at a time when Hastrup was ready and waiting. The reason for Nagel following you was to make sure you did what was expected. And last night, Hastrup knew you were going to be playing because Jodie told him. You invited her there, right?"

I looked at him with a new admiration. "Yeah, I did at that."

Duckworth almost wagged his tail. "See, it all adds up. You breeder boys will do anything for a pair of big tits, and I'll bet this Jodie girl has a tremendous set of hooters."

I chuckled and stubbed out my cigarette in the detritus of scrambled eggs and toast. "Okay, Sherlock, I have to admit that's a theory that fits the facts pretty well. And you're right about Jodie: she's no slouch in the mammary department. But all of that is incidental to my primary task—finding Terri McCulloch and getting Bishop's software back. It doesn't really matter who is or isn't protecting her, except that Mr. Hastrup's bad karma tests off the scale and he might need a little help finding redemption." I looked down at my watch. It was 11:20. "Time to breeze, boyo," I said.

Duckworth and I shared a cab as far as 8th and Minna. The Galaxy 500 already had two tickets on it, of course. I drove it back downtown and dumped it off in a garage near my building where they charged nearly as much as the tickets to park for eight hours. When I got to my office, Bonacker was at his desk with a young couple, going over auto insurance premiums on his computer terminal. He said:

"I'm sorry, I misunderstood you. I thought you said you were both over 30. That's going to change the quote a little bit."

This was Bonacker's standard bait and switch technique. When people called up for a quotation, he would "misunderstand" one of the parameters that affected the cost of the insurance to rig his quote so it undercut the competition. When the poor fools came running to his office to snap up their bargain policy, he would apologize, then crank the quote back up to full price. Most people went along with it because they couldn't afford to miss any more work and were tired of shopping around.

I made a snorting noise as I went by, and the young woman glanced up. "Don't worry about him," Bonacker put in quickly. "He's just here to water the plants."

I kept going to Gretchen's desk. She was wearing a tailored black pantsuit and she, too, was pounding on her computer. "Where's your watering can?" she asked. Then after getting a good look at my face: "You got beat up again, didn't you? Jesus Christ, August. When are you going to get on board the clue bus?"

"Probably not until it runs me down."

"Things like this make me so glad we never got married. I simply could not deal with the man I love continually treating himself to this kind of punishment."

"As opposed to your doctor friend who goes around all day with a lubricated rubber glove treating himself to enlarged prostrate feels?"

"That comment says more about you than it does Dennis. Of the two of you, who do you think does more to make the world a better place? I'll give you a hint: helping banks repossess poor peoples' cars does not make the world a better place."

"You could be replaced," I said peevishly. "Someone just asked me for your job, in fact."

"Who? That blonde bimbo you had in yesterday?"

"No, a different blonde bimbo — with a higher testosterone count."

"What?"

"Never mind. Look, let's call a truce. I appreciate your concern. I was just being jealous."

The Gretchen's expression softened, then turned into a smile. "You want me to do something, don't you?"

"Hey," I said. "That was a heartfelt expression of regret. But now that you mention it, get the number to a place called The Power Station and give them a call. Ask them if Mistress Tamara is working today."

"All right. But why don't you do it?"

"Because they might recognize my voice. If she's there, find out what her hours are."

"Will do. By the way, that guy Bishop has called you enough times to wear out the phone ringer."

"Imagine that," I said and went into my office. I flirted with the idea of blowing off Bishop, but he might have some new information, and I'd found it politic to make sure the client understood I was working on a case even when there wasn't a great deal of progress. In the end it didn't matter. The phone rang as I put my hand to it and Bishop started talking before I'd even finished hello.

"Well," he said. "Have you found her?"

"In a word, no."

Bishop cleared his throat savagely. "This is really beyond endurance. My lawyers tell me that Mephisto refuses to play ball. They are going ahead with plans to release the software next week. If I can't prove Terri stole the software and defrauded Mephisto, I'll have no choice but to involve the police and sue Mephisto for piracy. The whole thing could take years to resolve and I may never regain possession of my game."

"There's no guarantee that things will be any different once I locate McCulloch. In fact, there's every indication that she is going to fight us tooth and nail."

"What do you mean?"

I explained to Bishop about my run-ins with Hastrup last night and at The Power Station. I didn't tell him about Jodie's involvement and I didn't mention Nagel.

There was a heavy silence at the other end of the line. Finally Bishop said, "What are you, Mr. Riordan, a detective or a punching bag? Any fool can career across the landscape getting beat up. As far as I can tell, you've made no real progress on this case since the outset."

I got a little angry then. "Look, Bishop, I'm trying like hell to retain some sympathy for your situation here. But with your live-in call girls, your S&M spank-fests, your haughty, computer geek manner and all the physical punishment I've taken in the last 48 hours, it's damn hard to see why I shouldn't punch the ejector seat button and leave you to auger into the hillside."

"That's quite the vivid image you've painted for my predicament. And I'll thank you to keep your opinions about my life-style and personality to yourself." Bishop paused. "But I do appreciate that you've invested the case with all the physical vigor and intellect you possess. I further appreciate that there is insufficient time for me to engage another detective. So, I suggest that we leave the name-calling aside and focus on solving the problem at hand. What are your next steps?"

"Translation: you're an idiot, but I'm stuck with you. Way to kiss and make up, Bishop. I really ought to walk from this job. I really ought. But pass that. Next steps, you said. What do you know about a Todd Nagel, construction worker and Daly City resident?"

"Nothing. Should I know anything about him?"

"Not particularly. He just spent yesterday afternoon trying to crawl into my back pocket. What about Jodie and Lisa? Where do they fit into this mess?"

"Jodie and Lisa?" Bishop sounded flustered. "I wasn't aware they had any involvement. Apart from holding the same ... general position as Terri, of course."

"So neither is a particularly good friend of Terri — or to turn it around — is on particularly bad terms with her?"

"Well, Jodie came to us through Terri. That is to say, I hired Jodie on Terri's recommendation. I assume they are somewhat close. Lisa I hired as a replacement for Terri. I don't think they even know each other."

"What was Jodie's reaction when you fired Terri?"

"She expressed regret, but I believe she understood my reasoning. There had been repeated provocations with Terri, so I don't think it came as much of a surprise when I finally let her go. What's the point of these questions? Are the other girls implicated in some way?"

"No," I lied. "I'm just trying to cover some bases I probably should have covered at the outset. But it would be disconcerting to think that all your cuties were in league against you, wouldn't it?"

"Riordan!"

"Relax. You were owed a bit of needling. Now I'm headed out to have another go at finding McCulloch. Unless you have another inspirational message to impart, that is."

Bishop didn't rise to the bait. We said strained goodbyes and hung up.

Gretchen came in a minute later and told me that the word from The Power Station was that Mistress Tamara was not on call. That meant I was making a not-so-sentimental journey back to East Palo Alto. But before I left the office I opened the only locked drawer in my desk and pulled out a 9mm Glock automatic in a shoulder holster and strapped it on. I was tired of showing up at gunfights armed only with a winsome smile and a hardy handshake.

Chapter 13

blocked pawn

nOT MUCH had changed on Woodland Avenue since my last visit. The apartment windows still needed washing, the Chevy Impala was still on jack stands and the liquor store up the street was still happy to take my money. I bought a stale roast beef sandwich, coffee and a pint of bourbon and pulled the Galaxy into a choice spot across from the building.

There was no reason why Terri McCulloch shouldn't be home, except that the way my luck was running I couldn't imagine myself walking up to the door, ringing the bell and having her buzz me in. I went through the motions anyway — with the expected result. I went back to the car and sat, sipping the too strong coffee and chewing the leathery sandwich.

A female postal carrier came up and used a key to let down the front panel on the apartment mailboxes. She shoved mail into the individual boxes in a desultory fashion until she came to a large envelope that wouldn't fit. She tried rolling, folding and wedging it, and finally yanked it out of the box in disgust and dropped it on the front door step. She slammed the front panel shut, and wheeled her little satchel carrier past my car, muttering under her breath.

I said, "I guess that deal about rain, sleet and dark of night goes right down the tubes when you get a big envelope."

"Bite me," she said, and kept on going.

I tuned the radio to a jazz station for a while, but eventually killed it when they started to play too much fusion and I got worried about running the battery down. I smoked a cigarette & swigged some bourbon. An old guy with two miniature schnauzers straining at the leash went by. He called them "Duchess" and "Duke" and gave them biscuits from his pocket. Tenants drove up in beat-up cars and sat idling while the automatic gate creaked open to let them into the parking area. They parked, walked back up the ramp and activated the gate behind them before checking their mail and going into the building.

Several hours passed and it grew dark. Then it began to rain — hard. Water seeped in through a window on the driver's side that I could never get to roll all the way up. The bourbon gave out shortly thereafter and I was forced to bury the bottle at sea in the puddle of water that had formed at my feet.

By 11:30 I was ready to pack it in. No one who vaguely resembled Terri McCulloch had entered or left the building, and no lights were visible in the back window of the apartment I figured to be hers. I had my hand to the starter key when the headlights from a dark-colored BMW raked the windshield of my car. I ducked instinctively, then watched as the BMW angled into the parking spot directly in front of me. The driver killed the motor, fumbled around inside for a moment, stepped out into the road. It was Roland Teller.

Teller paused to turn up the collar on his raincoat and then slogged across the street to the entrance of the apartment building. Instead of buzzing to be let in, he surprised me by producing a key that unlocked the door quite handily. I tracked him through the glass panels of the lobby as he climbed the stairs. He disappeared down the second floor hallway, and a short time later a light came on in the back window I had been watching.

I played a little game of water polo with the whiskey bottle before deciding to go over and see what Teller was up to. After grabbing my set of burglary tools from the glove box, I pushed open the car door and sprinted across the roadway to the eaves of the covered parking area. I slithered over the gate and landed with a splash. A sheet of rainwater was advancing across the concrete floor, turning the mounds of oil-soaked cat litter under many of the autos into grimy little islands. I walked along the carport to the back of the building and went up the fire escape stairs to the second floor platform.

If I was hoping the damage from the other day had gone unrepaired, I was in for a disappointment. Not only had the doorknob been replaced, but a cheap-looking dead bolt had been installed above it. The pry bar would buy me exactly nothing, so I knelt in front of the door and began gouging away at the keyhole with a pair of lock picks. For a professional working in a dry, well-lighted setting, the miserable dead bolt would have taken about two minutes to open. For me — working by the light of a bare 30-watt bulb in a driving rainstorm — it took fifteen. By the time I lurched through the door, my suit jacket was plastered to my back and my knees were permanently tattooed with the sharp diamond pattern from the rusted metal flooring.

I rambled down the dimly lit hall, dripping water, caroming off walls. I reached Terri McCulloch's apartment and stood in front of it. Pausing to slip the 9mm automatic from its shoulder holster, I twisted the knob and nudged the door open slowly.

Roland Teller stood in the middle of the apartment facing the wall unit, his back towards me. In one hand he held a bottle of beer, in the other a framed photograph. I said:

"Simon says act surprised and foam at the mouth."

Teller probably didn't jump three feet. The photograph flew from his hand, cracking as it hit the floor. Beer from the bottle splashed him in the face. He stood tensely for a moment, then slowly craned his neck around to look at me. "Damn you, Riordan," he said sharply. "What in the hell do you think you're doing here?"

"Good job on the surprise, but I know you can foam better. A more important question is what are *you* doing here? Did you come back to renegotiate your deal with

Terri McCulloch?"

Teller turned full around and pulled out a handkerchief to wipe his face. "You've got yourself figured for a real smart monkey, don't you Riordan? You've always got some wise ass comment to make, or clever little stunt to pull. Well, you've just reached the limit with me, bucko. This one's going down on account for repayment."

I was wet, frustrated and more than a little drunk. It struck me later that Teller and I had more to gain by putting our heads together than duking it out — but that was later, much later. I shoved my automatic back into the holster. "If you're looking for trouble," I said, "I'm ready to introduce you."

Teller glanced behind me and smiled maliciously. "Meet some yourself."

There was a quick movement at the edge of my vision that I tried to dodge: no sale. Somebody landed a blow on the back of my head like a mine shaft collapsing. My knees buckled under me then and I tumbled down into darkness of the mine, Teller's harsh laughter echoing as I fell.

Chapter 14

teller leaves the board

"*A*RE YOU DEAD, or what?"

I pried open my eyes and squinted up in the direction of the querulous voice. I was lying on my back in the middle of Terri McCulloch's living room, the obese landlady from downstairs standing to one side, prodding my temple with her foot. She was wearing a loud green bathrobe that made me think somebody's shower curtain was missing. A wave of nausea rolled over me.

"Get lost Broomhilda," I growled, "you're making me sick."

"You've done plenty on your own to make yourself sick, I imagine." She kicked a little harder at my temple. "I was leaving anyway. I've got to go down and open the front door for the cops."

I watched her trundle out of the room and then rolled over on my side and levered myself up on all fours. My head throbbed like an oriental gong, and my stomach did the dipsy-doodle as I turned. I felt like a passed kidney stone. With a supreme application of will power, I sat back on my haunches and surveyed the room from an upright position.

If I wasn't completely sure why she had done so before, I now gained a full insight into the landlady's decision to call the police. Roland Teller's dead body lay smeared across the carpet not three feet away.

One arm was wrapped across his chest, the other, bent at the elbow, lay above his head. His legs were tangled in the cloth of his raincoat — a garment he hadn't been wearing when I surprised him. His face was a death mask done in white paraffin, the dull, half-open eyes like slits torn in a pillowcase. The obvious cause of death was a pair of neat bullet holes that pierced his thick, muscled neck just above the collar. The carotid artery had been cut, spilling rivers of blood onto his shirt and suit as he died.

Dark red blood. Not the shiny pink stuff Hollywood stunt men make from food dye and corn syrup, but the real stuff that flows out of wounds and clots and gets black and ugly and turns your stomach to look at. That kind of blood.

I didn't have the time or inclination to make a thorough search of his clothing, but I forced myself to pat down the pockets of his raincoat and suit jacket. I found a cellular phone, car keys, a roll of mints, a pocket comb, and oddly, a sealed business envelope with what looked like a ticket or coupon inside. I didn't know whether it was a ducat to this Sunday's Forty-Niner's game or 25 cents off my next package of dental floss, but I folded the envelope over and shoved it into my hip pocket.

Two uniformed bruisers on patrol car duty were the first to arrive. They swept into the apartment with revolvers drawn, arms extended and knees slightly bent, barking "freeze, police" at the top of their lungs. I was waiting for them in the middle of the room with my hands already laced behind my head.

"This is as cold as I get," I said cheerfully.

They showed me how much they liked that by shoving my face into the wall and putting a gun to my ear. The younger one patted me down, finding my 9mm in its holster and the set of lock picks I had used on the back door.

Fortunately, he overlooked the envelope I'd taken off Teller. After cuffing my hands behind my back, they frog marched me over to the dinette set and pushed me into a chair.

I gave them the *Reader's Digest* condensed version of the story, keeping Bishop's name and the exact reason for my visit out of it. Now that I was safely under wraps, the patrol cops listened and spoke with polite reserve, but their faces said they believed the things I told them about as much as they believed I was the King of Prussia. I had been through the story only one and a half times when two detectives walked in with the landlady in tow.

The one name Holtzman was short, red-faced and chunky. He had wispy blond hair and looked more like a donut cook than a police detective. Stockwell, his partner, was better typecast. He had a tall wiry frame, gray-flecked brown hair, and a face set in stone. His chin in particular looked hard enough to split logs. After speaking for a time with the patrol cops, Holtzman pulled the landlady into the kitchen for questioning and Stockwell came over to give me the benefit of his sunny disposition.

Stockwell wasn't a big fan of *Reader's Digest*, and evidently wanted something more along the lines of *War and Peace*. "Look Riordan," he said flatly, "I don't have time for hand-holding cheapie private investigators who are squeamish about giving out their client's name. Unless you supply the name of the person you're working for and the real reason you came up here, I'll be more than happy to let you take the fall on this one. We cops are kinda old fashioned in our ways. We find two guys in an apartment — one dead and the other carrying a gun under his arm — we just assume that the guy with the gun might've had something to do with the other guy being dead. It's crazy, but that's how it works."

"Come on detective, you know my gun hasn't been fired. Besides, those holes in Teller's neck weren't made with a cannon like mine. That's the kind of damage you get with a .22."

"So you brought a pea shooter in your sock and tossed it out the window just after you plugged him."

"Then there is the little matter of my being found unconscious by the landlady."

"Easy enough to fake for a clever Joe like you. And one thing you aren't gonna talk your way around is the lock picks we nabbed you with. That's breaking and entering and unlawful possession of burglary tools. I can have your license pulled for less than that."

I was beginning to see this was an argument I couldn't win. "Okay, I give," I said. "But do me the courtesy of keeping my client's name out of the papers. This is already enough to put me in real tight. I don't need to have him reading about himself tomorrow morning at breakfast."

Stockwell shrugged. "I'll see what we can do, but no promises. Now spill it."

I told him how Bishop had hired me to recover his software and how Terri McCulloch and Teller were involved, and about the conversation I had with Teller in his office. I explained that I hadn't been able to locate McCulloch up to now, and that a lot of her friends were doing their best to make sure I never did. I left out a few details here and there, such as the fact I had broken into Terri McCulloch's apartment on my first visit and found a .22 caliber revolver and that I had a piece of potential evidence sitting in my back pocket. Stockwell was particularly interested in my conversation with Teller. He had me go over it several times and asked me repeatedly if I was sure that Teller had identified Terri McCulloch as the individual he'd bought the chess game from. I assured him that Teller had picked McCulloch, but emphasized that he had apparently thought he was dealing with Bishop's legitimate agent.

When I'd finished telling the story for the third time, Stockwell rocked backed in his chair to think. Then: "You got any ideas on this?"

"None that you haven't thought of. If Teller was duped into buying the chess game from Terri McCulloch, then it figures he would go to see her about getting his money back once I tipped him to the play. He was probably waiting for her when I walked into the apartment. She arrived a minute later and bopped me over the head. Teller and she argued over the money, then Teller got too rough for her to handle. She shot him down and left me holding the bag."

"Yeah, the deck's stacked pretty heavy against her right now. I also like her for using the .22 caliber. That's a woman's gun."

It might even be *this* woman's gun, I thought. Sometimes I didn't know when to keep my own mouth shut. I said, "There's still a couple of things that don't quite figure though."

"I'll bite," said Stockwell.

"Well, first of all, how did Teller get a hold of the key to Terri McCulloch's apartment?"

Stockwell dropped the front legs of his chair to the floor abruptly. He leaned his forearms on the table. "That's easy, Riordan. They were playing house together. She gave him a copy of the key a long time ago. You said yourself that the landlady was complaining about all the visitors she had."

"Okay, point to you. His being hooked up with Terri McCulloch would also explain why he seemed so at home in the apartment — guzzling beer from the fridge and all. But the other thing isn't so easy to get around. I don't see her hitting me on the head from behind. One, she didn't have any real motive for it, and two, that's about the last thing in the world I would expect a woman to do in that kind of situation."

Stockwell chuckled. "You don't like the idea of it being a woman that knocked you out, that's all. Besides, she had a great reason for sapping you. She knew you were onto her game, so she wanted to make sure you weren't around to question her or stop her from pumping two quick ones into her boyfriend."

Holtzman had come back from the kitchen and was trying to get Stockwell's attention, so I decided to give it a rest. Stockwell got up to compare notes with Holtzman, and then the two detectives herded me and the landlady out of the apartment, down to a pair of waiting patrol cars. Several newspapermen converged on us as we came out of the building, but the detectives weren't talking for publication. A flash from one of the press cameras went off in my face just as I was being shoved — hands still cuffed behind my back — into the lead car.

We were driven to the East Palo Alto police station where Stockwell put me through my paces for two more hours. After a lot of warnings and tough talk about losing my license they released me. The landlady, it turned out, had been driven back to the apartment house an hour earlier, but an unexpected shortage of cars prevented them from providing the same service to me. I called a cab.

The driver was a chatty little bird who insisted on giving me his views on the rather arcane subject of women's fashion. After a great deal of study and close observation he had developed what he called "Hooper's three laws of women's wear." I can't remember what the first two were about, but the third sticks with me: all women's earrings that dangle from the earlobe look like fish lures. There seems to be something to that.

I picked up my car and drove back to my apartment in San Francisco. It was about 3:30 in the morning when I arrived. I stripped off my clothes and collapsed into bed like a demolished building. I fell asleep instantly, but the person who leaned on my doorbell less than one half hour later did not want me to stay that way. I pried myself off the mattress, donned a bathrobe and buzzed open the outside door. When a knock sounded on the apartment door I yanked it open, expecting to find Stockwell smirking like a hyena, having remembered just one more question he wanted to ask.

Chapter 15

terri comes calling

*t*HE TIGRESS on the other side of the doorway didn't resemble Stockwell even faintly. She was sleek and dark and radiated sex appeal the way a Franklin stove radiates heat. She just about wilted me. She wore a black bolero jacket made of ultra-suede with little puffs at the shoulders over a flame-colored silk blouse. A long string of onyx beads trimmed in gold lay in the deep valley between her breasts. Her hips were poured into black leather pants that merged at her ankles with a pair of short, black boots with pointed toes and long spike heels. She had fluffy black hair and dark eyes with lashes that didn't quite tickle her chin when she batted them.

She also had a pearl-handled .22 automatic pointed at an uncomfortable spot between my eyes.

"Terri McCulloch," I said, "or pushy Avon lady — which?"

"Not funny, Riordan," she said. "Not even mildly amusing. But we'll make allowances for the lateness of the hour." She lowered the gun to chest level and backed me into the apartment. "Now I want to know what happened tonight."

Standing less than a foot away, I caught the faint scent of her perfume. It was like breathing rarefied air at high altitude. "I'm sure I'd like to tell you," I said. "But I respond better to the carrot than the stick."

A smile tugged at the corners of her mouth. "Sure Riordan, I understand. I fuck you and then you tell me everything you know. Well here's a little down payment to loosen you up." She reached her fingers round the back of my neck and pulled my head to hers. Cushioning her lips against mine, she probed my mouth with a hot tongue that darted around like an agitated tropical fish. Her mouth tasted of fire & liquor. She stepped back when she was done and looked up at me with a kittenish expression.

Then she slapped my face.

"Plenty more where that came from," she said.

My face stung where she hit me and I felt hot and foolish. I grabbed for the gun and she danced out of reach.

"That was none too bright," she said. "Think you'd be any smarter if I opened a hole in your head for your brains to breathe?"

"If that's the same pitch you made to Teller, you were off by a good six inches."

Keeping the gun leveled on me, she kicked the door closed. "Shut up and sit down on the couch."

I backed into the living room and started to sit in the middle of the couch. "Not there," she said sharply. "Sit at the end near that monster speaker." She laughed. "You know, the era of the vacuum tube has come and gone."

"So has the era of the tough-talking, hard-bitten moll."

"And the new age bitch has taken her place." She reached behind her and produced a set of handcuffs. She slung them onto the couch. "Look familiar? Lock one on your wrist and the other through the handle of the speaker—and make sure they snap shut."

I did as she asked. The Altec Lansings have a metal handle bolted to either side to make them easier to carry, but they each weigh over 60 pounds. I wasn't going anywhere fast. I said, "I guess you're pretty handy with the restraints, Mistress Tamara."

"Can't have a party without them." She settled into a high-backed chair across from the couch. She held the gun casually, but there wasn't any doubt where the muzzle was pointing. "I wish I hadn't let Chuck talk me out of that session in the dungeon. I could have had quite a lot of fun with you." She looked me up and down and smirked, as if she knew all my secrets. "You could be broken, Riordan. Easier than you think. But the really surprising thing is you would like it."

It might have been the blows to the head, or the lack of sleep, or the mesmerizing, almost predatory nature of her attraction, but I halfway believed her. And it scared me. "What are you here for?" I said, wanting to change the subject.

"Like I said before, to find out what happened."

"Forgive me if I sound a little jaded, but it seems to me you're the last person in the world to be asking that question and I'm the last person in the world to be answering."

"Since I'm holding the gun, maybe you'd find it in your interest to get a little unjaded."

"I might. I might at that. But while we're on the topic of the gun, where did you get it?"

"It's my gun. I got it from my apartment — this evening."

"And having gotten it from your apartment, did you use your little gun to shoot Roland Teller — who was also in your apartment — twice in the neck?"

Terri McCulloch leaned forward in her chair and gripped the automatic in both hands. "You sure take some chances. If I had shot anybody, I'd have no compunction about ringing your sale up, too. There were *two* men lying on the living room floor of my apartment when I got there. You and Teller. I thought you were both dead, but you groaned when I lifted your wallet to check your name."

"What time did you get there?"

"It was around 12:30. I can't tell you the exact time."

"Let me guess. If you didn't shoot Teller, I suppose you're also going to tell me that you weren't having an affair with him."

"No. Of course not."

"Then what was he doing with a key to your apartment?"

She slammed the butt of the automatic down on the arm of the chair. "I don't know what Teller was doing with a key to my apartment," she said savagely. "What's more, I don't know what he was doing bleeding on my rug with two bullets from my gun. I don't know any of these things. Quit asking me all these mysterious questions and tell me what the fuck happened."

I didn't like to see her pounding the gun on things while

it was pointed my direction. "Don't slip your trolley," I said. "There isn't much to tell. I was parked out front waiting for you to show when Teller drove up. He went in through the front door and up to your apartment. I came in the back way and surprised him. We were snarling at each other when somebody hit me from behind, and when I woke up Teller was dead."

"And the cops think I did it?"

"They probably wouldn't except for three little things: motive, means and opportunity."

"Why don't you refresh my memory about the motive part. It seems to have escaped me."

"Does this ring a bell? You stole Bishop's chess software and peddled it to Teller, who thought he was buying legitimate goods. Teller found out he'd been cheated and came to you to get his money back. Things got out of hand and you killed Teller to keep the money. And, if one thinks the way a certain police detective named Stockwell does, we could add that you were having an affair with Teller, which explains how he had your key and would also cause Teller to be even more angry when he found he had been cheated."

She stared at me for a long moment. "Okay," she said. "I see what's going on."

"You gonna let me in on it?"

"No."

"This is going to sound trite, but if you really didn't kill Teller, the best thing to do is to turn yourself in and tell your story to the police. The longer you stay out, the worse it's going to look."

"Thanks for the sage advice."

I yanked on the handcuff in frustration. "You're standing in the boiler room of the *Titanic* with the water coming up to your waist. Whatever revenge you hoped to extract from Bishop by stealing his software is down the chutes at this point. At worst, you've helped his lawyers earn a fat fee for suing Mephisto to recover it. If you give up now and return the chess game to Bishop, I doubt he would press charges. Then assuming you're really in the clear on the Teller killing, you could walk away and everything would be jake."

She looked at me pityingly. "You're forgetting that Mephisto could still try to nail me for fraud. Besides, I never said I stole the software."

I squeezed my temples with my free hand. "Right," I said. "Let's just make a quick tally of the problems with that idea. First, you should have said, 'Who's Mephisto?' or something similar since I never mentioned them before. Second, Teller told me he purchased the software from you. Third, why send Hastrup and his band of hard cases after me as soon as I was hired? And fourth, there's the tired old business of what Teller was doing at your apartment with a key."

"Whatever."

"Sorry to be a bore. You mind telling me why you and Bishop had a falling out?"

She laughed. "Oh, Edwin failed to explain that, did he? He'd become impotent. Well, virtually impotent. It got to the point where the only way he could get off was in extremely submissive roles in S&M. He held me responsible for his condition. Said I'd emasculated him with my dominant sexuality, or some such thing. In the end he couldn't stand to have me around the house because he associated me so closely with his problem."

"*Were* you responsible for his problem?"

She leaned back in her chair and rubbed her knees

together slowly, looking at me from under her lashes. I vibrated like a tuning fork. "If little boys are going to play with fire," she said. "They may get burnt. Think you could handle the heat?"

I tried not to gulp. "I heard a different story," I said in a strained voice. "I heard you had a little too much Special K and went into a coma."

"A K-hole."

"A what?"

"When you overdose on K, you go into a K-hole. It's like you have tunnel vision. All your senses shut down except for what you can see and hear through the tunnel. But that's bullshit. I've never OD'ed on K."

"You sure seem to know a lot about it."

She stood up, still covering me with the gun. "Yeah, I know a lot of things about drugs and sex and inflicting pain. Anything else you'd like to get educated on? Ask me now because I don't intend on seeing you again."

There were a dozen more things I wanted to know, but I knew she wouldn't tell me. On a whim I said, "Just one thing: what do you have tattooed above your breast?"

Her lip curled provocatively. "Oh, you know about that." She undid the first three buttons on her blouse. She pulled the silk material aside, cupped her right breast, leaned down. She was wearing a black half-brassiere and I could see the dark brown semi-circle of her areola peaking out above it. Above that was a three-inch long tattoo of an insect done in dark green ink.

"It's a praying mantis," I said, surprised.

She straightened up and stepped back, rebuttoning her blouse. "You got it. Did you know that the female praying mantis will devour her mate after sex, if the male praying mantis is dumb enough to hang around? It gives her extra

nutrients to bear her children. Scientists say that by stud-
ying many generations they've found a trend that more
and more males are staying around to get eaten. In other
words, the males are being bred to sacrifice themselves to
the females through natural selection."

This time I did gulp. "If that's your world view, you
might want to get together with a bartender I met down
in North Beach."

"Huh?"

"Never mind. I just hope you're one half as tough as you
think you are, Terri."

"Wait and see." She stepped forward and shoved the gun
right under my chin. "Hold still now," she said, digging the
chrome barrel into my throat. She leaned over and I felt
her soft hair tickle my face. She flicked her tongue across
my lips, drew it broadly across my face to my ear. "Here's
a little something to remember me by," she whispered, her
breath warm and moist. She bit down violently on my earlobe. I yelped and felt the blood drip down my neck immediately. I shoved her away from me, forgetting the gun.

She wiped her mouth with the back of her hand. "Hope
you had your shots," she said. "Now don't go looking for
me anymore because next time I'll just bite your head
clean off. Just the way a mantis does."

I blotted my ear with the sleeve of my robe. "You'll have
a lot more people looking for you from now on. And tell
Hastrup and Nagel and that black guy to back off because
I'm through playing the patsy."

She looked at me with a queer expression. "You're not a
patsy, Riordan. You're a patzer. Look that up in your dictionary." She walked casually out of the room to the door.
"So long, my little patzer," she said, and slammed the door
shut.

spreading slightly, as a calyx. **c.** bearing the flower loose or dispersed, as a peduncle. [1610–20; < L *patulus* standing wide-open. See PATENT, -ULOUS] —**pat′u·lous·ly,** *adv.* —**pat′u·lous·ness,** *n.*

Pat·win (pat′win), *n., pl.* **-wins,** (*esp. collectively*) **-win** for 1. **1.** a member of a North American Indian people of the western Sacramento River valley in California. **2.** the Wintun language of the Patwin.

pat·y (pat′ē), *adj. Heraldry.* (of a cross) having arms of equal length, each expanding outward from the center; formée: *a cross paty.* [1480–90; var. of *pattee* < MF, equiv. to *patte* paw + -*ee*; see -EE, -ATE¹]

pat·zer (pät′sər, pat′-), *n.* a casual, amateurish chess player. [1955–60; prob. < G *Patzer* bungler, equiv. to *patz(en)* to bungle (cf. Austrian dial. *Patzen* stain, blot, *patzen* to make a stain) + -*er* -ER¹]

Pau (pō), *n.* a city in and the capital of Pyrénées-Atlantiques department, in SW France: winter resort. 85,860.

P.A.U., Pan American Union.

pau·a (pou′ə), *n.* a large, edible abalone of New Zealand, *Haliotis iris,* the shell of which is used in making jewelry. [1810–20; < Maori]

pau·cis ver·bis (pou′kis wer′bis; *Eng.* pô′sis vûr′bis), *Latin.* in or by few words; with brevity.

pau·ci·ty (pô′si tē), *n.* **1.** smallness of quantity; scarcity; scantiness: *a country with a paucity of resources.* **2.** smallness or insufficiency of number; fewness. [1375–1425; late ME *paucite* < L *paucitās* fewness, deriv. of *paucus* few; see -ITY]

Paul (pôl *for 1–3, 5;* poul *for 4*), *n.* **1. Saint,** died a.d. , one of the 12 apostles and missionary to the . **2.** Alice , author of several of the Epistles. Cf. Saul . Elliot (Harold), 1877, U.S. women's-rights (zhän), pen name of Jean , a male given name: from a meaning "little".

Paul I, **1.** died , pope 757–767. **2.** Russian, **Pavel Petrovich** , 01, emperor of Russia 1796–1801 (son of Peter) 1901–64, king of Greece 1947–64.

Paul II, (Pie) 1417–71, Italian ecclesiastic: pope 1464–71

Paul III, (se) 1468–1549, Italian ecclesiastic: pop

Paul IV, (a) 1476–1559, Italian ecclesiastic: pop

Paul V, (e) 1552–1621, Italian ecclesiastic: pop

Paul VI, (Montini) 1897–1978, Italian ecclesiast

Pau·la given name: derived from Paul.

Paul-B (ôōñ′), *n.* **Jo·seph** (zhô zef′), 1873–19 nd statesman: premier 1932–33.

Paul ndary giant lumberjack, an Amer

Chapter 16

**completely, irrevocably and
without remorse**

i WAS SO TIRED I didn't even bother with the handcuffs. I just swiveled around on the couch with my right hand above my head and went to sleep. It was 11:20 by the time I woke up.

The extra sleep must have done me good because I didn't feel nearly as bad as I had the day before. I unhooked the wires on the back of the Altec Lansing and lugged the speaker into the kitchen where I had a spare set of lock picks I kept in the drawer with road flares, duct tape and the largest collection of paper clips this side of the Mississippi. I dispatched the cuffs in relatively short order, and got some consolation from the thought that I now had a perfectly good set of handcuffs by which to remember Terri McCulloch — instead of just a nasty ear hickey.

The message light on my recorder was blinking faster than a shorted turn signal and it wasn't hard to figure who had called me so many times. I pressed the reset button on the recorder without listening to any of the messages and dialed Edwin Bishop's number. Jodie answered and I said:

"This is Pacific Gas and Electric. Is your refrigerator running?"

"No," she said. "I'm not going to catch it. Boy, August, are you in trouble."

"It's just a harmless crank call."

"You know what I mean. I'll go get him."

Jodie put me on hold and I was treated to several minutes of 18th-century violin concerto until that clicked off and Bishop's high-pitched voice came through. "Bishop here," he said.

"Hello Mr. Bishop. This is Riordan. I expect you've heard from Lieutenant Stockwell."

"Where have you been? I've called your office and home repeatedly."

"Today's the day I have my sea water colonic."

"I hope you find yourself amusing because I certainly don't. Where have you really been?"

"Asleep. Fast asleep."

"I see. I suppose that's not surprising. Well, let me say right up front that you are fired. Completely, irrevocably and without remorse — fired. Lieutenant Stockwell gave me a full account of the events at Terri McCulloch's apartment, and try as I might, I could not identify a single redeeming feature in the narrative. I told you I wanted to secure the return of my chess program without involving Terri or me with the authorities. Not only have you failed to retrieve my software, but you have managed to link

Terri and myself to a murder investigation. To top it off, the initial report of this disastrous performance comes not from my paid employee, but from a representative of the police department. You are a complete incompetent, Riordan. I am sorry I ever hired you."

"Yeah, that makes two of us. But you should take a clear-eyed view of the situation before you lay the whole piroshki at my door. The person who killed Roland Teller is the one who's responsible for your involvement in a murder investigation, not me. At the moment, Terri McCulloch is the leading candidate for that honor, as I'm sure the police have told you."

"That may be so, but none of it would have happened if you hadn't bungled the search for Terri. In any case, this debate has no bearing on my earlier statement. Our association is at an end. Good-bye Mr. Riordan."

"Hold it," I put in quickly. "One last question. You wouldn't happen to know what the meaning of the word *patzer* is, would you?"

There was a pause. "What an odd question. Is this another one of your little bon mots?"

"No. Straight goods. Just tell me what it means."

"A patzer is an inferior or amateurish chess player. It comes from the German word patzen, which means to botch or bungle. I believe that word came up earlier in the conversation, didn't it? Now, good-bye."

I kept my ear to the phone, listening to the buzz of the dial tone. I thought about Hastrup and Nagel and Terri last night, and I began to get very angry. I slammed the receiver down and a chunk of the plastic broke off and clattered to the floor. I was not walking away from this, Bishop or no. It wasn't about money, and it wasn't about doing the right thing, and it certainly wasn't something romantic like seeking the truth at all costs. No — it was about me not drinking myself stupid tonight in a shabby bar feeling like I was a loser.

I took a couple of deep breaths, ruffled my hair and went downstairs to get the afternoon paper.

When I returned, I made myself a cup of instant coffee and poured out a bowl of my favorite kiddies' cereal — the kind with the bright-colored marshmallows. I scanned the paper while I ate and found Teller's murder had been given prominent coverage in the Peninsula news section. The story was correct as far as it went, but a lot of the why's and wherefore's were missing. The tenant of the apartment was not named, nor was a motive given for the crime. Teller was identified as the victim of the shooting and was described as the savvy president of well-respected Silicon Valley software firm. I got credit for discovering the body and was nominated as a possible suspect in a quote from Stockwell. A nice 5x7 picture of me being shoved into the police car ran beside the article.

I showered and dressed, then got on the phone again to talk with Stockwell down at police headquarters. "You didn't waste any time getting hold of Bishop, did you?" I asked when he came on the line.

"No we didn't, and you're lucky that he corroborated everything in your statement or we would have hauled your ass down here pronto. Now what do you want?"

"I called to compare notes."

"I only compare notes with people I'm working with on an investigation. Yesterday was your last day on this case, so you don't have anything to compare. Get it?"

"Of course, Lieutenant. I understand. But have you figured out who shot Teller?"

Stockwell let out an exasperated growl. "Terri McCulloch shot him. We issued a warrant for her arrest at 8:00 AM this morning."

"Still gnawed by doubts, huh?"

"Go ahead, ride me. We have an eyewitness who puts McCulloch at the apartment house late last night. The landlady saw her go into the building at 12:25, and she saw her leave around 1:00. That timing fits with the information you gave us. In addition, we discovered that McCulloch has a .22 caliber hand gun registered in her name, and we found a cloth in her apartment with traces of gun oil, which suggests that a weapon had been kept there recently. Q.E.D. Case closed."

"I bet you found a lot more of interest in the apartment than an oil-soaked rag," I said.

Stockwell didn't say anything for a moment. Then he grunted. "Yeah, that was quite the collection. I guess you kind of made yourself more at home there than you told us. The landlady said someone recently busted the fire escape door, Riordan. If you really want us to tag you for it, I'd prefer a typewritten confession in triplicate."

"Sure, and people in hell want ice water. What about the chess game? Did you find Bishop's software in the apartment?"

"No, we didn't find any floppy disks, hard disks, optical disks, CD-ROM's, tape cartridges, PCMCIA cards or video tapes."

"What are PCM-whatever cards, and who said anything about video tapes?"

"That's the list Bishop gave us. Now look, I've spent more time talking to you than I do with my wife most nights. Think we could wrap this up?"

"Wait. What if I told you that Terri McCulloch came to my apartment last night?"

"Are you telling me she came to your apartment?"

"Yes. She was here."

"And?"

"And she said that she didn't shoot Teller and she didn't know who had."

"Oh, could she supply any information on the Kennedy assassination then?"

"Never mind, Lieutenant. It's just a gag."

"Call me when it gets funny," he said and hung up.

I pulled my lower lip out and let it snap back against my teeth. The business about the videotape was interesting. I wondered how Bishop would feel if he knew I still had the tape I had taken from Terri's apartment rattling around in the trunk of my car. That reminded me about another item I had taken from the apartment. I went to the bedroom and fished Teller's envelope from the pile of clothes I had dumped on the floor last night. I tore off the top of the envelope and shook out the paper inside.

It was not a ticket or coupon as I had thought, but a numbered claim check from a computer repair shop in the city. It was dated a week prior. I went back to the phone and called the shop.

"Good afternoon," answered a male voice. "PC Doctor."

"This is Roland Teller. I brought in, ah, some equipment last week and I wondered if it was ready." I read off the number from the claim check.

"Just a minute, sir." He was gone for less than a minute.

"Yes, Mr. Teller, your laptop is ready. We replaced the bad memory, so you're hitting on the full 64 meg now."

"Groovy," I said. "What are your hours today?"

"We close at eight tonight."

I told the man I'd see him well before then and hung up. It was too early in the day for whiskey, so I settled for a

Bloody Mary. I take mine without tomato juice and I substitute bourbon for the vodka. I paced around the living room with the drink, succeeding only in clearing a path through the layer of dust on the hardwood floor. I quit my trailblazing when the bourbon was gone and got in my car and drove off to meet the good PC Doctor.

Chapter 17

i'd rather be a hammer

POST STREET ends at Market in a crazy three-way intersection with Montgomery, causing cars to well up like water in a dammed stream. I was fourth in line at the light when I spotted Todd Nagel in my rear view mirror. He was two cars back in a yellow VW van, decked out in his backward baseball cap and mirrored sunglasses. As a professional tail, he was about as inconspicuous as a pimp at an Amish wedding.

When the light turned green I let the cars in front of me go through the intersection, blocked traffic until the signal turned a tasteful burnt amber, then gunned the motor and barreled across Market onto New Montgomery. Horns blared and a truck driver yelled an unscholarly observation about my genealogy, but as the Galaxy sailed past the line of taxis waiting at the Palace Hotel, I turned round and saw Nagel nicely snared at the intersection. The computer repair shop was just one block east on 2nd, but instead I took a quick right on Mission, cruised west to 3rd and then doubled back to Market. Nagel was nowhere to be seen by the time I came back through the Montgomery intersection, so I kept going to 2nd and buried my car behind a dumpster in a connecting alley.

The PC Doctor was housed in a small storefront with a bright orange sign that featured a dopey picture of a guy dressed up in a lab coat and stethoscope with a round mirror strapped to his forehead. He was putting a tongue depressor into the floppy drive of a personal computer that had an ice bag on top of the monitor and an unhappy expression on the screen.

A woman in a long, dirty coat made of fake fur stood by the entrance, hawking copies of the *Street Sheet* — a gritty little journal produced for homeless people. I told her to keep the paper for the next sucker, but dropped a dollar into her cup before going inside.

I passed the claim check over to the earnest-looking kid behind the counter who went to the back of the shop and returned with a laptop computer, placing it just out of reach in front of me. "Excuse me," he said. "I don't believe you are the same person who dropped the computer off. Did the owner ask you to collect it?"

I gave the kid an easy smile. "Sure," I said. "I work for

Mr. Teller. Didn't he call you? He said he was going to call and let you know I was coming by."

"Well, yes, he called. But he didn't say anything about sending someone else."

"I have the claim check, right? It's not like I stole it out of his pocket. But if you're not comfortable, I'll ask Mr. Teller to come by himself. I don't think he'll be too happy, though. He was counting on using that laptop." Just like he was counting on staying alive, I thought.

Another customer came into the store. The kid looked at him, then back at me, then made up his mind. "That's okay. If you will just sign the repair invoice so we have a record."

I told the kid I'd be happy to sign and forked over the 225 bucks he wanted for the repair. I left Todd Nagel's name on the invoice, tucked the computer under my arm and went back to my car to see what I could make of it.

I unfolded the hinged screen and punched the power button. The operating system booted up —Windows NT, as I was informed in large letters — and eventually the "desktop" came into view. There were graphic icons for a variety of applications — electronic mail, word processing, spreadsheets, overhead presentations and Internet browsing — and a corresponding set of data files. After a few minutes of nosing around, it became clear that I didn't really know what I was looking for. There were a number of game programs on the computer, but none of them seemed to be chess-related. Even if I did manage to locate the chess program, I wouldn't recognize the source code for it if it did a line dance across the screen. I powered off the computer with the idea of calling Chris Duckworth for a little expert advice. But before that, I decided Mr. Nagel's continued attentions required me to brush up on some of my home repair/do-it-yourselfer skills.

I called several hardware stores and a couple of lumberyards before I found what I wanted at a construction equipment rental place in South San Francisco: a gun used for driving nails into masonry and concrete. I put the gun and several of the explosive cartridges used to fire it into a burlap bag along with some three-inch masonry nails and dumped it in my trunk. Stopping briefly at my apartment to pick up the Glock automatic, I drove on to North Beach and parked in a choice spot on Chestnut Street, across from the entrance to The Power Station. I rounded up a 32-ounce beer in a giant go cup and a fistful of peanuts from a sports bar on Bay, and then went back to the car and settled in with both guns — nail and bullet — loaded and sitting on the front seat next to me.

It was pushing six o'clock and the sky was overcast and growing dark. Across the way, a tiny spot shown on the plaque with the club's name, and yellow light glowed from the high, industrial-looking windows of the first two stories. When I cracked the window so I could light a cigarette, I heard the elaborate clanging of a cable car bell as the conductor showed off for the tourists waiting at the nearby turn-around.

An hour went by with little activity. A cab pulled up to drop off a Power House patron — a fat guy with dark curly hair wearing chinos and a turtleneck — and two middle-aged women came out of the club arm-in-arm, tittering as they walked up the street. At about seven I saw what I was waiting for. A white van cruised the block towards Mason. There were no parking spaces along Chestnut, so the driver turned left at the corner and drove slowly out of view. I holstered the Glock and gingerly returned the nail gun to the burlap bag, carrying it with me as I double-timed it to the corner. The van was parked about 30 yards up on the right, and I arrived just in time to see Chuck Hastrup step out, slam the door and check to see if it was locked. He haltingly whistled the old Marty Robbins' tune *El Paso* as he ambled my way. I ducked behind a parked car and then snuck back to The Power Station, situating myself in the narrow alley between the old brewery and the adjoining apartment house.

I picked up Hastrup's whistling again, and gradually it grew louder. He appeared at the mouth of the alley just as he was struggling through the part of the tune where the cowboy meets Felina at the cantina. I had always found it a little too convenient that the girl's name rhymed with cantina, but at least it was better than Dagmar at the fern bar. I said:

"Howdy partner."

Hastrup turned. I landed a horrific punch that spread his nose like jelly on toast. His head snapped back and blood flowed from both nostrils. Stepping in close, I grabbed two handfuls of his wool blazer and brought my knee up on an express ride to his groin. He gave a strangled cry, lurched forward, toppled to the ground.

"Now tell me you're happy to see me," I said.

Hastrup responded with a moan and heaved a good quart of his dinner onto the sidewalk.

"You silver tongued devil, you. But I'd go easy on the menudo. Looks like it doesn't agree."

I retrieved the nail gun from the burlap bag, then grabbed Hastrup by the collar and dragged him into the alley. "Stand up," I said sharply, pulling him by the hair. He rose on wobbly legs and I shoved him against the brewery wall. I held the gun close to his face, the tip of the masonry nail an inch or so from his ear. His eyes got wide and pleading.

"Think of this as a sort of heavy duty stapler," I said. "And hold still or I won't be responsible for what gets stapled." I crammed the gun under his armpit, pulling the fabric from his coat and shirt so that it lay sandwiched between nail and concrete. Squeezed the trigger. The gun jolted with a flat report like a slamming door. A puff of dust blew out and the nail was buried the full three inches. Hastrup whimpered. A dark stain spread from his crotch like the Nazi blitzkrieg shown on the map of Europe. I reloaded and fired three more times, nailing him fast to the wall.

I stepped back and glared at Hastrup. His nose had swelled to a full-scale copy of Edison's first light bulb, the lower half of his face was streaked with blood, and his shirt was fouled with vomit. He looked like death on a cracker. "Chuck," I said. "I really can't begin to repay all the kindness you've shown me. But this is a first attempt. If you want to dissuade me from further efforts, I suggest that you answer all the questions I'm about to ask. *Comprende*?"

Hastrup looked up at me with unconcealed malice. He gathered saliva in his mouth and spat. The spittle dropped to the ground in front of me. "Fuck you," he croaked.

"I guess we were due for some spit. We've had just about everything else out of you." I walloped him twice in the stomach. His breath blew out and he lost his footing, leaving him thrashing on the wall like an insect pinned in a killing jar. I waited for him to collect himself, then pulled the Glock and pressed the barrel to the temple of his hanging head. "This one doesn't shoot nails, Chuck. Now why is Nagel still following me around? The cops have issued a warrant for Terri's arrest. At this point, I'm the least of her worries."

Hastrup temporized, then sputtered, "I don't know any-one named Nagel."

"Todd Nagel — a rangy-looking guy with baseball cap, mirrored sunglasses and VW van. You don't know him or recognize that description?"

"No."

"Then how did you know I would be at the jazz club?"

Hastrup lifted his head. "Dale and I followed you there from your apartment."

"Dale's the black guy?"

"Yeah."

"What about Terri's friend, Jodie? What's her angle? Are you sure she didn't tell you I was at the club?"

"Like I said: Dale and I tailed you there. I don't know anything about a Nagel or a Jodie. They must be imagi-nary friends of yours. Or maybe Jodie's the name of your inflatable doll."

I grabbed him around the throat and shoved his head against the wall. "You're the one who makes his living guarding perverts at club canker here. You know Jodie. She's a member or employee or something."

"Okay, okay," said Hastrup. He reached his hands towards his throat but thought better of it when I dug the gun into his temple with a twisting motion. "I know her — barely. Just to say hello. As far as I know, she isn't involved in ... in this at all."

"You're about as credible as Nixon's press secretary, you know that? Let's see how you do on this one. Where's Terri McCulloch?"

Hastrup shook his head, awkwardly. "Forget it. I'm not giving her up."

I tightened my fingers on his throat, but I knew I didn't have the steel to really put the screws to him. "How would you like one of those nails driven through your foot?" I bluffed. "You know I'm just looking for an excuse to tear you apart."

"Go ahead, you bastard. Think no one would hear me yell? You're lucky someone hasn't come by already."

"They'd only offer to lend a hand." I leaned into him, bringing our faces less than an inch apart. "Tell me where she is. She's going to get caught eventually. She's not worth getting maimed for."

"Big talk, Riordan. You don't have the stomach. You're nothing but a pathetic little man in a pathetic little business."

I released my grip on his throat and took a fist full of his thinning hair. I slammed his head against the brick wall. Again. "Tell me where she is," I screamed. I stepped back, trembling. Somehow the idea of bluffing was getting lost. Hastrup's head lolled and saliva dribbled from his mouth. "Fuck you," he mumbled. "I'm not giving her up. ...I love her."

I forced several deep breaths into my lungs. I needed to get out of there before I lost it entirely. "That's just great," I said after a moment. "A romantic thug. Have you two got your wedding pattern picked out? Something in a lovely black iron, no doubt."

I put the Glock back under my arm and gathered up the nail gun and the burlap bag. Hastrup watched me suspiciously, not believing I was finished. I patted him on the cheek, said, "That's right. I'm leaving you to your fate, pally. You're already in more kinds of trouble than I can think up. It's not for nothing she's got that bug tattoo."

I started to walk away, then turned back. "And Hastrup, don't ever come near me again. I'll give no more thought to emptying a clip into you than I would peeing on a urinal cake."

I went up the alley and across the street to my car. If I thought I was going to have the last word, I was wrong. Hastrup started yelling obscenities at me as soon as I put the key in the lock. I piled in the Galaxy, slammed the door shut, and slipped in a Miles Davis tape. With the volume cranked up, all I heard was Miles' cool trumpet as I oozed down the street.

Chapter 18

dead man's mail

CHRIS DUCKWORTH lived in a modest, Castro district Victorian in which someone had managed to find eight apartments. If Duckworth's was any example, the someone would have done better to divide the number by two. Duckworth lived on the top floor in a cramped garret directly under the roof.

I had called from a pay phone in North Beach to see if he would be willing to help me with Teller's computer. As it turned out, he was more than willing: he was positively eager.

"I can't wait to see what we find on that bastard's laptop," he said as he let me in.

"Don't get your hopes up," I said. "I couldn't find much. And you shouldn't speak ill of the dead."

"Yeah, right. I'll just dance the tarantella on his grave instead. You want a drink? I've got beer, wine and a bottle of rotgut whiskey some misguided soul gave me for Christmas."

"A tall glass of the rotgut, please. No ice."

Duckworth went into the kitchen and started pulling open cupboards and drawers and clinking glasses. I sat down with the laptop in a canvas director's chair and looked around. The place was decorated in quirky modern. There was a low couch with a fantastic curved back upholstered in a shiny blue material. In front of that was a round coffee table made of burnished aluminum, and on the walls hung a pair of spare line drawings that were either abstract nudes or renderings of the twisted wreckage of the Hindenburg — I wasn't sure which. There was also a fairly conventional table with a set of four chairs that had bright orange seat cushions. The kicker was a parking meter on a five-foot metal pole, embedded in a concrete block. It was rooted next to an arm of the couch, giving the impression you had to feed it for sitting time.

Duckworth came back from the kitchen and handed me a tumbler of caramel colored liquid. I sniffed it and took a sip. Jack Daniel's: a far cry from rotgut. "Nice place," I said. "But I wasn't aware the Department of Parking and Traffic was in the habit of loaning its meters."

Duckworth plunked down on the couch with a glass of white wine. He smiled. "It's possible they are not fully apprised of the arrangement. They were widening Church Street and my friend and I requisitioned this one from the fenced area where the meters were stored. Maybe like you requisitioned that laptop. Are the police in the habit of loaning out evidence in a murder investigation?"

"*Touché*. But right now there's nothing that says it's evidence of diddly-squat. I'll turn it over if we find anything relevant."

Duckworth took a sip of wine, pinkie finger extended. "August," he said. "I saw that article in the paper about Teller's death. The one with your picture. It said you were a suspect. You didn't really have anything to do with it, did you?"

I grinned at him. "Yes, once you told me Teller had fired you I went right out and plugged him. You're giving me too much credit — or too little. I try not to be on the business *or* trigger end of a gun if I can avoid it. Anyway, the person the cops actually suspect is Terri McCulloch. They're probably right, but I do have some evidence to the contrary."

"What do you mean?"

I told him about Terri's late night call at my apartment. I meant to stop at that, but couldn't think of a reason not to bring him fully up to date with the events of the day. "So if you believe Hastrup," I said at the end. "Nagel is an independent. And Jodie ... well Jodie is at least not working with Hastrup. She could still be working with Nagel and/or Terri or she could be on the level."

"How will you find out?"

"I think I'll tackle Nagel next. I know he lives in Daly City, so it shouldn't be too hard to locate him."

"While you chase down Nagel, why don't you let me check out Jodie for you, August? She'll have no idea who I am, so it'll be easy for me for me to sneak up on her and stake her out — or whatever you call it."

I held up my hand. "We've already been over this. I appreciate the offer, but this is the kind of work I have to do by myself. I'm not even getting paid at this point." I hefted the laptop. "Here's where I can use your help. Now how's about we do a little electronic gumshoe work?"

Duckworth reached over and took the laptop out of my hand. "Jeeze, August," he said with disgust. "Don't try to dress it up by calling it 'gumshoe' work. I'm not that gullible."

He put the computer on the coffee table and powered it up. I brought my drink and chair around so I could watch the screen while he worked.

"I couldn't find the chess program on the desktop," I said. "Of course, what I'd really like to find is the source code so I can bail myself out with Bishop."

Duckworth did some manipulations with the mouse and brought up a program called Explorer. He typed in some gobbledy-gook and clicked on a button labeled "Search."

"I just entered a search pattern to match the name of the chess program file," he said. "Not every application on a computer's hard disk has to appear on the desktop. If Teller wanted to be a little more discreet, he might have installed it in a way that kept it off. But even if he has the program, I doubt he will have the source. Teller wasn't technical enough to make use of it — and it really wouldn't make sense for him to go parading around with a valuable corporate asset like that loaded on his laptop."

As Duckworth was talking the computer popped open a

file folder with a graphic icon. "That's it," he said. He double-clicked on the icon and after a moment a chessboard was painted on the screen. "This is an alpha test copy. That may be why Teller didn't have it formally installed."

"Okay," I said. "Let me make sure I understand something. This is the same program you showed me at The Stigmata, even though it doesn't have all the virtual reality hocus-pocus."

"I could set up the board in the same position from Anderssen and Kieseritzky's 'Immortal Game' to prove it, but there's no need. I recognize the software. Like I said before, just because the user interface is different, doesn't mean the underlying smarts are different. Think of it like a brain transplant. The same brain can run the virtual reality version, the PC version, and in fact, there's even a third."

"What would that be?"

"It looks like a regular chess board with real chessmen, but there are pressure sensitive pads in the board to track the position of the pieces as you move them and a microprocessor that runs the software. But chess computers like that have been available for years. The new virtual reality interface is the thing with sex appeal."

"Yeah, maybe for nearsighted 14-year-old boys with bad skin."

Duckworth rolled his eyes. "It's just an expression. A marketing term."

"All right, enough about the attraction of modern technology. What about the source code? Is it there?"

"I don't think so. The search pattern I used before should also have found at least a few files in the source tree. I can try looking for any C++ files on the hard disk. I know the program was written in that language." Duckworth went through some more machinations with the Explorer program, but after waiting for a time with the cursor changed to an hour glass, the program spat back: "No matches."

He shook his head. "Sorry August."

I took a big slug of my drink. "I guess that's it, then. There's no point in giving the program we found to Bishop. You can't recreate the source code from a program, can you?"

"Nope. You can decompile it into assembly language, but that's not the same thing. But don't throw in the towel yet. Don't you want to see what else we can find?"

"Give me a for instance."

Duckworth picked up his wine and swirled it around. He smiled. "Well, I for one would have loved to have hacked Teller's e-mail while he was alive. I'm all the more interested now that he's dead."

"What? You mean you can dial into work and look at his e-mail messages?"

"No, we would have to have his password for that. But we can read any messages he might have retained on his laptop. You see, there're basically two kinds of e-mail programs: those that keep your e-mail messages on a central file server and let you read it from there, and those that copy it into a local file for you to view. At Mephisto, most everyone used the second sort, so it's entirely possible there will still be a snapshot of Teller's correspondence on the laptop."

I gestured with my glass. "Hack away, geek boy."

"Way to galvanize me into action," muttered Duckworth. As it turned out, there was very little action required. He simply located the e-mail program on the desktop menu and started it up. I was a little embarrassed

I hadn't thought of it on my own. The window for the program popped up, and we could see a listing of about a dozen e-mail message headers. Each header showed the message subject, the name of the sender and the date it was sent. I immediately saw two headers of salient interest, but Duckworth's eye was drawn elsewhere. "Look at that," he said. "The bastard wrote an e-mail about me." Duckworth double clicked on a header that had his name in the subject. Another window opened with the message:

To: nopenshaw@mephisto.com (Nancy Openshaw)
From: rteller (Roland Teller)
Cc: rteller (Roland Teller)
Subject: Chris Duckworth
Nancy,

As I have mentioned to you before, Chris Duckworth's behavior is often insolent and flippant, so much so that it borders nearly on insubordination. This morning as I came through the lobby I found him combing out a woman's blond wig on a Styrofoam head. When I told him that I didn't consider this an appropriate activity for the company receptionist to engage in, he told me "not to get my knickers in a twist" and suggested that he could comb out my toupee when he was finished.

I do not wear a toupee!

Nancy, as head of Facilities, all shared administrative personnel report to you, including Chris Duckworth. I expect that you will make clear to him that this sort of performance will not be tolerated. Furthermore, I strongly suggest that you place him on probation with the understanding that one more incident like this will result in his termination.

Thank you.

    --Roland

"I'm so misunderstood," sniffed Duckworth, and wiped an imaginary tear.

"Yes, I see how everyone misinterprets your attempts to reach out. Now if you are done wallowing in the artifacts of your wrecked career at Mephisto, I would be interested in reading the pair of e-mails Teller seems to have exchanged with Terri McCulloch."

Duckworth returned to the list of headers and double clicked on a message that had apparently been sent to Teller by Terri about two months prior. It read:

To: rteller@mephisto.com (Roland Teller)
From: mantis_girl@aol.com (Terri McCulloch)
Subject: Software Licensing Proposal
Dear Mr. Teller,
My name is Terri McCulloch and I represent Edwin Bishop. As I am sure you are aware, Mr. Bishop is a very well respected name in the software game industry. In addition to personally developing a number of extremely successful game programs, including the seminal video arcade game "Pest Control," he founded and took public the game company, Ajeeb, which today has a market capitalization of over $750 million. While Mr. Bishop has set aside the burden of corporate operational management, he continues to have a strong interest in game development. His most recent effort in this area is a computer chess program dubbed "The Turk," which we can say with confidence is vastly superior to any chess program on the market. Mr. Bishop has matched The Turk against several highly ranked Grand Masters in tournament play, with the result that The Turk has defeated the human players in eight out of ten games.

Mr. Bishop is now seeking a publisher to distribute his game.

He has a great deal of respect for Mephisto, Mr. Teller, and is particularly impressed with the user interface technology in your company's offerings. We believe that the marriage of The Turk's underlying chess strategy engine with your user interface technology would be an unbeatable combination.

With this goal in mind, Mr. Bishop has asked me to contact you to open negotiations for licensing his game to Mephisto. If you are interested, please respond by return e-mail and suggest a time when we might meet for a demonstration of the program and an initial discussion of terms.
Thank you for your consideration.

> Regards,
> Terri McCulloch

"There's your smoking gun on the software theft," said Duckworth. "If you needed one. What's with McCulloch's 'mantis girl' e-mail alias do you suppose?"

"You don't want to know. Let's take a gander at the next message."

Duckworth brought up the text:

To: mantis_girl@aol.com (Terri McCulloch)
From: rteller (Roland Teller)
Cc: rteller (Roland Teller)
Subject: Re: Software Licensing Proposal
Dear Ms. McCulloch,
Thank you for your recent e-mail regarding the possibility of licensing Edwin Bishop's new chess software. While I respect Mr. Bishop's work and would very definitely be interested in exploring an arrangement to license the game, your method of approach is little unusual.

I'd like to suggest that you call me at the Mephisto offices so that I can get a better understanding of your authority to negotiate on Mr. Bishop's behalf. I'm sure you can appreciate that it would be very easy for someone outside Mr. Bishop's circle to send an electronic mail message claiming to negotiate for him, especially as he is not a public person and tends to reclusion.

Also, as you are perhaps aware, Mr. Bishop and I once had a business dispute of a relatively serious nature. Therefore, I am somewhat skeptical of his interest in negotiating with me now.

In any case, I will look forward to your call.

Best regards,

Roland Teller

Duckworth leaned back on the couch and locked his hands on top of his head. "Hmm," he said. "I guess Teller wasn't quite so dumb after all."

"Yeah," I said. "I'm sure he was fine until he talked to McCulloch — and more importantly — saw her. Then she probably put a collar on him and led him around the block on a leash."

"Ha! And you still don't think she murdered him?"

"I never said I didn't think she murdered him. I just said there was some evidence to the contrary."

"You should get a job in physics splitting atoms," said Duckworth. "You do a great job on hairs."

"Right. You got any more tricks in your bag?"

Duckworth sipped his wine, and then began manipulating the mouse and the keyboard. "There are two more things we can try that might be of interest. First of all, we can bring up his word processing program. Nowadays, almost all word processors keep track of the last four or five files that you've edited on the file menu. If we see anything interesting we can bring up the document and look at it. Sort of like pressing the redial button on a phone."

A word processor came up on the laptop screen. Duckworth went to the file menu and clicked the left mouse button. A list of four files was shown at the bottom of the menu before the exit option:

1 C:\DOC\Company Address.doc

2 A:\To-Do.doc

3 C:\DOC\Bishop Agreement.doc

4 C:\DOC\Board Meeting.doc

Duckworth immediately selected the "Bishop Agreement" document. "File not found," came the response.

"Nuts," said Duckworth. "He must have deleted it."

"If it was the contract for licensing the software, I'm almost surprised he had a copy in the first place. You'd expect the company lawyers would prepare that."

"He could have asked for a soft copy to review," said Duckworth reasonably. "Or it might have just been the rough terms for the agreement — not the final contract."

"Yes, I suppose. What about the to-do list? Can we look at that?"

"Sorry, August. The entry references the floppy drive and there's no floppy loaded."

"Okay, what was your second idea?"

"It's similar. We can bring up his web browser and look at the 'bookmarks' he's set up to see what web sites he's been visiting." Duckworth killed the word processor and double clicked on the icon that represented the World Wide Web browser. As it came up, the program complained that the computer wasn't connected to the

Internet, but Duckworth was still able to select the Book-marks menu entry. He laughed when he caught sight of the listing:

1. http://www.playboy.com
2. http://www.penthouse.com
3. http://www.animal-instincts.com
4. http://www.bootybarn.com
5. http://www.pantyman.com
6. http://www.girlswithgirls.com
7. http://www.pornobuffet.com
8. http://www.pussy4free.com

"It's all the same with you breeder boys," he said. "Big tits make the world go round."

"I don't even want to know what *you* think makes the world go round." I slugged down the rest of my drink and stood up. "Thanks for your help, Chris. I'll be sure to give you a whole chapter in my memoirs."

Duckworth chuckled. "If you want, I can hang onto the laptop and do some more digging. There may be other stuff I could turn up with a little more time."

"No, given what we found, I think we have to turn the computer over to the cops." While Duckworth powered off the laptop and folded it up, I walked over to the parking meter and plunked in a quarter. "There's a little hard currency for your efforts," I said.

"My appreciation knows no bounds," he said and passed over the computer.

I said good-bye and drove home to my first night of normal sleep in what seemed like a very long time.

Chapter 19

daly city bondage

i HAD SEEN Todd Nagel's address when I looked at his wallet at Fisherman's wharf, but I could not recall the street or the number. Finding them turned out to be as easy as calling information and asking. He lived in the 300 block of Palisades Drive, a street that paralleled the Pacific Ocean in the northwest part of town, less than two miles from the San Francisco city line.

I was feeling well rested, well breakfasted and peaceful, so rather than jumping on the freeway with all the morning commuters, I got on Geary and drove west to Point Lobos and the start of the Great Highway, which ran north and south along the beach. I drove south past the Cliff House and the ruins of the Sutro Baths, through Golden Gate Park and by the Dutch Windmill that looked out on the area where the Bay to Breakers race finished, down a long stretch of the highway — where sand dunes and bicyclists bundled against the morning chill were the main features of interest — onto Skyline Boulevard, past Lake Merced and the attendant golf courses and across the line into Daly City. The sky and ocean remained a featureless gray, and there was a heavy moisture in the air that had me running the creaky wipers on the Galaxy the whole way down.

Nagel's house was in a neighborhood filled with houses exactly like his. It was a two-story California stucco special, with the bulk of the living space layered on the second floor above the garage. The main things that distinguished the house from the rest on the block were the fresh yellow paint job, the well manicured lawn with a plot of yellow and purple flowers I didn't know the names for, and a "For Rent" sign tacked on the garage door. I couldn't see into the back yard, but from looking at a map I knew the lot must butt against a strip of parkland that ran along the ocean in this area. Daly City was not exactly a top-drawer address, but given the ocean view, the size and the condition of the property and the general prosperity of the neighborhood, this was a house that must rent for at least $1600 a month. Somehow Nagel and $1600 a month did not seem to go together. I wondered if the landlord was trying to evict him so that he could rent the place to a better prospect.

I walked across the lawn on irregularly shaped flag-stones to the side of the house where a flight of stairs led up to the door on the second floor level. The door was painted purple and had a buzzer in the middle. I pressed my elbow against the holstered Glock for reassurance and then leaned on the doorbell. The bell made an interesting mechanical chime, but more interesting still, the door slipped the latch and swung partially open. I nudged the door open further with my foot and called out:

"Candygram. Candygram for Mr. Nagel."

If Nagel was there, he wasn't answering. He also wasn't making use of any furniture. With the exception of a half-filled plastic trash bag and a discarded light bulb, the living room I looked into was empty. I stepped inside. The carpet still had depressions from a couch and other furniture, and several logs remained stacked in the grate of the fireplace. A large window at the back of the house looked out on the yard, and beyond that, a green strip of bramble and eventually the beach and the ocean.

I moved across the room to the adjoining breakfast nook and kitchen. Here there were more signs of recent occupancy — and even more recent departure. There were no pots, pans or food in the cabinets, but coffee grounds covered the floor, a box of partially eaten donuts sat on the counter and the refrigerator had a moldering pizza from a popular chain. I went out of the kitchen and down the hallway to the bedrooms. There were two of these, and both were stripped bare. I was just ducking into the bathroom for a look-see when I heard a muffled thumping noise.

It seemed to come from below and behind me. I slipped the 9mm out of its holster and retraced my steps to a

closed hallway door I had bypassed on my way to the bedrooms. The noise was much louder here. I gripped the
knob, turned it carefully, pushed the door open. It gave on
darkness and a set of concrete steps leading down. I
flicked on the light and the thumping noise got louder,
more urgent. A kind of strangled bellow joined with it.
Going down the steps, I found myself in a utility room at
the back of the garage. The room had concrete walls, a
concrete floor with a drain, and along one wall were a
washer and a dryer. Along another were a metal sink and
a tall wooden cabinet. The noises came from the cabinet.

Aiming the Glock in front of me, I jerked open one of
the cabinet doors. Chris Duckworth lay face down on the
floor. His hands and feet were hog-tied behind him with a
good ten yards of duct tape, and his mouth was taped shut
with a strip that ran all the way around his head. He was
wearing a gray sweat suit. His eye looked up at me with a
wild expression, and he tried to say something through
the tape that might have been my name. I said:

"Don't get up on my account."

He said two words with urgency that probably ended
with "you." My first instinct was to free Duckworth, but I
didn't want to end up in the cabinet next to him, so I told
him to hold tight for a minute and went through a door at
the back of the utility room that led to the garage. There
were no cars, and more importantly, no Todd Nagel lurk-
ing in the shadows waiting to jump me from behind. I
went back to the utility room, locking the door to the
garage behind me.

I holstered the automatic and fished out the Swiss Army
knife I had on my key chain. The little blade from the
knife was sharp, but its small size made it hard to put any
muscle behind the strokes. I concentrated on the band of

tape that held Duckworth's arms and feet together. When I finally sawed through it, his legs dropped like a wooden dummy's, knocking over the mop and bucket in the far corner of the cabinet. He groaned through the tape. I freed his hands and feet, then rolled him out of the cabinet onto the concrete floor. He sat up with his legs in front of him, rubbing his hamstrings with hands that shook visibly.

"I think you better do your mouth," I said. "Pulling off that tape is going to smart."

Duckworth nodded his head in agreement and groped around the ring of tape to find the edge. He picked at it ineffectually until I finally got tired of watching him, brushed his hands away and yanked off a foot or so of tape. This uncovered his mouth, but left the strip that went around the back of his head all too firmly in place.

"Jesus H. Christ!" he yelped. "I was getting to it, August."

"Yeah, and the polar ice caps are melting — but I haven't bought any water wings."

He rubbed his face. "At least I won't have to wax my mustache for long while."

"How about that. Now, I think you have a bit of explaining to do."

He looked down and away. "Yes, I suppose I do," he said and picked at the tape on his wrist. "Well, I decided you could use some help after all, and I selected Nagel instead of Jodie. I got his address from directory assistance, and then came down here early this morning. I was watching the house from my car at about 7:20 when Nagel came out and started loading stuff into his van. He brought out several loads, then closed the van door like he was finished and went back into the house. With the 'For Rent' sign and all, I thought he might be moving and I didn't want him to get away. So I snuck up the driveway where the van was parked and started letting the air out of his tires. I figured that would slow him up enough for me to call you to come down and apprehend him."

"I think you've got me confused with Dick Tracy. What were you going to do? Call me on your two-way wrist radio?"

"Come on, August. This is not a joke."

"Bingo. My point exactly."

Duckworth looked up at me. "I know what you're saying. And believe me, I'm never going to do anything like this again."

"Glad to hear it. So what happened next?"

"You can probably guess. I got a little too absorbed in my task, and the next thing I knew, Nagel had come up behind me with a knife the size of a curling iron. He put the blade under my chin and said, 'What do you think you're doing, faggot?' I was petrified. I couldn't think of a single word to say. Nagel didn't wait for an answer. He frog- marched me into the garage and through to this room and bound me up with the tape. Then he shut me into the closet and switched off the lights. A little while later, I heard his van start up and I figured he had gone. At that point, I really began to worry. I didn't know if you or anyone else would come to the house for days. I had horrible cramps in my hamstrings, and I imagined myself starving to death, locked up in that claustrophobic little space. You can't know how relieved I was when I heard someone walking around upstairs. I think I would have lost my mind if I had stayed there even 30 minutes longer."

I felt bad for being flippant earlier. "Sorry," I said.

"You know where you find sorry, don't you?" said Duckworth. "In the dictionary between shit and syphilis. But it's not your fault. You did your best to warn me off."

"Well, don't take it too hard. It could have just as easily happened to me. What else did Nagel say to you?"

"*Nada.* He didn't seem particularly surprised or angry to find me here, either. He was very efficient and dispassionate. Like he was pulling a tick off his pet dog or something."

"Hmm," I said. "Then here's an interesting question: how do you think he knew you are a little light in your loafers?"

"What a sensitive way to phrase it, August. Why did he call me a faggot, is that what you mean? I don't know. I may be a little fey when I'm not in drag, but most straights don't pick up on it. Especially when I'm doing something butch like letting the air out of tires. What's your point?"

"Just this: Nagel must have already known who you are. Which means that he was following me one of the times you and I met."

Duckworth shivered. "Then he knows where I live, and he could come back and do something else to me."

"I doubt it. If he were going to do anything particularly nasty, he would have done it when he ran into you here. And he wouldn't have left you at the house to be found."

Duckworth pressed his fists into his eyes and rubbed them. "I suppose. Let's get going. I don't want to stay another minute longer."

I pulled him to his feet. With the fragments of duct tape hanging from the back of his head and all four limbs, he looked more than a little ridiculous. "You go ahead and take off. I'm going to nose around a bit more."

Duckworth nodded his head, the duct tape fluttering like a kite tail. "Knock yourself out," he said.

I walked him out through the garage and watched him get into his car and drive off. He was still a little shaky, but I didn't think he would have any trouble making it home. I went back inside and dumped the plastic trash bag in the living room onto the floor. It was pretty slim pickings. There were beer cans, a couple of football magazines, a torn tee shirt, bubble wrap, a roll of duct tape with about an eighth of an inch left and a greasy red and white cardboard bucket with crumbs of fried chicken in it. Donuts, pizza and now this. Here was a guy who actually ate worse than I. You had to be impressed.

I went out the front door, down the steps and through a gate at the side of the house. A strip of concrete had been poured next to the foundation and corded firewood was stacked under the eaves beside a gas barbecue grill covered with a tarp. There was also a large plastic garbage can on wheels. I pulled out the pair of trash bags I found inside and plopped them onto the concrete. They were wet with dew and stunk to high heaven. Using the blade from my penknife, I slit them both open and stirred through the contents with a stick of kindling from the woodpile.

There was more evidence of Nagel's fast food diet, and of a recent oil change: four empty quart containers and a discarded filter. But mixed in amongst the debris of bad meals and auto maintenance were some of the personal papers I was looking for. I found and extracted a soggy credit card bill, several pages from a Pacific Bell phone bill and a bent manila folder. The folder was of immediate interest as it contained a set of newspaper clippings going back almost ten years — all dealing with the meteoric Silicon Valley career of Edwin J. Bishop. I shoved the bills into the folder with the clippings, and cleaned up the trash as best I could. Then I made another pass through the garage, but didn't find anything of interest.

The last thing I did before getting in my car to drive to East Palo Alto was to note down the telephone number written on the rent sign. I hoped that Nagel's landlord would be more helpful than Terri McCulloch's had been.

station break

fOR A COMMUNITY that had led the nation in murders per capita several years running, East Palo Alto's police station was surprisingly modest. It was shoehorned into the first floor of a stark office building from the mid-seventies that lacked any trappings of municipal pride. There was a McDonald's directly in front of the building on the corner of University and Bay, and as I came through the drive up window, I could see the tiny stable of squad cards behind a rolling gate in a fenced section of the parking lot.

I parked on the far side of the building and sat in the car while I wolfed down my hamburger and coffee. I puzzled over the steady stream of people with books going in and out of the entrance, until I noticed a sign that indicated the East Palo Alto library was also housed here. The night Stockwell had brought me here from the Woodland Avenue apartment house I was taken handcuffed through the prisoner's entrance at the rear and didn't have the opportunity or presence of mind to take in such details. I locked up the Galaxy and went through the double glass doors, taking Teller's laptop computer with me.

The police department was at the back, past the city council chambers and something called the "Community Room." I pushed through another glass door with the city emblem on it and walked up to the tiny reception desk. To the right, on the other side of a swinging half door, I could see into the squad room and a maze of partitioned cubicles. A large black woman in uniform sat behind the desk. She was in her mid-thirties and looked like she didn't put up with any sass. She gave me the kind of stare Hitler would get at a Bar Mitzvah.

"August Riordan to see Detective Stockwell," I said.

She nodded curtly and picked up the phone. "Lieutenant Stockwell, there's a Mr. Riordan to see you," she said. She listened for a moment, nodded, looked back at me. "He says to tell you that I'm to kick your ass through the McDonald's arches if you don't clear out of here in 30 seconds."

"Tell him it's not a gag. I really need to see him."

She complied with my request and a moment later Stockwell came charging up to the half door from inside the squad room. He was wearing a dress shirt that had been given to him many Christmases ago with the sleeves rolled past his elbows. A striped tie that was narrower than *Gentlemen's Quarterly* said it should be this year was knotted loosely around his throat. His hair was disheveled and he had a twisted red plastic coffee stirrer clamped in his teeth. He looked every inch the harried, underpaid cop that he was. "Come on, you," he said through pursed lips.

He led me back to a cubicle where you couldn't swing a 38-inch baseball bat unless you choked up. There were a couple of metal chairs that seemed even harder than the ones in my office and a scarred wooden desk with all the usual office junk. A picture of a very attractive woman with two cherubic kids stood to one side in a clear plastic frame.

"You've a very handsome family," I said, trying to soften him up.

"That's not my family, you moron. I bought the frame today — the picture came with it."

"Oh."

He took the plastic stirrer out of his mouth and grimly tied a knot in the middle of it. He pointed with it at me. "I'm going to give you a little lesson in the realities of East Palo Alto police work. And for once, you're going to shut up and listen."

"If you say so."

"Yes, I do. I'll bet you think I'm pleased to be assigned to a high profile case like the Teller killing. I'll bet you think I'm putting all my time into it expecting to break it big and make myself a name in the department. I'll bet that's what you think, huh?"

"I guess you're looking for a straight man here, Stockwell. Okay, sure, that's what I think."

"Well, you're wrong. I wish to God Teller had gotten his ten blocks west in white-bread-with-mayo Palo Alto. I would have dragged his corpse over the line if I thought I could have got away with it. A rich, prominent Silicon Valley executive shot dead in East Palo Alto is the last thing we need. Not here, not now. We already got more than we need. We got drugs on every corner. We got black gangs. We got Latino gangs. We got turf wars, robberies, muggings, knifings and drive-by shootings with all the trimmings. We got 17-year-old hookers propositioning customers while they wait in the McDonald's drive through — right in front of the police station. We got bars with blue lights in the bathrooms so the junkies can't find their veins to shoot up. And we got the rest of the frightened citizenry sleeping in their bathtubs at night so the stray bullets don't kill them in their sleep. We got all that on the smallest tax base of any city in the area, and as a result, a totally undermanned and under-gunned police force that can't even afford shotguns in all the patrol cars."

"Understaffed," I said.

Stockwell looked at me stupidly. "Huh?"

"You should have said understaffed. Undermanned is not politically correct."

Stockwell threw the plastic stirrer at my chest. "Fuck politically correct. Did any of what I just said register with you? Or have you been too occupied monitoring my goddamned word choice."

"I get it, Lieutenant. You're too busy keeping your head above water to make the Teller case a priority."

"No," said Stockwell. "I don't have a choice about the Teller case. It is a priority. I've been told that personally from the mayor on down. I also happen to have about 12 other cases that are priorities, including a double homicide of two five-year-old kids. But that's not the point. The point is I'm too busy keeping my head above water to waste time dicking around with you. I thought I had made that crystal clear the last time we talked."

"Things have happened. Things you should know about. Look, I'm trying to do the right thing here, but you sure aren't making it very easy."

Stockwell took a deep breath and let it out slowly. He folded his arms and sat back in his chair, looking me over.

"What's your grift, Riordan? Bishop told me he fired your ass. Why are you still nosing around in the embers?"

I wasn't sure how much I wanted to let my hair down. I said, "When I took this case I told Bishop that I had re-solve — resolve in spades. Let's just say I know I haven't played this one as smart as I could and I don't want to walk away with the score as it stands. I'm going to see it through."

Stockwell shook his head. "That's putting a pretty face on it, Riordan. You feel like you've been made a fool of and you want to get even. It's that simple. Problem is, there's no one to get even with. Not really. The only thing that's left to do is clean up the mess: find Terri McCulloch and put her in jail. Any chance you had of doing what Bishop really hired you to do is long gone."

"Some of what you said is true, but not all. I think there's more to be done than just clean up. For one thing, there are still players flitting around who aren't on the program."

"You mean Nagel."

"For one."

"Okay, let's dispense with the quilting circle chit-chat and get down to it. Just what do you have for me?"

"Right. Exhibit A: Roland Teller's laptop computer." I set it on the desk in front of him.

Stockwell stared down at it like it was a ticking bomb.

"Just where in the hell did you get this?" he demanded.

"At a repair shop," I said. "Where it was being fixed. Because it was broken."

"There's cause and effect for you. It was at a repair shop because it was broken. We've been looking all over for this thing. Teller's wife and the people at Mephisto told us he used it heavily, but nobody could locate it among his other possessions. How did you know to get it from the shop?"

"I swiped the claim check off his body the night of the murder."

Stockwell reddened and pulled savagely at his tie. "That's it, Riordan. That's the I-beam that breaks the camel's back. I've turned a blind eye to all your other shenanigans, but tampering with evidence in a murder investigation — I'll not lie down for that. I'm throwing the book at you."

"Calm down, Stockwell. Don't inflate your air bag. I didn't tamper with anything, and in a way, I did you a favor. The computer was at a shop in San Francisco. I can just imagine the kind of cooperation you would get from the big, tough SFPD when you called them to retrieve it. They probably would have kept it for weeks and then maybe held a press conference to toot their own horn. And there's not a thing you could have done about it."

Stockwell looked at me sullenly and I could tell I scored a hit. "Okay," he said. "I'm not saying you're right, but it could be that this will make things a little easier. But if I find you've twiddled so much as a single bit on this computer, I'll—"

I cut him off. "I know," I said. "You'll have my nuts for neckwear — or something equally colorful. I didn't touch the computer. But on it you'll find an e-mail from Terri McCulloch pitching Bishop's software to Teller."

"Ah-ha."

"There's also one back from him that says he needs some proof she's legit."

"Yeah, well, that was before she got to swallowing his sword. After that, he'd be putty in her hands."

"So you're sticking with the theory they had an affair. What does his wife say about that? Did she think Teller was fooling around?"

Stockwell avoided my eyes. "There we get into a little of that extra helpful SFPD cooperation you were talking about. Teller's widow lives in the City — in Pacific Heights. I couldn't get her to come down here so I had to go up there to interview her — in the presence of a San Francisco detective and her high priced lawyer."

"Yeah, so?"

"So Teller made some big contributions to the mayor's reelection campaign, and the mayor let it be known that the widow is to be treated nice. I only got a half hour with her and I didn't get answers to half the questions I asked."

"Including the one about the affair?"

Stockwell ran his fingers through his hair. It didn't make it any less disheveled. "She says they were separated. She says she wouldn't know if he was seeing anyone else."

"But you didn't believe her."

"No."

"What else did she say?"

"Nothing more that I'm going to tell you, Riordan. Now have you shot your wad or are you now going to pull the address where Terri McCulloch's gone to ground out of your ass?"

"No, I'm not. But Chuck Hastrup knows."

"Says who?"

"Says him. We had a little, ah, meeting of the minds,

and I got that definite impression. It would have taken bamboo under the fingernails to get anything specific, but maybe you'd have more luck with him."

"That will involve still more cooperation from the San Francisco cops. They've questioned him once already, and they're supposed to arrange a meet for me tomorrow morning."

"Might be a good idea to put a tail on him."

Stockwell found a scrap of paper and made scribbles on it. "Let me just write that down so's I don't forget," he said.

"Put a t-a-i-l on him. Golly, Riordan, you're good."

"You'll need a wider tie if you're going to be witty and debonair, Stockwell."

Stockwell picked his tie off his stomach and looked down at it. "What? What's wrong with it?"

"Nothing. It was a cheap shot. Look, there are a couple of other things I need to tell you and they both pertain to Nagel. First off, he's still following me around. Like I said before, if we really are at the mopping up stage with this business, then tell me what's his angle? And by the way, Hastrup says he doesn't know anything about Nagel either. Second, he's flown the coop. I went down to Daly City this morning and he had just moved out of the house he rents there. As in just this morning."

"Okay, I already alerted the Daly City cops about him, and they were at least a little more polite than the SFPD. I'll follow up."

"Thanks."

"Don't thank me, Riordan, because I'm not doing it for you. I'm doing it because it's my job. Now this is the last time I'm going to warn you: butt out. If I find you sniffing around my heels once more, I run you right in. And you know I've got more than enough to make it stick."

I stood up and reached my hand over the desk to Stockwell. He hesitated a moment, then shook it. "Thanks for your time, Lieutenant," I said. "I can thank you for that, can't I?"

He looked at me sternly. "You're still not having any, are you Riordan? You still think you're going out there to tilt at windmills. So be it. Maybe some time in the sneezer will do you good."

I went out of the squad room through the half door to the reception area. The big black woman was still behind the desk. I told her Stockwell would have been happier after all if she had kicked my ass through the Golden Arches. Her face assumed the sympathetic expression of a granite headstone, and I went out of the building to my car.

Chapter 21

party time in pac heights

i DROVE BACK to San Francisco and double-parked on Ellis behind my building. That was definitely thumbing my nose at the parking gods, but I didn't plan to be in my office long and I hoped the press placard would keep the meter maids at bay for the duration of my visit.

Mercifully, when I got upstairs Bonacker was nowhere to be seen. I found Gretchen at her desk munching on a tuna fish sandwich with a lot of sprouts and other weedy stuff sticking out of it. She was wearing a black body stocking and a pair of black jeans. Her hair was pulled back in a short ponytail tied with a gold ribbon.

"Hi Auggie," she said between bites. "I see the bruises on your face have turned a lovely putrid green. For you, I believe that's the equivalent of rosy cheeks and a healthy glow."

"Thanks for noticing," I said dryly. "I wonder what signs your urologist friend looks for in his patients. Rosy cheeks might be one at that."

"Don't start with me, August."

I held my hands up in a placating gesture. "Just returning serve. Any messages?"

"Tony Lutz called about a gig tomorrow night. They're playing at Undici and he wants you to sub for Howie."

"Undici — good. You can't get a string bass up in that loft, anyway. Electric's the only choice."

"Why? What's wrong with your bass?"

"Nothing. I just took it in to have the keel hauled. Do me a favor. Call him back and tell him I'm on for the gig and get all the details."

"Okay. And don't think I'm buying that keel hauling business."

I grinned at her and set Nagel's phone bill and the slip of paper with the landlord's phone number down next to her tuna sandwich. "Thanks," I said. "You're a doll. Just two more things. Go through that phone bill and find out who all the numbers belong to — particularly the ones in the Bay Area. Just dial and ask if you have to. Second, give that other number a call. It's from a 'For Rent' sign on a vacant house in Daly City. Find out anything you can about the prior tenant, a Mr. Todd Nagel. I especially want to know his forwarding address."

"Oh, joy. Another career enriching assignment."

"Better than filing insurance forms for Bonacker."

"Barely."

I thanked her with more fervor and went into my office. I didn't expect Teller to be listed in the San Francisco phone directory, and a quick check confirmed my expectations. Plan B in cases like these was to call an acquaintance I had at Pacific Gas and Electric. This was usually cheaper than bribing someone in the Department of Motor Vehicles and didn't involve suborning a state employee — something I try to avoid. I got my man, Jason Jones, on the line and he looked Roland Teller up on his computer.

"Sweet," he said. "You're rubbing shoulders with a better grade of people, August. The deadbeats you typically have me run are almost always behind on their utility bill — if we haven't cut 'em off already. This here's a Pac Heights address. In that part of town they spend more on personal trainers and pet psychologists than they do on electricity. Of course, I should point out that the bill for this little domicile topped $600 last month."

"I'll take the address and phone number," I said. "And hold the jaundiced commentary on the life-styles of your betters."

Jason dictated a phone number and a Lyon Street address to me, finishing with: "And August, please do try to avoid an embarrassing reoccurrence of the sort of problem I alluded to earlier: late payment. I expect to receive my 50 bucks in the next couple of days. Or else."

"Or else what?" I said, winding him up.

"Or else you may experience a sudden and unexplained service outage at your own apartment."

"But that would be misuse of your authority."

"Ain't it the truth," he said cheerfully.

I hung up on him and hustled downstairs to my car. There weren't any tickets on it, but a bulky UPS driver in those ridiculous brown shorts they make them wear was eyeing the car with uncharitable thoughts in his heart. I had blocked his delivery truck next to the curb.

"Hey," he said. "You can't just double park wherever you like."

I said, "Write that one down and tape it to your rear view mirror."

I piled into the car and maneuvered it through downtown traffic to Pine Street. I headed west on Pine all the way to lower Pacific Heights and then went north on Lyon and started up the hill. Pacific Heights wasn't called that for nothing. As I crested the rise at Pacific Avenue I could see the steel gray waters of the Bay, dotted with sail boats and cut here and there with the white wake of a tug boat or a ferry heading across to the green foothills of Marin County. I had lost track of the street numbers, but I guessed I was in the right vicinity, so I coasted a block further to where Lyon and Broadway both dead-ended and parked at the corner.

This was quite the neighborhood. Lining Broadway to the right were some of the most expensive houses in Northern California. They were all shapes and styles — like crazy capped teeth done by different dentists in the same mouth. To the left was the boundary of the Presidio, the sparse branches of wispy cypress trees overhanging the rough rock wall that delineated it. In front of me was a stone balustrade with a break in it for stairs that led sharply down the hill and the resumption of Lyon Street. From the head of the stairs I could see the pink-hued rotunda of the Palace of Fine Arts, the full sweep of the Marina neighborhood that the 1989 quake had damaged so badly, a thicket of masts from the sailboats tied up at the yacht harbor and so on to the Bay. Runners doing stair work charged up and down the steps, and a couple sat on the balustrade alternatively admiring the view and chewing each other's faces.

I trudged back up the hill and soon realized that the rambling Mediterranean style house on the corner was the one I was after. The Broadway Street side was a towering wall of terra cotta that rose up from an ivy covered slope. Screened by eucalyptus and oak, it had a number of false balconies with black-trimmed windows set just under the tile roof to take in the view. Along the Lyon Street side grew more oaks and a monster bottlebrush tree. Coming up the sidewalk, I passed a short drive that led to an opening in the wall for a one spot garage and following that a stout wooden door with a weathered brass plate that read, "Tradesmen's Entrance." I wasn't settling for that, so I went further along the walk until I came to a broad drive paved in brick leading to a courtyard nestled between the wings of the house. Arcaded galleries ran the length of each wing, and at the far end of the courtyard was another, much larger garage with a Lexus and a BMW parked inside. The front door was positioned midway down the near gallery, through an arch partially covered with ivy.

There were flashier houses in the neighborhood, but this one had a 1920's elegance that wasn't breaking a sweat to show its class. I was surprised. I had expected something much more parvenu from Teller.

I rang the bell and after a long wait a blonde woman holding a wineglass opened the door. A snow-white terrier shot out from behind her and attached itself to my trouser leg. "Who are you?" asked the woman in a soft voice.

"Buster Brown," I said. I pulled my foot forward, drawing the dog with it. "And this is my dog Tige."

She gave me a weary smile. "I don't think so. Tige was a pit bull. Not that I'm old enough to remember such things." She addressed the dog. "Ransom, get back in the house. Right now."

The dog relented and trotted back into the dark interior. I leaned down to put the cuff of my trouser leg right, and gave the woman a once over as I straightened up. She was fairly tall and thin — with hips that were a little wider and an ass that was a little flatter than she probably would have liked. Her skin was pale, her mouth and nose small, but her eyes seemed very wide and very green. I had a sudden flash of her as a child, and I guessed that she had been beautiful, but that time and hormones had taken her away from that innocent perfection. She was still a handsome woman. On closer inspection I realized that her hair was not a solid blonde, but was more of an ash blonde with blonder highlights. She held her wineglass in both hands, and there was something curious and graceful about how her long fingers curled around the bowl of it. She was wearing a black and white silk dress with a pair of black flats and sheer white stockings. I guessed she was about 40.

"Actually," I said. "My name is Riordan. August Riordan. Are you Mrs. Teller?"

She hesitated a moment before speaking. "Yes," she said. "Please excuse the dog, Mr. Riordan. He doesn't get enough exercise. I do hope you're not selling anything."

"No, I'm not. I'm investigating the death of your husband."

More hesitation, then: "But I've already spoken with several of your colleagues. The most recent, I believe, was a Detective Stockwell."

"I know. I met with him earlier today. I'm not a member of the police force, Mrs. Teller. I was hired by Edwin Bishop. As you I'm sure you know, Mr. Bishop had some business dealings with your husband — dealings of a somewhat disputed nature. The McCulloch woman, in whose apartment your husband's body was found, was a former employee of Mr. Bishop."

The woman in front of me sighed, and her face took on a far away look. For the first time I realized she was tranquilized to the gills. "And you are the detective that found my husband. I understand now."

"Yes. I know this must be a very difficult time for you Mrs. Teller, but I was hoping you could see your way clear to answer a few questions. I can't change what's happened, but there's some reason to believe that the interpretation of events the police have is not correct. I'm not convinced that your husband, well, that your husband—"

"Was sleeping with Ms. McCulloch? It was clear Detective Stockwell thought so." She brushed a non-existent hair from her face. "I've promised to go to this wretched open house. I'd sooner walk barefoot over hot coals, but I'm very active on several charitable boards and in spite of what's happened, I can't afford to drop out of the circuit altogether. And, to be brutally honest, I don't want people gossiping about me in my absence. Anyway, I must leave in another 15 minutes. I'll give you that much time if you like."

"Thank you. I appreciate it very much."

"Please come in, then. I'm having some wine and cheese to fortify myself for the party. Would you care to join me?"

I made a show of glancing at my watch. "I don't know," I said. "It is a little early in the day for cheese."

She laughed. It was a pleasant sounding laugh but it seemed to take a lot out of her. She looked at me thoughtfully. "I have a better idea. Come with me to the open house. We can talk there."

"Would that be a good idea?" I sputtered. "I'm sure your friends would think it odd that I came."

"They might think it odd, but you would be ever so helpful as protection. So, what do you say? I'm leaving now with or without you. Your only chance to talk is to come along."

"You want to use me for protection? From what?"

"From the Pacific Heights Inquisition. From the false pity and sympathy that will flood over me the moment I walk through the door. I guess you could call that using you, Mr. Riordan, but after all, you wish to use me as well. A fair exchange of services — that will be our goal. And from what I've seen of your rather rough-hewn wit, I don't think you will disappoint."

"Great. Just let me know when to spit on the carpet. That ought to be rough hewn enough for them. Are we walking or driving?"

"I suppose we could walk, but I'm not really in the mood for fresh air. Do you have a car? Would you mind driving us?"

"Yes to the first question and no to the second," I said.

She went back into the house, leaving the door open. I waited outside. She returned a moment later with a purse and a long coat, which she had draped over her arm. She locked up and we walked down to the Galaxy, where I opened the passenger door for her.

"What in the world happened to your back seat?" she asked as she sat down.

"Back seat?" I said. "There's no back seat on these babies, Mrs. Teller. It's a two seater sport model."

"Here I thought a Galaxy 500 was a family sedan. We're just going up the street to Broadway and Steiner. And perhaps you shouldn't call me Mrs. Teller. My first name is Margaret. Do you mind if I call you August?"

"That'd be spiffy." I started the car and pointed it down the street. This was going to be a trip of about six blocks. "Who are our hosts?"

"There's only one. His name is Brad Wilford. He's just gotten back from an archaeological dig. His house is being refurbished so he's leased the penthouse suite in an apartment building during the construction. This party is a sort of combination house warming and 'Hello, I'm back in town' for him."

"So he's an archeologist? Where was he working?"

Margaret Teller let out another heavy sigh. "Yes, he's an archaeologist, a mountain climber, an artist, a bicycle racer, a professional student and a one time fiancé of mine. His family has money, so he's never actually held a paying job. He just dabbles. I don't know where the digs were exactly. Somewhere in the Middle East."

I was stuck behind a pickup truck with lawn equipment and bags of cut grass. As it crept to a stop at intersection in front of us, I had a sudden desire to jump out of the car and leap on to the back of it. I wasn't liking the set up for this party at all.

We drove several more blocks in silence until we came to Steiner. Margaret Teller said, "Here we are," and gestured to the left. On that side of the street was five stories of squat, cream-colored brick building. Two valets in short red jackets stood in front on the walk. Another came up to the car window. "Are you here for the Wilford open house?" he asked.

I nodded, and he told me to pull my car around to the other side of the street. I did so, and the two guys on the sidewalk decanted Margaret Teller out of the Galaxy while I fended for myself. If they thought the car didn't belong in the neighborhood, they didn't say anything.

At the front door was another guy in some kind of servant get up. He held open the door for us and gestured to the elevator. Standing there was yet another guy in uniform. He smiled, told us to get off on the top floor. As the doors pulled back at the end of the ride, a sixth person in uniform — this time a middle-aged Latino woman — led us down a short corridor to the only door in the hall. She pulled it open and held it while we walked into the room beyond.

"What," I said. "No announcement as we enter?"

Whatever response Margaret Teller made to that was lost in the suffocating yammer of 30 or 40 people who had already availed themselves of at least two cocktails apiece. We were in a wide open room with a wall of glass at the back — affording an excellent view of the Bay — several pieces of heavy furniture pushed against the sides, and an expensive looking oriental rug that covered all but a thin margin of the hardwood floor. There was nothing special about the people except that they talked a little better, dressed a little better and rattled a little more jewelry than an equivalent number of the general populace pulled at random off Market Street. I snagged a pair of champagne flutes from a silver tray being circulated by another servant, and returned to Margaret Teller's side to await developments. They weren't long in coming.

A gangly, yeasty-looking guy who was balding in back made a show of catching Margaret's eye from across the room. He arrived next to us with a hang dog grin and some crumbs from a *hors d'oeuvre* trailing down the front of his well-pressed cambric shirt. "Margaret," he said. "I'm so glad that you made it. I'm so sorry about Roland. How are you holding up?" Then, seeming to notice me for the first time, "Oh, pardon me. I'm Brad Wilford." He put out his hand.

I gave him my name and shook his hand, despite its seeming lack of endoskeleton.

"I'm fine, Brad," said Margaret Teller. "At least for now. Dr. Hines has taken pity on me and refilled my Valium prescription. I can cope as long as those hold out."

Wilford reached across to take Margaret's upper arm and squeezed it. "We'll have dinner soon and talk." He gave me a twitchy glance. "Things will work out for the best, believe me. I know they have when I've faced hardship. To be honest, I didn't achieve the success I'd hoped at the site in Syria. But I've already found a new lease with my digital photography. You'll find something too."

"Yes, Brad," said Margaret with another sigh.

Wilford glanced at me again. "Well, I must circulate. Please take care of yourself and I will call you soon." He started to leave. "Oh, and nice to meet you August."

After he had gone, I said, "Sorry. I don't think I'm much help."

"No, you were a great help," said Margaret. "Didn't you see how rattled he was by your presence? He can't figure out what you're doing here but is too polite to ask." She tilted her head back and downed the remainder of her champagne. Tears squeezed out of the corners of her eyes. "The idiot. As if taking up something like digital photography could replace a husband."

"Maybe this isn't such a good idea," I said, suddenly developing a case of the guilts. "Maybe we should leave. My questions can wait until another time."

Margaret Teller shook her head and dabbed at her eyes with a knuckle. "No, I've got to run the gauntlet sooner or later. It's best to get it over with."

The "gauntlet," as she put it, consisted of a string of encounters with eight or nine more people. Three of them were former beaus, including another man to whom she had been engaged. When I questioned her about the high density of ex-boyfriends she explained:

"Wealthy society in San Francisco is very insular. We like to think we're big town stuff like New York or even LA, but we're not. We don't even have the heritage like Boston — we just pretend to. What you end up with is this little group of people throwing parties for each other, writing articles in *The Nob Hill Gazette* about each other and sleeping around with each other. We're more inbred than the Appalachian hillbillies — and a damn sight less honest about it. That was one of the reasons I married Roland. He wasn't part of this — at least, he wasn't at the beginning. When I met him he was like a breath of fresh air: a self-made man who worked hard for a living and wanted — I mean *really* wanted — to raise a family."

I was eager to get her talking about Teller, but at that point a couple came through the door that made Margaret wince visibly. "This is where you might want to spit on the rug," she said.

"Who are they?"

"It's Milton Carroll the Third and the woman he's currently seeing, Erica Stevens. I went to school with her. He comes from a family of very successful writers, and he tries hard to wear the mantle, but the truth is he's nothing but a hack. His last effort was a coffee table book about tequila. He's a horrid, unctuous man. I was once in a group therapy with him and he confessed to the group that he was stalking his former girlfriend because she dumped him. He expected, no, he demanded our sympathy for his actions."

Carroll and Stevens made straight for Margaret as soon as they spotted her. He was a short man of about 45 years with a fringe of brown hair surrounding an oddly shaped bald head. His features were heavy and plain, and he was wearing a blue blazer with tan slacks. The woman seemed to be about Margaret's age, but she was working harder to hide it. She had dark hair and dark skin and was wearing a dress that showed a little too much of her meager breasts. She looked about as hard to get as the time of day.

"Margaret," said Milton Carroll effusively. "I want you to know how wretched I feel about Roland's death. You must be absolutely devastated. Still, you've managed to make it out in public before the funeral — and with an escort no less. What strength you must have. Bully for you, Margaret."

"The coroner is holding Roland's body," Margaret Teller said almost inaudibly. "We can't have the funeral until it is released."

"My God, you've really have been through a lot, haven't you?" said Erica Stevens, putting her oar in with a vengeance. "First the news that you can't have children, then the separation, now this. I guess you are just inured to heartache, dear."

"I'm sure friends like you have done a lot to help," I said

quickly. Stevens got a funny look on her face as she thought that one over. "Say," I said to him. "Aren't you Milton Carroll the Third?"

Carroll grinned and puffed up about three sizes bigger. "Yes, that's right," he said.

"Your father was quite the writer," I said with enthusiasm. "Must be hard to follow in his footsteps. What was it William Faulkner said? 'Nobody is going to remember William Faulkner's son,' or something like that. Still, I just saw a book of yours."

"Oh?"

"At a garage sale. I had no idea tequila was made from cactus juice. Fascinating stuff."

Carroll got an expression like he'd eaten some bad kimchi and maneuvered the conversation to a close. He and Erica Stevens walked off. Margaret Teller watched them go with more tears welling at the corners of her eyes, but she said, "You are like a nuclear retaliation. I should have ordered a preemptive first strike."

"I don't know. A punch in the mouth would have been more effective — and satisfying. Now, how about we go somewhere quiet where we can talk?"

We wended our way through the social register until we found a small, unoccupied study at the back of the penthouse. I closed the door on the buzz of the cocktail party, and we sat down on a green leather sofa in front of a fire going great guns in a marble-mantled fireplace.

"This is much better," said Margaret Teller.

"Maybe you won't feel that way after I start grilling you," I said.

"No. Anything would be an improvement over what I went through out there."

"Yeah. I guess so. You mentioned earlier that you were

attracted to Roland Teller because he wasn't part of San Francisco society. How did you meet then?"

"He came to a party for the opening of the opera. A lot of executives from the Silicon Valley make it up for the opening. I mean, few men really *like* the opera — certainly Roland couldn't have cared less for it — but the opening is always a big thing. This party is hosted every year by a group of young business professionals. There are always a lot of single people there and it's a good opportunity to meet someone."

"Erica Stevens said that you were separated. May I ask why?"

Margaret Teller looked down and pulled at an upholstery button on the sofa. "It's not what you think," she said. "It's not because he was having an affair with another woman. One reason was the strain my inability to have children put on the marriage. We both wanted so very badly to raise a family and I had gotten to the age where getting pregnant was no mean feat. Roland was several years younger than I, you see. But that wasn't the underlying cause. The underlying cause was those people out there. Those lovely people out there." She brought her eyes up to mine. "In fact, it's not overstating it to say that they are responsible for his death."

"I can't even see your dust on that one."

"They warped him. When I met him he was a relatively unsophisticated man who had made good by hard work and perseverance. I was part of this world, true, but he was not. But the more contact he had with it, the more the Pacific Heights crowd let him know in subtle — and not so subtle — ways that he wasn't quite their caliber of person. He became very sensitive to slights — both real and imagined — at home, in the work place or on social occasions. And to change his standing in their eyes, he started doing everything he could to accumulate and flaunt more wealth and social position. I had money from my family and he amassed quite a respectable fortune from his business, but it wasn't enough. We over-extended ourselves to buy that mansion — it cost well over five million dollars — and he started running his business ruthlessly and without regard for risk, trying to squeeze as much income as he could from it."

"I think I know where you're going with this. You're saying he wouldn't have made the deal for Bishop's software if he wasn't so concerned about the bottom line."

"Not that he wouldn't have made the deal. It would have been an eminently reasonable thing to do. But he never would have negotiated with this Terri McCulloch person. He knew there was something wrong about her from the start. In fact, he told me he had broken off negotiations with her at one point."

"So you spoke about it?" I said.

Margaret Teller nodded and looked into the fire. "Yes, we still spoke regularly even during the separation. He said that he'd had a meeting with her and he came away very skeptical that she had the authority to negotiate for Bishop, even though the software she demonstrated was impressive. Later, he told her that he wasn't interested."

"When did he change his mind?"

"I'm not entirely sure. The only hint I had was several weeks later when he told me that he had a big money maker at work, and he hoped that it would redeem him in my eyes." She stifled a sob and looked up at the ceiling. Now the tears were really flowing. "He still hadn't gotten it. He still thought I was judging him the way everyone else in Pacific Heights did."

Watching this was no fun. Everything I'd seen of Teller said he was a horse's ass, but there must have been something decent in him to evoke this sort of response. Or maybe she was crying for herself. There was a pile of cocktail napkins on the coffee table in front of us. I took one off the stack and handed it to her, and then patted her shoulder awkwardly.

So what if our goofy host, Brad Wilford, chose that exact moment to stick his head in through the study door. There wouldn't have been a good time. "What kind of shenanigans are going on in here?" he said affably. "Oh — Oh, it's you, Margaret, please excuse me."

Margaret Teller stood up quickly, dabbing at her eyes. "No need to apologize Brad. I was just crying on August's shoulder." She looked over at me. "But I think perhaps we should go. I'm no good to anyone at this point."

We said our good-byes to Wilford and went back through the penthouse and down to the street. The party crowd had thinned out, but those who were left had compensated by cranking up the volume of their cocktail chitchat in direct correlation to the number of drinks they'd imbibed. Outside, it was growing dark and a stiff breeze had come up from the Bay. The valet on duty said, "Oh, you had the old Ford, didn't you?" before I even approached him.

When he brought the car around, I tipped him two bucks and told him that I preferred the term "classic" to "old." I drove Margaret Teller back to her house, and then got out to walk her to her door. We hadn't spoken since we left the study, but as we came under the arch at the front entrance, I said:

"Sorry to keep hammering on this. But in terms of actually pulling the trigger, you don't have any reason to doubt

that Terri McCulloch is responsible. I mean, Roland did-
n't say anything to you about anyone else who was involved in the deal?"

Her face seemed very pale in the darkness. "No," she
said. "I'm satisfied she killed him. I think Roland decided
to buy the software from her, even though he knew it was
stolen. I doubt he even pretended to believe her. My guess
is he told her right out that he thought he was buying
stolen property in order to get the best deal from her. He
was just that driven to make money."

"But how could he expect that Bishop would hold still
for it? And if he had bought it from McCulloch with the
understanding that it was stolen, why would she later kill
him?"

Margaret Teller let out another sigh. A sigh that had the
weight of all her suffering behind it. "I'm just guessing,
Mr. Riordan — I mean — August. But what could Mr.
Bishop do but take Roland to court? It would take years
to settle, and by then, Roland would have reaped most of
the benefits from being first to market with a unique
product — even if he lost the suit in the end and had to
compensate Mr. Bishop. As a matter of fact, Roland and
Bishop once had a dispute over a similar matter. Bishop
claimed that Roland's company had copied the user interface for one of his games. Roland told me it all came to
naught because Bishop's counsel advised him against
bringing any action. The cost and the risk of a judgment
in Roland's favor were just too high.

"As to why Terri McCulloch would kill Roland, many
reasons occur to me. She wanted more money. She was
angry that Roland had implicated her. Perhaps Roland
even refused to pay her the sum they had agreed. I just
know one thing for certain. They did not have a lover's

quarrel. Roland had changed, but he would never have had an affair behind my back."

I took a card from my wallet and handed it to her. I said, "If there's ever anything you need..." On impulse, I leaned over and kissed her cheek. Her skin beneath my lips felt soft — and very cold.

I turned quickly and walked out of the courtyard. On the drive home I felt oppressed by a vague sadness that even *The Happy Horns of Clark Terry* could not stave off.

home on the range

i HIT THE BOURBON hard when I got home, and the next morning I didn't exactly spring out of bed to do aerobics with the pretty girls wearing spandex on the TV fitness show. However, I did pay careful attention to their routines — particularly the stretches — while sitting on the couch in my boxer shorts eating raw Pop-Tarts. Who knew when I might get religion and take up strenuous exercise? I wanted to be prepared.

I was tearing open a second foil package of Pop-Tarts when the bell from downstairs went off. I got up from the couch and buzzed open the door without thinking too much about it. Then I remembered the consequences of a similar decision just three nights ago, and I went back to the bedroom and got the 9mm out of its shoulder holster where it hung on the bedpost. As I pulled open the apartment door in response to a sharp tap, I leveled the Glock at the belly button of the person in the hallway with a strawberry Pop-Tart clamped in my teeth.

"Don't shoot," said Lieutenant Stockwell. "I get killed in San Francisco by a guy in his underwear eating toaster pastry, Saint Peter's gonna send me straight to hell. There's no such thing as mitigating circumstances on a deal like that."

I lowered the gun and bit off the chunk of Pop-Tart I had between my teeth. I chewed it carefully and swallowed. "Sorry. I thought you were the Girl Scouts. They've really stepped up the pressure on the cookie racket lately."

Stockwell bulled through the door and closed it behind him. He was wearing a dark blue suit with a tie that came closer to being fashionable than the one from the day before. His eyes measured the place. "Jesus, Riordan. This dump is messier than my teenage kid's room. And what the hell are those things?" He pointed at the Altec Lansings. "Loudspeakers from the Paleolithic age?"

I turned heel on him and went into the bedroom, where I put the gun back in its holster and threw on my ratty bathrobe. When I returned, Stockwell was sweeping Pop-Tart crumbs off the couch preparatory to sitting down. He looked edgy and uncomfortable. I pulled the high-back chair around to face him and fell into it.

"So," I said. "Did you come by to pass on some decorating tips, or did you have something else in mind? Yesterday you said you were too busy keeping your head above water to waste time dicking around with me. And then, by golly, you show up at my door. Miles out of your jurisdiction, even."

"Sure, rub my nose in it. I didn't have to come here, and I damn well don't have to stay. But if you'd keep your trap shut for a minute, there might be some advantage to it."

"All right, Lieutenant. I'm listening."

"Chuck Hastrup is dead."

I whistled under my breath. "How'd he get it?" Then after thinking a bit: "Hold on. You members of the fraternal order of law enforcement don't think I had anything to do with it, do you? Because if that's your idea of an advantage, I don't see it."

"Got a guilty conscience, Riordan? They did tell me he has a broken nose."

"Nobody dies of a broken nose. A broken neck, a broken heart — maybe. But not a broken nose. Now what's the story?"

"It's simple. He went to a South San Francisco shooting range this morning, rented a handgun, shot three rounds at a range target and then put the gun under his chin and capped himself."

I looked at Stockwell carefully. It occurred to me that this was some sort of trick. "No," I said. "I don't believe it. That's like a rattlesnake biting itself."

"If you don't believe me, then maybe you'll believe the videotape from the surveillance cameras. The whole thing is recorded on the first ten minutes of today's log." He stood up suddenly. "They're holding things for me down at the range. Throw on some clothes and you can see for yourself."

This was getting stranger and stranger. "Why? Why include me on this?"

"I've got my reasons. For now, let's just say that I need somebody who can ID the body. All we've got to go on is the stuff from his wallet. Let's go, Riordan. Chop-chop."

I got up and went to the bathroom. I did what I could at the basin with a wash cloth and a comb and then put on some clean clothes. Stockwell was pacing up and down in the living room when I came out.

"Come on," he said. "We'll take my car."

We went out and I locked the apartment door. As we were hustling down the stairs, I said, "I think I should just meet you there. That way you don't have to drive me back to the city."

"No. I don't have time for fooling around with two cars. And I don't want you showing up there first."

"Why ever not?"

Stockwell stopped short on the stairs and I almost ran into him. He looked back at me. "Listen. Taking you to a crime scene isn't exactly playing it according to Hoyle. It's better if the South City cops think you're a detective on the EPA force. I don't want you to lie about it exactly, but I also don't want you to do anything obvious to tip them off. Get it?"

I patted him on the shoulder. "I feel so proud. It will be an honor to serve with you on the East Palo Alto force, Lieutenant."

"Shut up."

Stockwell had an unmarked Chevy that had seen better days. I let him ball himself up in San Francisco traffic trying to find one of the few freeway on-ramps they hadn't torn down with quake damage. After he got done cursing and pounding the dash, he finally did something productive and hit the siren and then I directed him down 4th and the entrance to Highway 80. From there we got on Highway 101 south and drove less than five miles. The shooting range was on the freeway access road on the northbound side. It was one building in a strip of pre-fab tilt-ups that lined the road, and there were two South San Francisco patrol cars, an obvious unmarked car and an ambulance parked in front.

Stockwell flashed his badge to a uniformed cop who was

guarding the door and asked for somebody named Lewinski. The cop said, "Yeah, they been waiting for you. He's in
the office, talking to the manager. It's the door behind the
front desk, just inside there."

We went into the building. On the right was a reception
counter with a cash register and a sign-in sheet. Behind
that was a wall with cubbyholes — some open, some covered by locked doors. The open ones had earmuffs for protecting your hearing while shooting. I assumed the locked
ones had guns for rent. Hanging from the ceiling was a
TV monitor that cycled through different views of the
shooting range every few seconds. One view showed a police officer looking down at something on the floor, just off
camera. Stockwell and I went around the counter and
through a door that opened in the back wall.

Two men were in the room beyond. One was sitting in
an elaborate ergonomic chair behind a modern looking
desk. He was bald, fat and had a pitted face with a thin
black mustache like a skid from a bicycle tire. He didn't
look too happy. The other man was slouched in a plain
chair in front of the desk, a leg dangling elaborately. He
had blond hair cut like a Marine's, a pinched nose and a
big, sloppy body.

"You the guys we're waiting on?" said the fat guy peevishly. "'Cause I got a senior's tournament in an hour, you
know. I can't have those gray hairs waiting out in the parking lot while you haul the stiff out in a body bag. What
would they think?"

"They might think they were witness to a tragedy of the
sort caused by unrestricted access to handguns in Ameri-
ca," said Stockwell.

"Yeah, right," said the fat guy. "More likely they'll just
pee in their Depends and cancel the tourney. And I can't

afford that. So let's snap it up with this fancy-schmancy detecting. The guy took a gun and blew his brains out. How hard can it be?"

The blond guy stood up to face us. "I'm Lewinski. You Stockwell?"

Stockwell said he was and shook hands with Lewinski. "This is Riordan," said Stockwell, almost reluctantly.

That earned me a handshake with Lewinski too. Lewinski gestured to the man behind the desk. "Meet Mr. Frankel. He's the manager of the shooting range. That gives him a particular interest in seeing that the wheels of justice turn quickly."

"So I noticed," said Stockwell. "How about we go and look at the body so you can move it out. Then we can take a gander at the other stuff."

"Fine by me," said Lewinski. "This way to the main attraction."

We went out of the office in a small procession and around the reception counter to a corridor that ran along the front of the building. We passed through a heavy door and continued down the corridor until we came to a set of stalls that looked out onto the range. Each stall had a pulley gizmo running along the ceiling to the back of the building to move paper targets to and from the range. There were also controls for running the pulley in each stall and a metal bucket sitting on the floor in front to collect expended shell casings. There were numerous signs urging shooters to practice the NRA rules for handgun safety and reminding them to dump their shells in the bucket and not on the floor. The lighting was an intense florescent that made my hangover reassert itself with a passion. The thing on the floor didn't do a whole lot of good either.

Chuck Hastrup had fallen backwards after he shot himself, and as a result, was lying face up with his arms and legs spread like a kid making angels in the snow. He was wearing the same white clothing he was on the night he jumped me, but there was nothing else angelic about him. Under his chin was a nasty, blackened hole with a trickle of dried blood that ran down his neck and led to a coagulated pool on his sternum. A strip of adhesive tape over a misshapen nose marked his last encounter with me. His eyes were wide open in a startled expression, and he had a shrunken, wizened appearance that made him look like an old man who'd been surprised in a horrific fall down the stairs. As for the top of his head, it simply wasn't there.

The cop I'd seen on the TV monitor was leaning on the counter of the stall in front of Hastrup, watching our approach. A couple of paramedics sat on a bench further down the corridor, their wheeled gurney standing next to them. One of us in the procession — very likely me — must have looked a little green, because the cop waiting for us said:

"Please be sure to place your expended shell casings — and the contents of your stomach — in the metal buckets, not on the floor."

"Thank you for that, Beauchamp," said Lewinski. He turned to us. "The lab ghoulies have already come and gone, but this is pretty much how we found him. Does he look like the guy you're interested in?"

Stockwell looked over at me. "That's him," I said. "Or at least most of him."

"Yeah, well, they already cleaned up the rest of his brains," said Lewinski. "Sorry about that. We also got his wallet, some other stuff in his pockets and the gun he rented: a Ruger Blackhawk .44 Magnum."

"Christ," said Stockwell. "He used enough gun, didn't he? Isn't that one of those Wild West revolvers?"

"That's right," agreed Lewinski. "They rent all kinds of shit here. And if you look above you at about 11 o'clock you'll see where the slug went into the ceiling, still zipping along after it took off his brain pan."

Stockwell and I looked up at the hole. It was about a foot away from one of the surveillance cameras. "Ain't physics wonderful?" said Stockwell. "What's next on the tour?"

"We can show you the video tape, I guess," said Lewinski. "Then you can look at the stuff we took off the body." Lewinski shouted down to the paramedics, "Okay, you guys can take him now."

One paramedic started wheeling the gurney toward us, while the other stood up and looked at Lewinski with a wise-ass expression. "So Sarge," he said. "You want us to say he died on the way to the hospital like usual so you don't have to mess with the paperwork?"

Lewinski reddened. The cop leaning on the counter smothered a grin. "That little bastard," said Lewinski in an undertone. "You know how it goes: if they die in the wagon it saves you about two hours of paperwork. So, once in a while we'll get them to take a fresh one on board and say he croaked on the way. Nothing like this of course."

"I know the drill," said Stockwell.

Lewinski and Stockwell started back up the corridor, but I lingered to talk to the paramedics. "You guys know Ronan O'Grady in San Francisco?" I asked them. "He's in your biz." O'Grady and I had played jazz together in a couple of pick-up sessions.

Both men had come up with the gurney now and were

pulling on rubber gloves. The one who had mouthed off said, "That Irish pirate? Of course we know him. We see him drinking at the Rat and Raven almost every week."

"Well, tell him Riordan says hello." I looked down at the gurney where the plastic body bag was already unzipped and waiting. A tag on the zipper said, "Caution, Bio-Hazard."

"What's with that tag," I asked, curious.

"It's nothing," said the other paramedic. "It's standard operating procedure nowadays."

"Hey Riordan," yelled Stockwell from the door leading to the reception area. "Let's get with the program here."

I jogged up to the door. "Gee," I said when I reached him. "I hope you're not gonna report me to the chief of detectives."

He glared at me and mouthed the words, "eat shit."

Lewinski was waiting for us in the reception area when we came through the door. He was monkeying around with a videotape machine on a shelf below the counter. "Now," he said. "I think I've got it cued up to the place we want. Take a look at the monitor."

We did — and it wasn't pretty. Watching Hastrup kill himself was twice as bad as looking at the dead body afterwards. The tape had a gritty, surreal, this-can't-be-happening aura. It reminded me of the footage from the Vietnam War of the South Vietnamese officer executing a Vietcong prisoner.

As the tape started Hastrup was loading the revolver with cartridges from a box. The gun was a monster: black, long-barreled with the distinctive curved hammer of a western-style six-shooter. Hastrup snapped the cylinder of the gun in place and pressed a button to send a paper target attached to the pulley mechanism to the back of the

range. He didn't appear nervous or tentative in any way —
just another pedestrian day on the shooting range. He
fired three rounds at the target, pausing to take careful
aim before each shot. There was still nothing out of the
ordinary about his actions, except that he hadn't bothered
to put on hearing protection before shooting. Then, in one
movement — as if part of a standard routine — Hastrup
took the gun with both hands and shoved its barrel under
his chin. Given the placement of the camera, all we could
see was Hastrup standing upright, his elbows sticking out
at his side, his head tilted back slightly. It almost looked
like a yoga position.

Until he pulled the trigger.

The top of his head vaporized in an instant and Hastrup
seemed to jump backwards as the force of the slug
launched him off his feet. The camera shook as the bullet
embedded itself in the ceiling. Then there was nothing
left but a wisp of drifting smoke. The body and the blood
and the viscera on the floor could not be seen.

Lewinski shut off the videotape machine. We all stood
silent, avoiding each other's eyes.

"My God," said Stockwell finally. "Talk about being cold-
blooded. He did it like he was flipping a light switch."

"He probably knew he was being taped," said Lewinski.
"Wanted to put on a good final show."

"I was wondering about that," I said. "Why do they run
the cameras in here?"

Lewinski smiled grimly. "Guess you haven't been reading the police wire much, bud. Shooting range suicides
are the new thing. There's been about four in the last year.
The range owners have put in cameras to monitor the customers, but it really doesn't do much for prevention. Ends
up being a good way for the owners to protect themselves
from lawsuits, though. Hard to argue that your loved one

died as a result of negligence when you look at something
like that."

"You probably don't have a lot of loved ones in the first
place if you do that to yourself," said Stockwell. The paramedics came by with the gurney and wheeled Hastrup out
the door into the parking lot. Stockwell watched them absently, then said, "Okay, let's wrap this up. You got the
stuff from the body, you said. No suicide note, I take it."

Lewinski kicked at a gray evidence lockbox on the floor.
He opened the hinged lid and took out several plastic bags
containing personal articles. "No," he said. "No note. We
got his wallet, keys, some change and some breath mints.
That's it."

"Breath mints," I said. "Then it's true what they say. It is
always important to have fresh breath."

Stockwell looked at me with a martyred expression. "I
knew you weren't going to let that one pass." He turned
back to Lewinski. "The keys fit any of the cars in the lot?"

"No, there were no cars we couldn't account for after we
sent all the other customers packing. The manager thinks
Hastrup may have taken a cab here anyway."

"I suppose that makes sense," said Stockwell. "Why
leave any more loose ends than you have to. Well, how's to
rifle the wallet. Or have you already done that?"

"Sure, we looked through it. It was pretty slim pickings."

Lewinski put on a pair of plastic gloves from the lockbox and took the wallet from its bag. He pulled out all the
cards, money and other papers it contained and spread
them on top of the counter. He was right — it was pretty
slim pickings. I saw just two things of interest: one was a
snapshot of Terri McCulloch very similar to the one
Bishop had given me, and the other was a business card.
The card was for a guy named Dale Pace who was in the
used car business. Hastrup had said the black guy who

helped work me over was named Dale, so I figured it belonged to him. I pointed at Terri's picture. "There's your gal, Stockwell."

"Yeah," he said. "I know it. Can you flip it over for us, Lewinski? I want to see if there's anything written on the back."

Lewinski flipped it and the back was clean. "That it?" said Lewinski.

"Just let me copy down the stuff off the business card and you can pack it up," said Stockwell. He took a small notebook and pen from his breast pocket and wrote down the information. "Wait a minute," he said. "Riordan, you know who the card belongs to?"

"Yeah, probably. I think it's the guy who, ah, participated in the assault and battery with Hastrup."

"Great. Thanks for coming across with that so quickly."

"Don't worry, Lieutenant. I would have told you back at the station house."

Stockwell narrowed his eyes at me. "Okay, I think that covers it for us," he said. "I appreciate your holding things until we got here, Lewinski. I'll be in touch about the lab work and such."

Lewinski took off the plastic gloves and reached over to shake Stockwell's hand again. "No, problem. Happy to help. Good luck on the Teller kill, and I'll give you or Riordan here a call when we get the lab work back."

"Call me," said Stockwell quickly. "Riordan isn't going to be working on the case any longer."

"Yep," I said. "Got me a cush assignment guarding the Mayor's eighteen year old daughter. You see, she's been getting these threatening calls from—"

"Let's get going," said Stockwell. He hustled me out the door and we walked back to his car without any more conversation. Once inside, I said:

"Okay, let's have it. You didn't take me down here to be a nice guy. Maybe you needed me to identify the body, but that could have waited."

Stockwell rubbed his face with both hands and looked out the window, not seeing anything. I noticed for the first time how worn he looked. "I need to go over something with you," he said. "There's been a development. A development that doesn't exactly fit with my take on the homicide. Nothing totally out of whack, you understand, but enough to get me thinking." He looked over, expecting me to say, "Neener-neener," or some other equally mature remark in the I-told-you-so line.

I was tempted, but I didn't want him to clam up on me. "What kind of development?" I asked.

"I got the lab report back from the murder scene. They dusted for fingerprints like they always do. Hers are all over the apartment, of course. Teller's are there in several places: the refrigerator door, the beer bottle, the photograph you said he was holding when he walked in."

"But not enough places for him to have been over there before. Not enough places for him to have been having an affair with her."

"Yeah, probably," said Stockwell. "But that's not where I'm going with this. If they were having an affair, they could have been meeting in hotels. Who'd want to have sex in that dump? No, the point is they found another print. A print that we can't identify."

"You're sure it's not one of mine?"

Stockwell snorted. "No, it's not yours. Of course we did find yours all over the fucking place, Riordan. If we were going by volume, you'd be the one having the affair with her."

I knew better than to respond to that. "All right, then. So what's the big deal on the mystery print. Could have been left by a friend. Could have left been the landlady — she seems like the sort to snoop."

"The big deal is it was found on the framed photograph that Teller was holding. The photograph — you may not have noticed — that was back on the shelf by the time we got to the apartment. And it ain't the landlady's."

"I see what you're driving at. You think someone else was in the apartment that night and picked up the photograph and put it back on the shelf. I suppose that could be. It could also be Terri McCulloch put it back that night, and the print is from a friend who had handled it before."

Stockwell pounded on the steering wheel. "Here I am providing evidence to shore up your cockamamie theory of a different killer — one, by the way, that I still don't buy — and here you are arguing the other way. The print was found on the surface of the photograph, under the place where the glass broke off. And it seems to be fresh."

"Oh."

"Believe me, I know that doesn't prove anything conclusively. We don't know how long McCulloch had the photograph, who developed it, who framed it, etc. But what I need confirmed is that you really did see Teller drop the photograph and that neither of you picked it up and put it back on the shelf."

"He dropped it all right. And neither of us was exactly in a good housekeeping frame of mind. It stayed on the floor for as long as I stayed conscious."

Stockwell took in a deep breath and let it out slowly. "Okay then," he said. "Thank you."

"You got any other niggling contradictions you want to talk over?"

Stockwell gave me a searching look. "Chuck Hastrup's do-it-yourself brain surgery in there isn't a contradiction?"

"Sure. I said as much in my apartment, didn't I? You think it's tied in with Teller's murder?"

"Well, I'm sure as hell going to check his prints against the one on the photograph. Maybe he was the one who came up from behind you at McCulloch's place. Maybe he whacked Teller that night and got to feeling guilty about it later."

I mulled that one over. It was an idea that had crossed my mind. "I like him because Terri McCulloch has used him for all her other heavy lifting," I said. "But I can't see him offing himself over guilt. And that photograph. He could—"

Stockwell cut me off. "Don't say it. He could have put his print on there before. Give your skepticism a rest, will you Riordan? I'm not building the whole case around the photo."

I let him cool off. "Anything else?" I asked after a decent interval.

He started to say something, then bit back the words. "No, that's it." He put the key in the ignition switch and started the motor. "Let's blow," he said abruptly.

There was clearly more that was bothering Stockwell, but I didn't have much luck wheedling it out of him on the drive home. I regretted my remarks about the photograph because it made him reluctant to discuss anything else I might judge far-fetched. He did tell me that no one had brought in Todd Nagel for questioning, and that the Bay Area — and now state and nation — wide hunt for Terri McCulloch had turned up exactly zilch.

Stockwell dropped me off in front of my building at about 1:30. I did my ritual with the Samuel's Jewelers street clock and then rode the elevator up to my office.

Chapter 23

honest dale's used cars

*b*ONACKER was talking on the phone when I walked in. He was dressed casually in a faded polo shirt with the logo of his insurance company over the pocket, and a pair of khaki pants. He gave me an energetic military salute as I walked by, and I heard him say into the phone, "So, the hippie takes off his mask, and says, 'Surprise, I'm the hippie.' Then the nun takes off *her* mask and says, 'Surprise, I'm the bus driver!'" He guffawed. "I'm the bus driver," he repeated gleefully. "Get it?"

I walked past Gretchen's desk, which was unoccupied, and into my office. On my desk was a bud vase with a single pink rose. Beneath the vase was a handwritten note from Gretchen. It read:

Auggie,

If you can't have rosy cheeks, then how about a plain old fashioned rose? And I don't want to hear any complaints about
women giving men flowers. Didn't anyone ever tell you not to
look a gift bud in the pistil?!

I told Ben I was taking the rest of the day off (time for a little
retail therapy), but I did check into the things you requested.
Here's the scoop:

You're on for the gig at Undici this evening. Tony wants everyone there by 6:30. You're supposed to play four sets, and he
expects you'll be out of there by 1 or so.

Todd Nagel's landlord has no forwarding address for him. He
says Nagel was a good tenant and always paid his rent on time.
However, Nagel only gave him a few days notice before he
moved out.

I checked through the phone numbers on the bill you gave me.
Most of them were pretty innocuous (if you think $200 worth of
1-900 phone sex numbers is innocuous), but it does appear that
Mr. Nagel called Terri McCulloch's home number several times.
He also made a lot of calls to a number with a Woodside prefix
— not Bishop's — that I can't track down. It never picks up when
I call, and it's not shown in any of the reverse directories we
have. Maybe you have some other tricks up your sleeve?

Take care of yourself!

xoxoxoxo,
Gretchen

It occurred to me — not for the first time — that Gretchen
was better than I deserved. I picked up Nagel's phone bill
from the desk where Gretchen had left it and glanced at
the number she had highlighted. It had an 851 prefix like
Bishop's, but apart from that, there was nothing familiar
about it. I folded up the bill and put it in my breast pocket with the intention of getting Stockwell to use his official
connections on it. Then I pulled out the yellow pages to

refresh my memory on the address that went with the phone number and place of business I'd seen earlier today on a business card. Chuck Hastrup's friend Dale was running a nice half page ad to remind me that Pace Auto Sales and Brokerage was located on Market Street, just east of Laguna. I jotted down the street number and went out of the office.

Bonacker was still talking on the phone as I walked by. There was a concerned look on his face. He said, "Hey, come on, I'm Catholic myself. I went to Saint Ignatius and was taught by the sisters and everything. There's no reason to cancel your insurance policy over a little joke. As a matter of fact, my good friend Father Murphy told it to me in the first — Hello? Hello?"

I jumped on the number 8 bus just outside the building and rode it straight down Market to Laguna. Dale Pace's used car emporium was on a narrow lot that ran under an elevated portion of Highway 101. There was a Quonset hut at one end for washing and prepping the cars, and a trailer on a raised platform at the back that housed the office. A tattered line of plastic flags was strung from the trailer to the hut — like colored pennants on a sinking yacht. There were about three dozen cars for sale, all of them five or more years old, and none of them costing much over $6000. It looked like the kind of place you bought your car if you were on your way up in the world — or were well on your way down. The oppressive rumble of freeway traffic fell on me like a weighted net as I came onto the property.

To my extreme right was a young couple eyeing a middle-aged Toyota with skepticism. In front of them stood a glib-looking man in a checked sports coat and a black turtleneck. He had bushy black hair, a black mustache and he smiled a lot and made tight gestures with fingers extended as if he was coiling yarn. I left them to their rituals and made a beeline for the door of the trailer. Inside, there was a lot of dust, linoleum, low wattage lighting and a couple of desks. Behind one of these sat Dale Pace. He glanced up as I walked in and immediately jerked open a drawer and began groping for something at the back. I pulled open my jacket with my left hand and wrapped my right around the exposed butt of the Glock automatic. "It doesn't have to be this way," I said. "But if you insist on swapping lead, you're going to be doing a lot more catching than throwing."

He looked at me impassively and slumped back in his chair, his hands folded on his lap. "If you think I'm going to hold still for more of that crazy shit you pulled on Chuck, best you take your piece all the way out and see can you find the trigger."

I let my arms go back to my side and walked deliberately over to Pace's desk. There were several pictures of him in a Steeler's uniform on the wall behind, and a game ball resting on a stand on the bookshelf to one side. Pace was in shirt sleeves and a tie, and from the junk on the top of the desk, appeared to have been working on the company books. I sat down in a chair by the desk. "I came to talk," I said. "That's all."

"That ain't necessarily better," he said. "Because I don't have a whole heck of a lot to say to you. Unless you are in the market for a car, that is."

"No. No cars. I took the bus today. *Viva* public transportation and all that. Have the cops been here yet?"

Pace took his time with that one. "So you filed a complaint, did you? Seems to me what you did to Chuck pretty much evened things out. Or did you figure you still owed me?"

"I owe you both plenty more as far as I'm concerned. But Chuck has put himself in a position where he is no longer eligible to receive payment. He committed suicide this morning. Blew his brains out at a shooting range in South San Francisco."

Pace brought a finger up to his mouth and bit off a hangnail. He turned his head and spat out the harvest.

"You'll have to excuse me," I said. "I'm not used to coping with a display of such unvarnished grief."

"I'd be an idiot to take your word for it," said Pace. "But if it is true, then it don't surprise me in the least. He was heading for a fall — no question."

"Why?"

"'Cause he got himself wrapped up with that bitch. She manipulated him all to hell. Had him run interference for her. Had him drop the hammer on you and all sorts of other shit he never would have got involved with on his own. He thought it was true love. She thought it was a convenient way to scrape the mud off her shoes."

"But that doesn't explain why he killed himself. Not really. Did McCulloch dump him?"

Pace shook his head. "No. I mean, I don't know, man. Hard to dump someone exactly when you're hiding out from the cops. He must've got fed up with it is all. He must have finally seen for himself what she was doing to him. Took a look in the mirror one day and didn't like the thing staring back at him."

"I don't believe it. There's gotta be something else: drugs, financial problems, culpability for a big crime. Something."

Pace cracked the knuckles on his huge hands absently. "Hey, it don't make a never-no-mind to me what you think. I'm not even sure I believe he's dead. I'm just telling you it wouldn't surprise me."

"Did he shoot Roland Teller? Could that be what was eating him?"

"No, he did not shoot Teller. I think you got a wrong idea about Chuck Hastrup. He isn't — or wasn't — the killer type. He could be mean, sure. You can't play defensive lineman in the NFL and not get a little mean. But on his own, he was basically a pretty good joe. He used to do volunteer work for the Big Brothers, donate blood, all sorts of do-gooder crap. Then he met her. She warped him something terrible — but not enough to kill."

"So what's your excuse?"

Pace smiled broadly. "Oh, I'm naturally bad. No one's fault but my own. If I'd been working you over that night, you would still be in the hospital counting doctors' fingers, as in, 'How many am I holding up now, Mr. Riordan?' But when I do shit, I do it for me. I don't do it because some bitch squeezes my dick and pats me on the head."

"You helped Hastrup that night. That wasn't for you."

"That's different. I used to play ball with him. And you'd already knocked him around pretty good earlier in the day. I didn't want him getting busted up any more."

I should have let it go, but I said, "For someone who was so all fired eager to protect him, you sure don't seem very upset now to hear that he's dead."

Pace went rigid in his chair. He seemed to grow larger. "I already told you: I don't necessarily believe word one that you say. And if you expect me to start bawling or some shit like that after you come waltzing in with a loaded gun, you got another thing coming. I'd written Chuck off anyway. That McCulloch bitch took away his manhood."

That was almost exactly what Terri McCulloch said Bishop had credited her with. "If that's the case," I said. "Why don't you tell me where she is?"

"And why don't you fly around the room with jet farts out of your ass?" Pace laughed. "I can't is why. Chuck never told me, and I never asked. Truth be known, I don't think McCulloch even told him where she was."

"But she did call him after the murder?"

"So he said. Look, it's not like I've been living with the guy. He called me once after you did your thing on him with the nail gun to give me the heads up. He said he talked to the bitch and he started to lay on the sob stuff about what a shitty deal she got, but I told him to can it. I didn't want to listen to that load of boohoo."

I picked up a rubber band from Pace's desk and began twanging it like a bass string. I let my eyes wander up to the pictures of him in uniform. "I remember you now from the Steeler's," I said. "You were a heck of a line-backer."

Pace grunted noncommittally, but I could tell he was pleased. "Well, them days are long gone. I wished I had a tenth of the money I made back then. I wouldn't be sitting in a trailer on a used car lot talking to you. But the coke and the women bled me white — so to speak. That's why I don't have much patience for Chuck. He's too old to be making those kind of mistakes with his life."

Pace looked down at his lap and seemed to go away for a moment. "You giving me the bona fides on this thing with Chuck? About him killing himself."

"It's true. You'll probably be having a visit from a cop named Stockwell as soon as he can line up some coopera-tion from the SFPD." Then, to explain the connection: "They found your card in his wallet."

"So you're not filing charges on the shit that went down outside In the Key of G?"

"No. There'd be a list with about twenty guys ahead of you if I started filing charges on everyone I tangled with.

Stockwell's an EPA cop, anyway. It wouldn't do any good to take it to him."

"Well, I'm not sorry we racked you up. That was just the way it was. But I am sorry I smashed your bass. I snuck into the club while we were waiting and I heard you play. You weren't half bad — for a white boy."

"Thanks. Crawford is the one with the juice in that band, though. While we're talking about the club, mind if I ask you one more question? Then I'll get out of your hair."

Pace rubbed his shaved head. "Lucky I'm not a sensitive person or I mighta taken that for a crack. Go ahead, ask your question."

"There was a girl at the club that night named Jodie. She works for Edwin Bishop like Terri McCulloch used to. Do you know where she stands in all this? Did she have anything to do with you guys finding me at In the Key of G?"

"You must be the kind of guy that asks for double bags at the grocery store, Riordan. Chuck told me you wanted to know about her. All I can tell you is that she's a friend of Terri's, and Chuck said that she and Terri weren't getting on so well since Terri left Bishop. But she didn't have nothin' to do with us being at the club. We tailed you there from your apartment." I started to say something and Pace raised his hand. "And don't ask me about that other dude you mentioned to Chuck because I don't know nothing about him neither."

"Nagel's his name. But that's not what I was going to ask. I was going to ask why Terri and Jodie weren't getting on."

"Who knows, man? Think I pay attention to crap like that? It was just some shit Chuck said while we was freezing our asses off in the van waiting for you to show. It wouldn't surprise me that they weren't so hot for each other now. One of 'em lost her job and the other one kept it. Envy, that's what that's called."

I stood up. "Thanks," I said. "I appreciate the information."

Pace got up too and put out his hand. I shook it. "Oh yeah," he said. "I'm happy to help a guy that lets me know I'll be catching lead as he comes through the door."

"Well, I didn't exactly think you were reaching for a number two pencil."

"You got that right, Riordan. Watch your back now."

I went out the trailer door. The salesmen and the couple I'd seen earlier were just coming up the steps. I left the door open and the salesmen slipped through behind me. "Dale, I've got some bad news," he said in a loud voice from inside. "The Hendersons here have just about *stolen* a car from us."

I flagged a cab on Market and rode back to my apartment. I tried calling Jodie at Bishop's mansion, but I got the answering machine twice and the third time Bishop himself picked up — and I had no intention of talking to him. Just for yucks I tried the number from Nagel's phone bill. It didn't pick up at all.

I thought about calling Margaret Teller, but I wasn't sure what I would say to her. I wondered what made me think of her at all. When I got bored asking myself questions I couldn't answer, I took a long, hot shower and changed for my gig at Undici. At around 6 o'clock I carried my electric bass and amp down to the Galaxy 500. The first drops from some nasty looking storm clouds flattened against my windshield as I rolled down Post Street.

checked

*t*HE GIG WENT WELL. Tony Ruelland's group, Zugzwang, was cut a little too much in the pattern of fusion groups like The Yellowjackets to suit my reactionary tastes, but I enjoyed having the opportunity to do some slap-plucking, and Tony gave me a good lead on a replacement for my string bass. I got home about 1:30, too wired to go straight to bed. I was drinking bourbon and listening to Zoot Sims's 1952 recording *Zootcase* when the phone rang.

I uncoiled from the couch and walked over to the phone. I had a sudden feeling of edgy apprehension: like I'd seen a violent flash of lightning and was bracing for the accompanying clap of thunder. The display from my caller ID showed the person phoning had blocked his line, which only added to my misgivings. I picked up the phone and put the receiver to my ear without saying anything. It was a cell phone connection, but apart from static, nothing came through — not even breathing. I waited for what seemed like a very long time — gripping the phone tightly, staring at my shoes — and finally gave in. I said:

"You never let me get a word in edgewise."

A voice came on, deep and somewhat muffled. It seemed familiar and then it didn't. "Package for you, Riordan. Hotel Cavalier on Eddy at Taylor. Room 312. It's perishable goods so snap it up." The line switched off with a metallic snarl.

I put the phone down and massaged the back of my neck. Eddy at Taylor was the heart of the Tenderloin. I could imagine few places worse to go running off to in the middle of the night. The only good thing about it was that it was convenient. Given the marginal placement of my own apartment, the Hotel Cavalier would only be about six blocks south and east.

For no good reason that I could see, I decided to go. I went to the closet and got out my raincoat. I shrugged that on, and then yanked the Glock from its holster and dumped it in a pocket. I felt undergunned — or more accurately, just plain scared — so I pulled the lockbox from underneath my bed and took out my Smith and Wesson .38 revolver. That went in the other pocket. It didn't help much with being scared, but at least I wasn't lopsided. I put on a beat-up fedora and left.

Outside, storm clouds still spat rain and my breath billowed in front of me as I walked up Hyde. In a strange form of natural selection, the character of the neighborhood changed the further I got in the Tenderloin. It went from a broad mix of shops, restaurants, bars and apartment houses to the specialized amalgam of sleazy adult bookstores, massage parlors, residence hotels and fly-by-night auto repair shops that was better adapted for survival. Few people were out and about, but there were plenty of bodies curled in doorways, covered in blankets if they were fortunate or cardboard or newspapers if they were not.

When I got to Eddy I took a left and continued on past Leavenworth and Jones. Part way down the block between Jones and Taylor was a tiny city park. Notorious for drug and prostitution traffic during the day, even now there were groups of people huddled under trees, smoking cigarettes and taking pulls from bottles wrapped in brown paper. One of the city's new pay toilets stood at the perimeter near the street. The toilets had been acquired from a company in France, were self-cleaning and were supposed to solve the problem of public facilities in San Francisco as they had in Paris: with economy, decorum and Gallic *je ne sais quoi*. As I walked by, the door to the green, oval-shaped structure lurched opened and out tumbled a middle-aged black man with his pants around his ankles. He hit the ground with a heavy grunt and the bottle he was holding slipped from his grasp and rolled past me into the gutter. Somebody in the park yelled, "Yo, Jerome! Your bottle or your pants — you best be holdin' on to one of them." Stifled laughter followed.

I detoured around the man and crossed the street to where I could see the words Hotel Cavalier written in a faded script on a dingy, narrow building sandwiched between a head shop and an adult bookstore. A metal grating covered the entryway to the building, but the door to the grating stood wide open. Likewise the front door itself was ajar. All this seemed a little too convenient. I put my right hand in my raincoat and took firm hold of the automatic, snicking off the safety with my thumb. Then I stepped inside.

There was a minuscule lobby lit by a dusty, art deco chandelier that had spots for five bulbs with two missing and one burned out. A threadbare carpet stretched tight over too much rubbery padding covered the floor. It was like walking on a sponge sausage. To the right was a barred window with a narrow counter looking into an office. No light came from the office and no one was sitting at the desk inside. A staircase with a carved oak banister and solid streak of black grime running along the wall at waist level opened in front of me. I crept up the stair, staying close to the banister so that I might be harder to spot from above.

The second floor landing had a tile floor with dust balls the size of hens eggs, cluttered with a ruined bicycle and a rusted folding cot that wouldn't have opened if you used a hydraulic jack. A quick check confirmed the rooms on the corridor were numbered in the 200's, so I continued up the stairs. Thus far I'd seen no one and heard nothing — not even a muted TV. The third floor landing was as cluttered as the last with the added attraction of floor tiles chipped out of the grout. I went down the hallway on spongy carpet, watching the even numbered rooms on the right. 312 was next to a busted ice machine filled with empty Chinese food containers, dead soldiers from the Mogan David platoon, and a savory scattering of used condoms. I saw light coming from the bottom of the door of 312 as I tapped on it with the butt of my automatic.

There was no response. I cleared my throat to speak. It seemed like I hadn't talked since I changed the shelf paper in my kitchen. "Open up," I said. "The fall guy is here."

Still nothing from inside. In true fall guy fashion, I took hold of the doorknob and twisted. It wasn't locked, but then it wouldn't be. I gave the door a shove and jumped to one side, dodging the spread of buckshot I knew to be coming.

None obliged me by coming. The door hit the interior wall with a crash and rebounded part of the way back. I pushed the automatic across the threshold and craned my head around the doorframe to see into the room.

Terri McCulloch was sprawled facedown on a bare mattress in a cheap iron bedframe. One arm flopped over the side like she was trailing her hand in the wake of a canoe. On the floor, a few inches from her outstretched fingers, was a hypodermic syringe. Her face was flattened against the mattress and the flow of saliva from her gaping mouth had darkened the fabric in an irregular stain. Her hair was a tangled mop, the tips of it damp with sweat or rain. She wore black panties and black socks and nothing else. I swept into the room and searched it, still wary of being jumped from behind. No one was in the bedroom or the closet, and the revolting little bath was home only to fat, shiny roaches. I closed and bolted the room door and went to the woman on the bed. The pulse in Terri McCulloch's neck throbbed when I touched it, but it seemed very slow and irregular. Lying next to her was a leather purse as big as a knapsack, and next to that a number of items that had spilled from it. One of these was a spoon with a blackened bottom and a handle bent in a flat ring. A crust of brown scales adhered to the bowl, residue from the heroin Terri McCulloch had shot in her veins. Of more immediate utility was a cell phone — very possibly the one used to call me.

Without bothering about fingerprints, I grabbed the phone from the bed and dialed 911. I told the emergency operator to send an ambulance to the hotel for a drug overdose victim. She asked me to stay on the line so she could collect more information, but I told her there wasn't any and hung up.

I shook the remaining contents of her purse onto the bed. Terri's pearl-handled automatic, a disposable lighter, some currency and several white packets that looked like drugs fell out. The last thing to come cartwheeling down was a flat card about two inches by three. I retrieved it from the side of Terri's leg where it had landed. It had the letters "PCMCIA" printed on it, along with "Flash Memory Card" and "256 MB." This looked like an item from the list of computer media that Bishop had given Stockwell. I slipped it in my hip pocket behind my wallet and then pushed the rest of the stuff back in the purse, covering my hand with the material from my raincoat so as not to leave prints.

I looked down at Terri McCulloch. I wondered if there was anything I could do before the paramedics arrived. She hadn't ingested the heroin so there was no point in trying to make her to throw up. I could try slapping her and marching her around the room, but I suspected that was only done in Hollywood movies to make with the dramatic scene.

I settled on flipping her over so that she might breathe easier. She made a blubbering noise as I turned her and I noticed for the first time that her left arm, which had been hidden under her body, had a rubber tube tied around it. A puncture mark was visible above the tube on top of a distended vein. I pulled off the tubing and covered her with my raincoat, as much to keep her praying mantis tattoo and pierced nipples from my view as to keep her warm.

I spent the next few minutes pacing back and forth in front of the bed, pausing occasionally to check if she was still breathing. A heavy pounding on the door put an end to that. "Did somebody here call for an ambulance?"

yelled a voice in a faint Irish brogue.

I unlocked the door and pulled it open. Standing in the hallway was a stocky paramedic with red hair, a florid complexion and freckled horse teeth. It was my friend Ronan O'Grady. Behind him was another uniformed paramedic: a bulky woman with shoulder length black hair, no makeup & a butt big enough to smother a grizzly.

"God's teeth!" said O'Grady. "What are you doing here?"

"If we had two hours I would tell you. Your meat's over there. And she's not looking any too good."

O'Grady swaggered through the door like Marshal Dillon and went over to the bed. His partner manhandled a gurney in from the hallway. O'Grady picked up Terri McCulloch's limp arm to check her pulse and then got a small flash from his belt to shine in her pupil. "Sure, it's as bad as you could wish for," hissed O'Grady. His eyes strayed to the syringe where it still lay on the floor. "It's heroin, is it then?"

"Yeah. The spoon she used is on the bed."

The female paramedic was rummaging through a medical bag on top of the gurney. She pulled out a syringe of her own and passed it over to O'Grady without being asked. O'Grady found a choice vein in Terri McCulloch's right arm and plunged the hypodermic home. He yanked the raincoat off her and roughly maneuvered her arms to the center of her torso. "Come on," he said to me. "Take her feet and we'll swing her onto the stretcher."

As we hefted her off the bed, the silver rings in her nipples flashed in the thin light from the ceiling fixture. Bent between us like a deflated air mattress, she looked weak, pale and feverish. We placed her down carefully on white sheets and O'Grady's partner pulled a blanket over her and buckled two nylon straps across her body.

"Right," said O'Grady. "Let's roll."

"What about the IV?" asked the woman.

"Fuck the IV. We'll start it once we get her in the wagon. Now move."

The two of them maneuvered the gurney out the door and into the hallway. As they raced toward the stairwell, I yelled at their backs, "Can I ride with you to the hospital?"

"No," said O'Grady, lifting the gurney to start down the stairs. "You have to wait for the cops."

"My favorite thing," I said, but they had already gone out of view.

A door across the corridor opened and out stepped a sleepy old geezer in a tee shirt and boxer shorts. His hair stood up like dead weeds, and he'd left his teeth soaking in the glass. "What's going on?" he asked.

"Drug overdose," I said. "You know the party in this room?"

"Yah, I seen her." His words were slurred without his dentures. "She can make even my old pecker snap to."

"Great. Something to look forward to in my golden years. You see anybody else go in or out of this room tonight?"

The old guy scratched his crotch thoughtfully. "Thought I mighta heard somebody a while ago, but I didn't get up to check. There's always some damn thing going on around here."

I heard the tromp of feet on the stairs and the old guy and I turned to see the hats of two uniformed officers rise over the banister. The old man said, "Better you than me, son," and ducked back into his room.

I stood my ground in the corridor as the cops approached. As it turned out, they were like scout ants sent to find food at a picnic. They were quickly joined by two more patrol cops, and after I explained that the woman who OD'ed was Terri McCulloch — chief suspect in the

Roland Teller murder — there were soon plain clothes officers, lab technicians, and eventually a Captain of Detectives. They cordoned off the room, took photographs, collected samples of the heroin, dusted for prints, interviewed people on the hotel corridor, and most of all, grilled the heck out of me.

By four AM I'd been taken down to headquarters and my story of being alerted to Terri McCulloch's whereabouts by a mysterious phone caller was being received with fresh skepticism by an entirely new set of faces. Somewhere along the way I got permission to make a phone call myself, and I used the privilege to leave a message for Stockwell at his office. At the very least I owed him a personal call, and in any case, I didn't trust the San Francisco cops to get the story to him promptly.

When dawn came, I was sitting in an interrogation room by myself with my head cupped in my palm and a Styrofoam cup of coffee on the table in front of me. Without non-dairy creamer, it tasted like lukewarm tobacco spit. With it, lukewarm tobacco spit and flea powder. I amused myself by stirring the coffee and watching the undissolved creamer flakes swirl around like a stars in a muddy little galaxy. Eventually, I must have nodded off. The next thing I knew a rough hand was shaking me by the shoulder. "You're free to go, Riordan," said a voice.

I looked up and found a weathered cop with gray hair combed straight back standing over me. He had suspicious eyes and if he knew how to smile it would only be from reading about it. I stood up wearily and slung my raincoat over my shoulder. I walked to the door of the interrogation room and pulled on the knob.

"By the way," said the cop behind me. "Terri McCulloch died this morning at 4:36. Heart just stopped. Nothing they could do."

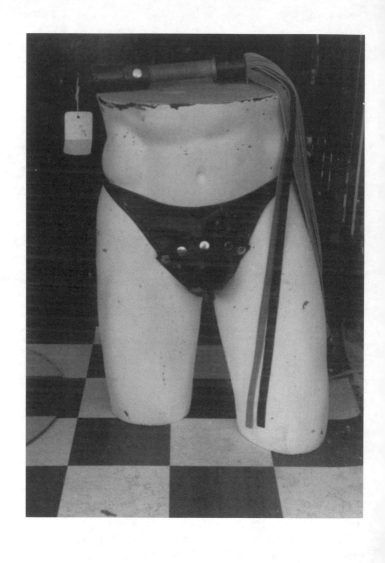

Chapter 25

home movies

fOR THE SECOND DAY in a row, Stockwell interrupted my morning routine — this time by waking me up. The phone rang angrily. I fumbled the receiver off the prong and laid the cool plastic against my cheek, not raising my head from the pillow. "Yeah," I grunted.

"How're the Pop Tarts this morning?" asked Stockwell in a too loud voice. He sounded like a guy who'd had a full night's rest, a nice breakfast and a kiss good-bye from his wife. I hated him.

"I haven't gotten that far."

"Tsk, tsk, I hope I didn't wake you up."

"No, it's like Neil Young says: rust and Riordan — we never sleep."

"Well, I called you to thank you for telling me about McCulloch. You beat the SFPD by six hours and the *San Francisco Chronicle* by four."

"Guess I'm getting good at finding dead bodies. The College of Mortuary Sciences ought to follow me around."

"Maybe they should. But Terri McCulloch wasn't actually dead when you found her."

"No, she wasn't. That just shows the depth of my talent. I can find 'em even before they go."

"I suppose you can at that." He paused. "Well, be seeing you. I'd tell you to keep your nose clean, but there ain't a big enough handkerchief."

"Wait," I said. "That's it?"

"What else would there be? 'Roland Teller's Murderer OD's in Tenderloin Hotel.' That's the *Chronicle* headline this morning."

"You believe that? What about all your complicated theories from yesterday?"

"What you said. Just complicated theories. It wasn't Hastrup's fingerprint on the photograph in Terri McCulloch's apartment. We ran it."

I sat up in bed, putting my feet on the cold hardwood floor. "Doesn't anyone care about the identity of the guy who phoned me last night? That seems like a pretty big loose end to tie up before declaring victory."

Stockwell grunted. "I don't think that's such a big mystery, do you? Who else would know where Terri McCulloch was hiding out besides Chuck Hastrup? His friend Dale. If you hadn't gone over to his car lot yesterday and muddied the waters before I could talk to him, he might have told us where she was in time to save her."

"He admits he called me, then?"

"Yeah, the San Francisco cops sweated it out of him. He says he went over to confront her about Hastrup's suicide and found her on the bed. He didn't want to be left holding the bag, but he didn't want to see her get away or die so he passed the buck to you."

"How do you know that he didn't pump her full of dope himself? He might have killed her because of Hastrup."

"Now who's making with the complicated theories, Riordan? A guy like that would have killed her with his bare hands, or shot her or knifed her. He wouldn't mess around with something vague and inexact like a drug overdose. And even if he had, he wouldn't have called you. He would have just let her die in the hotel by herself. She probably wouldn't have been found for a week."

"If you say so."

"Yeah, I do. I've been given the word from high to close this case, and I'm more than happy to. You should be happy too. You've been bending the rules like cooked spaghetti. Nothing I could nail you for exactly, but it was only a matter of time. In fact, it wouldn't surprise me if you walked off with more evidence from that hotel. Hang it up now, Riordan. It's time. This is the best outcome you could hope for."

"I thought you called me to thank me, not lecture me."

Stockwell growled into the phone. "I knew there wasn't any point in telling you to keep your nose clean. Call me when you're humping for bail. I'll chip in a quarter." He slammed the phone down.

I hung up at my end and fell back in bed. Staring at the ceiling, I thought about all the things I should have done differently. It was hard to count that high. Then I thought about the things that were left. That was a much shorter list. I needed Duckworth's help again to see if Bishop's software was on the PCMICA card I had taken from the hotel. If the source code was there, I would return it to Bishop to try and dig myself out of that hole. If not, I didn't see any point in giving it to the cops. It would just make more trouble for me — especially after Stockwell's irksome remarks on the topic of stolen evidence. The last thing I could think to do was look up Ronan O'Grady and find out more about Terri McCulloch's death.

I reached into the night stand drawer and fished out a pack of desiccated cigarettes. I lit one and took a pull. The old tobacco burned like a fuse. I watched as the smoke from the butt curled and eddied up to the ceiling fixture. Thinking about Terri McCulloch reminded me there was an item rattling around in my trunk that I'd never taken time to fully review: the S&M tape of her and Bishop. I decided I would add that to the list of TBD's. It seemed unlikely there was anything on the tape that would bear on the case, but in spite of Stockwell's exhortations, I wasn't ready to hang it up entirely. Besides, it'd be stupid not to give the tape a quick run through after taking the trouble to nick it from the East Palo Alto apartment.

I was pulled sharply out of my ruminations by the cigarette. It had already burned down to my fingers. I cursed & stubbed it out violently like I was mashing a scorpion.

I cleaned up and got dressed and then walked over to Postworth to have a late breakfast while I read the paper. The afternoon *Examiner* was already out, but it hadn't seen fit to alter the *Chronicle* headline Stockwell dictated to me in any significant way. "Teller Murder Suspect Found Dead. Heroin Overdose in Tenderloin" was how it read. The reporting on Terri's discovery was pretty thin. Dale Pace was not mentioned at all, and I was referred to only as a "San Francisco Private Detective." Much more substantive was the discussion of the significance to the Teller case. The SFPD spokesperson made it clear that the department considered the case to be closed, and found plenty of juicy credit to baste themselves in. Poor old Stockwell only got his name in print one time, and that was in a quote thanking members of cooperating police forces. It sounded like the winning pitcher thanking the batboy.

On my way home I snagged the videotape from the Galaxy's trunk. It was a little worse for wear — one corner of the plastic housing had chipped off — but I figured it would still play. At the apartment I got the tape in my VCR without problem and rewound it to the beginning. I didn't want to miss the socko opening scene.

The tape began as I remembered: in the dungeon with Bishop in fetters on the wooden wheel and Terri flaying away at his butt with a birch rod. He made every bit as much noise as before, but with the benefit of a full play through, I also got to hear Terri's contributions. In a continuing patter, she barked a series of orders, observations and questions at him like a perverted drill sergeant. "You like this, don't you Edwin?" she said. "You need this ... you can get hard now, Edwin. ... I give you permission ... only I decide what you do with your cock ... it's mine ... relax your cheeks ... give yourself up to the rod," and so on.

It didn't take very much of this to send me scrambling for the remote and the fast forward button. I thumbed it down and watched as McCulloch whipped Bishop's butt in herky-jerky movements like a mad woman. In a minute or so, the scene changed abruptly. I lifted my thumb.

Bishop and McCulloch were still in the dungeon and Terri
was wearing the same thing: black leather corset, black
boots and the satisfied expression of a woman who enjoys
her work. Bishop, however, had a whole new look. He was
standing upright, firmly shackled to the concrete wall by
wrists and ankles. A cushioned support at kidney height
was visible on either side of his hips. The apparent goal of
this was to thrust his pelvis forward, bending him off the
wall like a sail in the wind. But that was just the half of it.
Wrapped tight around his scrotum was a black leather
strap. Attached to that was a black iron chain — and dangling from the chain was a metal ball the size of a shot
put. I pressed my knees together and grimaced in sympathetic pain.

In spite of the medieval torture, or perhaps because of
it, Bishop had an erection. I'm not usually one to comment on the physical endowments of others, but if Bishop
was an Oscar Meyer Wiener, he would definitely be a
cocktail frank. Terri stood in front of him, batting his dick
around with crimson-clawed hands the way a cat bats an
injured mouse. She said:

"Now your little soldier is standing at attention. But
only because I ordered it. Isn't that right, Edwin?"

Bishop looked over at her. "Yes mistress," he answered
miserably.

McCulloch grabbed a tuft of Bishop's underarm hair
and yanked it. He yelped like a kicked dog. "Answer more
promptly. And keep your eyes down." She cuffed Bishop's
dick particularly hard. "I think he's ready for some action.
Let's see, what will it be?" She reached between her legs
and undid several snaps. The bottom half of her costume
fell away, leaving her naked from the hips down. Her
pubic hair was trimmed in a narrow stripe.

"A frontal assault?" she said, and rubbed herself suggestively. She passed the hand that had been between her legs under Bishop's nose and then licked her fingers. Bishop whimpered. "A sneak attack?" she continued. She stood with her back to Bishop and bent over, spreading the cheeks of her ass. Bishop's eyes grew wide behind his glasses. "Or an amphibious landing?" She turned to face Bishop and made exaggerated licking motions inches from his face.

"Yes," she said. "We'll do the amphibious landing. Let's just hope your little pecker doesn't get swallowed in the stormy seas." She kneeled in front of Bishop and took hold of the chain between his legs. Tugging down hard on it, she pulled the head of his cock to the level of her mouth. Bishop groaned and scrunched his eyes tight. She teased him for a while with her tongue, and then took him all the way into her mouth. Things finally seemed to be going well for Bishop. Terri's head went up and down rapidly while he made inchoate huffing noises in response.

Then she bit him.

Her head stopped mid-stroke, her jaws clenched and suddenly Bishop screamed like he hadn't screamed before. For a horrible moment, I thought she had taken his penis clean off. I fingered my earlobe where McCulloch had bit *me* and thought, "There but for the grace of God..." I saw that I was wrong, however, when she stood up smiling. Bishop's dick was still firmly attached, but there was blood dripping from it in fat drops that fell lazily to the floor. Terri lips glistened with it. She leaned over and kissed Bishop hard on the mouth, marking him too.

"You've got to expect a few casualties in any action, don't you, Edwin?" she said.

She didn't wait for a reply, but took her left leg under

the knee and swung her foot up to the wall, planting her spiked heel just under Bishop's arm. Then she reached for his cock and slid on top of it. Her ass was a thing to behold as she moved up and down with the ponderous rhythm of a cricket pump. The metal weight oscillated between their legs in counterpoint, the amplitude of its swing increasing until it pounded the concrete wall like a wrecking ball.

Bishop at first seemed stunned by this "frontal assault," but very quickly adapted to the new state of affairs. Once again, he began to make noises of obvious pleasure. They rose in frequency and volume in synch with the swinging ball. As things reached a crescendo, Terri commanded, "Beg for it, Edwin. Beg me to let you come."

Like the obedient dog, Bishop repeated, "Please Mistress, may I come ... please Mistress, may I come," until he was overtaken by orgasm. At the end of it, he hung limp from the chains with his chin on his chest and his hair pasted with sweat to his forehead. The ball drifted back and forth like a metronome left running after the song has finished.

Terri stepped off Bishop with the casual ease of an expert horsewoman. She took hold of his right nipple and tugged on it. She said, "Next time you will pleasure *me*, you miserable slave." Then the screen went blank.

I hit the stop button on the remote control. I ejected the tape from the VCR and walked it out to the apartment corridor where there was an opening for a garbage chute that emptied into the dumpster below. I broke the tape in two on the lip of the chute and dropped both pieces down without ceremony.

I went back to the apartment. I felt like I needed another shower, but I settled for double bourbon.

guinness, o'grady and me

i WENT to my office. Some new business had come in that seemed closer to my speed — employee background checks — so I did what I could with the phone to get the ball rolling. The client was yet another high tech software firm, and it didn't take much checking to find that their candidate for VP of Marketing had a little problem with sexual harassment. Although no one in any official capacity would speak for the record, an HR director at a company where he had worked let slip that another ex-employee might share a tale or two. Turned out the guy had taken his direct reports sailing on the bay to celebrate the completion of a project, and with the benefit of a few wet ones down the hatch, had attempted some maneuvers with female employees that didn't have much to do with steering the boat.

I took it as far as I could without leaving the office, and then called the ambulance company where O'Grady worked. The dispatcher told me that O'Grady was off, and the best place to look for him at this time of day was a bar. That was a search I could really work up some enthusiasm for, but before I set out, I called Duckworth and made an appointment to meet him after he finished the early show at The Stigmata.

I knew from the paramedics at the shooting range that the best place to look for O'Grady was The Rat and Raven. I'd been there a few times, and had read in one of the San Francisco weeklies that it had been selected "Best Bar to Get Hit in the Head with a Dart While Coming Out of the Men's Room" in the annual "best of" issue. As that dubious distinction suggested, it was a somewhat cramped place modeled loosely along the lines of an English pub. They had an excellent selection of beer on tap, however, and that and the allure of being able to claim you were going out for "a little R & R" proved difficult to pass up for its young, mainly working-class clientele. It was located on 24th Street in the heart of a popular neighborhood known as Noe Valley.

I asked the driver of the cab I took from the office to wait while I checked in the bar for O'Grady, but as soon as I stepped out I spotted him through the window at a table near the front. I paid off the cabbie and went inside. Very few people there were heeding the Surgeon General's warning about smoking — and if he had anything to say about listening to Jimmy Hendrix at high volume, they were pretty much ignoring the hell out of that too. O'Grady was sitting on a stool at a high table with a group of five people: three men and two women. Several were wearing paramedic uniforms, and they were all nursing a pint of dark beer. The foamy remnants of a pitcher of Guinness Stout stood in the center of the table. O'Grady had a flush on his face and he was telling a story in a loud voice between drags on his cigarette. He said:

"So I ask them how it happened. Now your man — he is in too much pain to talk. And your woman — well, she knows her husband blames her and she don't want to say anything that will add to her troubles."

"Quit building it up, Ronan," said a man sitting across from O'Grady. "Just tell us what happened."

O'Grady smiled and took a big swallow of beer. He set his glass down and looked around the table with an amused expression. "Well, as I told you, they were an older couple. The wife still liked to use that aerosol hair spray that comes in a can. She's in the WC getting ready for their night out, but she can't get the hair spray to work. It's clogged, you see. She's shaking the can and shaking the can and still nothing comes out. Finally she gets the idea to ream out the nozzle with a pin. She does that, but then she gets to worrying that the spray will come out too fast. So instead of chancing it on her hair, she lifts the lid of the toilet and aims it into the bowl. It sprays out fine, and she puts down the lid and finishes getting ready.

"Now the husband has been pacing outside in the hallway, puffing away on his cigar. He has to take the devil's own crap and the wife has been in the bathroom for nearly an hour. Finally she comes out, and he rushes past her, drops his trousers and settles onto the can. But there's no ashtray about, see, and his cigar ash has gotten long, so he parts his legs and flicks it down between his thighs. Well, the ash is burning and it ignites the hair spray that the wife has sprayed in the bowl. It goes up like a fireball, and whether from the force of the explosion or from the pain, the husband launches off the toilet and hits his head on the edge of a cabinet above him. And that is how when I arrived I found your man with third degree burns all over his arse, his pants around his ankles and a four inch gash in his head."

O'Grady's companions pounded the table with their glasses and laughed appreciatively. I had to chuckle myself. O'Grady downed the rest of his beer, and finding the amount remaining in the pitcher insufficient to meet his needs, slipped off his stool and went up to the bar for a refill. I came up beside him and said:

"This round's on me, Ronan."

O'Grady turned sharply and stared at me a little bleary-eyed. "August!" he said, slapping me on the back. "I'm going to look under the bed tonight before I go to sleep. The way you keep popping up, I won't be surprised to find you there."

I smiled. "The last time was a coincidence. This time I went looking for you. I wanted to talk to you about the woman you picked up at the hotel."

"She's dead, August."

"I know. I thought you could tell me more about how she died."

"Was she a particular friend of yours?"

"No. No friend at all. But she was important to a case I've been working on. If you read the paper today you know what it's about. It's mostly over, but I wanted to tie up the lose ends."

"I don't mind talking if you don't mind listening. But since you're buying, why not get two pitchers: one for us and the other for that pack of troublemakers at the table."

I bought two pitchers as O'Grady suggested and we took ours to a corner table by the window. O'Grady poured the Guinness slowly, being very careful to let the foam settle just so, and then took a sip from his glass. "It's crap," he pronounced.

"What do you mean?" I said. "I thought all you first generation turf gobblers loved this stuff."

"Jesus above. Don't be calling me a turf gobbler. That's reserved for the hicks — as you would say — from outside of Dublin, and most especially for people from Cork. I'm direct from Dublin, as I think I've told you. Anyway, the problem is not with Guinness in general, but with this Guinness in particular. It gets ruined coming over. This tastes nothing like what you get from a pub in Ireland."

"At least it's not in cans."

"Now you are blaspheming. So what is it you want to know in return for your beer?"

"Well, I'm not sure. Maybe you could just tell me what happened after you left the hotel. I gather she didn't die in the ambulance."

"No, she didn't, but she certainly tried. She stopped breathing almost as soon as we had her downstairs and we had to put her on the respirator. You saw me give her the shot in the hotel room?"

"Yes."

"That was something called Nalline. It's a drug that neutralizes the narcotic effect of heroin. If you give it to someone quickly enough, it will bind with the heroin in the blood stream and bring the patient out of their coma. It works so well at times that a patient can wake up angry and frustrated because you've completely destroyed his high. It's ironic — you have someone who almost died from an overdose and he's already craving another fix."

"But that's not what happened with Terri McCulloch."

"No. She had too much dope in her system for too long

a period. That was why her breathing stopped. In high doses, heroin has a paralytic effect on the respiratory response. Still, we kept her going with the respirator and started a Nalline IV drip, so she had a fighting chance. I was a bit surprised when I heard that she had died at the hospital."

"Why?"

O'Grady took out a penknife and scraped idly at the wooden table. "Oh," he said. "A couple reasons. The first is that in spite of all your 1960's rock stars and such OD'ing on heroin, not that many people die from an overdose these days if they receive medical attention. So the odds were in her favor, even if we did get to her late. The second reason is that she seemed to me to have stabilized by the time we got her to the hospital. I thought she might have turned the corner."

"What happened then? Why didn't she pull through?"

O'Grady set the knife aside and picked up his glass. He swirled the beer and looked down at it thoughtfully. "I don't want you to misunderstand me. I thought the odds of her living were better than her dying, but they weren't so much better that I would have bet money on it. And I don't mean to imply that the hospital staff mucked up her treatment. But given the circumstances, there are one or two things I can imagine that might have tipped the scales against her."

"Okay, let's have 'em."

"Well, it occurred to me later that there might have been some other drug mixed in with the heroin. Some people do speedballs, which is a mixture of heroin and cocaine. The problem in treating a speedball overdose is that Nalline has no effect on the cocaine. Once you suppress the effects of the heroin, the cocaine comes blasting through with a vengeance."

"But no one dies of a cocaine overdose."

"Sure they do. Especially if their body has been weakened from a disease or congenital defect. And there you have my other idea. It's possible the girl had an underlying medical problem that compounded the overdose. In the end, her heart just stopped. Could be she already had a cardiopulmonary defect."

I shook my head. "From what I saw of her, she was pretty damn vigorous. But how could we find out for sure — I mean, about other drugs or medical problems."

"I'm surprised at you, August. Wait for the autopsy, of course. That or talk to the hospital staff. They might have run blood tests for the drugs or detected other health problems."

"I like the hospital angle. You took her to Mount Zion, right? You chummy with anyone on their staff?"

"What? Are you joking? I know all the ER staff. Penny Waller — she's a particular friend of mine at Mt. Zion."

"Great. How's to take a quick trip over to Mt. Zion and talk to her?"

"Right now? There's no chance of that, man. I see enough of emergency rooms without using my free time to visit them."

It took some arm-twisting and the promise of more Guinness Stout, but eventually I managed to get O'Grady bundled into a cab headed in the direction of the hospital. We pulled up in the broad drive of the emergency entrance and I paid off the driver. Ronan jumped out and strode through the automatic doors to a reception desk just inside. When I caught up to him, he had already established that Penny Waller was in a staff lounge a short way up the corridor. He bulled through the lounge door without knocking.

It opened onto a narrow, brightly lit room that had a glass-topped coffee table and a pair of worn couches covered in green plaid. At the back was a kitchenette with a sink, coffee maker and a tiny refrigerator. The only person in the room was a bored-looking woman with short hair dyed a shade that only occurs in nature on fire engines. She was wearing an austere hospital pantsuit that didn't completely obscure a lush figure. Her eyes were startling china blue, she had a silver stud in her left nostril and she was sitting on a couch using a slight overbite to good advantage on a juicy red apple. She looked to be in her mid-twenties and the tag on her breast read, "Penny Waller, RN."

She took one look at O'Grady and said, "Scat! Shoo! Go away! I'm on my break. Don't you dare bring any business to me."

"Relax, darlin'," said O'Grady. "You can see that I'm not in uniform. The fact of the matter is, we're here for a small favor — and it has nothing to do with new patients."

Waller eyed us skeptically. "I can smell the beer on your breath from here, Ronan. This isn't another one of your crazy scavenger hunts is it? The things you paramedics think of when you get drinking. 'Do you have an x-ray of a guy with a gerbil up his butt, Penny? Do you have some of the pubic hair they shaved off the mayor before his hernia operation, Penny?' Sheech. You guys need to grow up. Who's your friend there, anyway?"

If O'Grady was the least little bit embarrassed, he didn't show it. He dropped on to the couch across from Waller. "His name is August Riordan, Penny dear. He's a great drinker, a mediocre jazz bass player, and a bad detective. The terrible thing is, he makes more money from the

third than the second. The result is a set of warped priorities. Rather than drinking or bass playing, he fritters his
time away chasing clues."

Waller put the apple down on the table. She looked up
at me while working on a back tooth with the nail of her
pinkie finger. "Damn apples," she said after a moment. "I
only eat them because they're supposed to be good for
you." She flicked a particle of apple peel across the room.
"Clues. What kind of clues?"

I said, "I want to look at the medical file of the woman
Ronan brought in last night. The one who died."

"And why would that be?"

"I want to find out how she died."

Waller shrugged elaborately and glanced over to
O'Grady. "She OD'ed on heroin. What's to find out?"

O'Grady gave me a hand. "I'm afraid I suggested there
might be some complicating factors," he said. "We'd like to
see if they ran any tests on the pharmacology or diag-
nosed any underlying health problems."

"This *is* just like one of your scavenger hunts," said Waller. "What do you think, I can go up to ICU and just ask
them to hand over the file? Besides, they probably sent it
to the coroner's already."

"If the file is gone, then of course there's no help for it.
But where's the harm in borrowing it for a short while if
you find it's still there? I would regard it as a particular
favor, Penny. It's the quickest way to restore me to my bar
stool, and get the great white detective out of both our
camiknickers."

"He wouldn't be in *my* cami-whatever's if you hadn't
have put him there." She stared at Ronan defiantly and
then snapped her eyes over to me. "Okay, I'll go look. But
only because I have a soft spot for tall men with dark hair

and pale complexions."

O'Grady laughed. He said to me, "I believe that was a reference to you. God gives all his creatures the means to get by. In your case he's compensated for your lack of brains with an appearance that is inexplicably attractive to emergency room nurses."

Penny Waller giggled and left the room. She came back a few minutes later carrying a pink file folder. "Here it is. They were holding it for the results of some lab work they ordered last night. Came back too late to do her any good, I guess." She passed the file over to O'Grady. "You can hang out here and read it. Don't even think of taking it out of the building. I've got to go back on duty, so when you're finished drop it off with Ellen at the front desk."

"Thanks very much," I said. "I doubt there's anything of interest, but I just felt like I had to touch all the bases."

Waller nodded and put her hand out for me to shake. "No problem. Maybe next time you play somewhere, you can invite me to come. I like jazz — as well as tall, pale men with dark hair."

"Done," I said, and shook her hand. My eyes and O'Grady's tracked her shapely posterior out the door.

"Well, there you are, August," said O'Grady. "You've made a new friend."

"I'd like her better if she didn't use her nail for a tooth-pick."

"Don't be getting above yourself. Penny Waller is a jewel of a girl. She's just a little earthy is all."

O'Grady began thumbing through the file. I looked over his shoulder while he read, but I didn't get very much from what I saw. There was a page on the top with hand written notes. Below that were various forms with text printed by a computer, a long strip of graph paper with what I assumed was output from a heart and respiration monitor and a log of some sort with annotations made every half-hour. The last entry was made at 4:30 am.

"So," I said. "What do you make of it?"

"Well, I can tell you that she died of massive pulmonary edema. Basically that means her lungs filled with fluid, and the resulting strain on her lungs and her heart eventually did her in. It happens sometimes with heroin overdoses, although doctors don't really know why. Some people think it's triggered by the stuff they cut the heroin with — which is often quinine — and some people think it is caused by mixing the heroin with other drugs or even alcohol."

"Is there anything to show that there were other drugs in her system?"

"It does appear she'd been drinking, at least. There's a test here that shows her blood alcohol level was .10 percent when she was admitted. Nothing that says she'd used coke or barbiturates, however. The best way to double check would be analyze the stuff left in the syringe or run a urinalysis during the autopsy."

"They also got some unused packets of drugs from her purse they could check. What about other health problems? You said something about a cardiopulmonary defect at the bar."

"Well, I don't see anything to indicate a problem like a bad heart valve. There is one thing that's a little odd. They ran a blood test on her and her T-cell count is somewhat depressed."

"What's that mean?"

"It means she might have had some sort of infection. The count is still above 500, which is not way out of whack, but it could indicate the presence of a viral respiratory infection, bacterial pneumonia or even TB. If she had any of those, it would definitely have contributed to the pulmonary edema." O'Grady stared down at the folder and seemed to drift off.

"What?" I said. "What are you thinking?"

"I'm thinking that a low T-cell count can also be an indicator of HIV. You know that intravenous drug users are a high risk group."

"Did they run an AIDS test on her?"

"No, you can't do that without a patient's written permission. Since she never regained consciousness, they wouldn't have been able to get it. But I wouldn't want us to jump to conclusions. A T-cell count like that might indicate nothing more than a bad flu. And in the end, it is still secondary when it comes to determining the cause of death. To quote our friend Penny, 'She OD'ed on heroin. What's to find out?'"

I mulled that one over a bit. "Okay, I'll throw in the towel. Her death just seemed a little too convenient. I guess I wanted to find some evidence of poison or other foul play."

"The only foul play around here, lad, is the continuing lack of liquid refreshment. I suggest we repair to the nearest pub and remedy that situation post haste."

O'Grady and I left the hospital and walked up Divisadero to a bar on the corner at Pine. I split another pitcher with him, listening to the story of how he and his partner had a contest giving CPR to an 80 year old man who'd been dead for 20 minutes by the time they got him strapped in the ambulance. The goal was to see who could drive the dead guy's pulse rate the highest on the ride to the hospital. O'Grady claimed he won by sending it to 200, which he said was twice as high as the guy ever got when he was alive.

I left O'Grady in the company of Mr. Guinness for my appointment with Duckworth at around 9:30.

Chapter 27

queen to queen's knight one

"*i* THINK you've got the real deal this time, August," Duckworth said looking at me in the mirror of his cramped dressing room. He was perched on a stool with a laptop computer balanced precariously on top of a crossed leg. Swathed in a red silk gown with gold swirls embroidered throughout the bodice, he had accessorized with matching red pumps, diamond earrings and a short black wig with ludicrous spit curls that clung to his cheeks. Overall, he looked like a young Liza Minelli with too much time on the bench press. "The card appears to have the source code on it, as well as a compiled version of the game. Of course, I really couldn't say for sure that all the source code is there unless I tried to recompile it. I don't have a C++ compiler so I can't do that for you now." He ejected the PCMCIA card from a slot in his computer and passed it back to me.

"Really?" I said. "All that on this little card? It doesn't need batteries or moving parts or anything?"

Duckworth shook his head and his diamond earrings shimmered. "Nope," he said. "It's called flash memory and I don't really understand how it works, but somehow it stores information nonvolatilely without consuming power. As long you don't step on the card or drop it in the sink, anything you write on it is retained for as long as you want. The only downside is it is pretty expensive. A card that holds over 200 megabytes like that probably goes for at least a thousand dollars."

"A thousand dollars. Terri McCulloch certainly didn't have that kind of money to fling around. She must have stolen the card from Bishop when she took the software."

"That makes sense. He's the sort of guy who would have all the latest toys. I doubt he would have used the card to archive his source code, though. I'm sure he has tape drives, optical storage devices and all sorts of other paraphernalia for that. Still, it would be a very handy way for Terri to make off with the chess program. Light, compact and easy to conceal."

"You're right about that," I said, slipping the card into my breast pocket. I looked down at the table in front of Duckworth and picked up an eyelash curler from the clutter of makeup, brushes, powder puffs and lipsticks. "This looks like something Terri McCulloch would have used in her dungeon. Aren't you afraid of pulling your eyelids clean off?'

Duckworth smiled. "It seems more medieval than it is. You should try tweezing your eyebrows. Now that's torture."

I returned the curler to the table. "I guess that's all I needed. I'm taking the card back to Bishop tomorrow if he'll agree to see me. And that will be the end of that."

"But what about Nagel? You never did find out what he was up to."

"No, I didn't. I'm not going to worry about it. That reminds me: did you get all the duct tape out of your hair?"

Duckworth brought his hand up to the back of his head almost involuntarily. "I had to douse it with lighter fluid for a good half hour, but it finally came out." Duckworth looked at me solemnly. "I guess this is good-bye then."

I chuckled. "Don't make it sound so dramatic. But thanks for all your help, Chris. I really appreciated it."

Duckworth stood up. Even in his heels, he only came up chin high. I watched as his eyes filled with water and his lower lip trembled. "Would you mind giving me a hug, August?"

I hesitated, and then awkwardly reached round to hug him. He hugged back with a fierce strength, and planted a blubbery kiss on my neck. "I'm going to miss you."

"Cut it out," I said. "We'll get together again." I broke the clinch and stepped back. "Maybe we can do a brother/sister act. Me on bass and you on vocals."

Duckworth smiled weakly. Streaks of mascara-stained tears rain down his face "Yes, I'd like that."

I walked over to the dressing room door and pulled it open. "By the way, Chris," I said. "You look swell in red."

Chapter 28

bishop's gambit

i CALLED Bishop the next morning. Once I got it into his pointy little propeller head that I actually had his software in my possession, he agreed to see me. Eagerly. I told him I would stop by around mid-day. But before heading down to Woodside, I took another walk through the Tenderloin to get to San Francisco's new main library at Larkin and Grove.

The librarian said I didn't look like a man who would be greatly interested in chess, but she agreed to help me use the computer-based card catalog to dig up a few books on the subject anyway. I put in several hours beneath a mural depicting the driving of the solid gold spike reading about famous games in chess history. I returned the books to the librarian when I was finished and admitted that her estimation of my interest in chess had been about right.

The sun had burned off the morning clouds and fog by the time I pulled into Bishop's driveway. The house appeared freshly scrubbed, and the surrounding grounds seemed as green as the emerald in the Buddha's belly button. The bell played the same waltz as last time, but I still couldn't place it. Jodie answered the door wearing another swimsuit. This one was a dark, one-piece number that was cut so high on her hips it almost exposed ribs. Flying in the face of sound structural engineering practices, a flimsy netting that exposed a great deal more than ribs had been used throughout the top of the suit.

"Hello August," said Jodie soberly. "Things didn't work out very well, did they? Edwin says Terri brought it all on herself, but I can't help but feel bad."

"Really?" I said. "That's white of you. Is the big fella around?"

An odd expression settled on Jodie's face. "He's on the phone. He told me to take you to the study to wait 'til he gets off the line."

"Lead on."

I followed a few steps behind, watching her taut calf muscles flex and release as she sashayed down the marble hallway. She dropped me off in the same study chair as before. Looking around, I realized for the first time that the chessboard next to Bishop's desk was actually a computer with pressure sensitive pads of the sort Duckworth had described. I fiddled around with the switches until some lights came on, and then made some trial moves with the black pieces and watched as the computer responded. I had been going at it for about fifteen minutes when a voice from behind interrupted:

"What's the damage?"

I looked up to find Bishop standing at the door in a bathrobe and sandals. Jodie was just behind him. "I'm ahead in captured pieces," I said, "but I understand you can't always judge by that."

"Yes, it depends on the circumstances. We're going out to the hot tub. Would you care to join us?"

"Thanks but no thanks. I didn't come prepared."

"I'll be happy to loan you a bathing suit."

The thought of me trying to squeeze into one of Bishop's swimsuits was laughable. "No, I'll have to pass."

Bishop made a dismissive gesture. "Well, come out with us anyway. We can talk while Jodie and I soak."

I got up and followed them out the study door, down the marble hall to an adjoining hall that led to a back door. The door opened onto a vast redwood deck that was laid in a parquet pattern and extended from the house in multiple tiers. Wrought iron lawn furniture was scattered across it on various levels, and planter boxes with carefully trimmed Japanese bonsai were set along the edges. We followed the course of a winding stair to ground level and then went along a flagstone path into a group of oak trees. The hot tub was in the middle of a large clearing, set flush into a redwood deck and covered by an octagonal pavilion. The tub itself probably wasn't big enough to hold the killer whale show at Sea World.

Bishop opened the hinged doors that covered the tub,

stripped off his robe and stepped inside. Jodie paused to flip the switch that controlled the jets and then followed him into the bubbling water. Bishop eased his arm around her as she settled in. "This is the life, eh Riordan? You should have taken your chance when you had it."

"Yeah, it seems I miss a lot of chances."

Bishop gestured to a small clasp envelope I had carried from the car. "So, you have my chess software in there, do you? I did notice a PCMCIA flash card had gone missing, but I couldn't be sure that Terri had taken it."

I opened the envelope and pulled out the card. I held it between my thumb and forefinger and turned it slowly like I was admiring a thing of great beauty. "I still can't get over these cards," I said. "They say the more advanced a technology is, the more it seems like magic to the uninitiated. Well, these babies seem pretty magical to me. But to answer your question: yes, I'm told by someone who's up on this stuff that your source code is on the card. I guess it's pretty valuable to you now. Being your only copy and all."

"It's immensely valuable. In fact, I'd appreciate it if you would return the card to the envelope and place it on the deck. I wouldn't want to handle it with wet hands."

I looked down at Bishop. His pale skin and spindly build made me think of a plucked squab being parboiled. I leered at him and calmly flicked the card into the water. A strangled cry erupted from Jodie.

"What in the hell do you think you're doing?" thundered Bishop, but made no effort to retrieve the PCMCIA card. It fluttered to the bottom of the tub, a dark square visible through the bubbling water next to Bishop's overgrown toenails.

"If I wanted to be poetic, I'd say I was returning a red

herring to the sea."

Bishop's eyes bored up at me. He pulled his arm out from behind Jodie's shoulder. "You're going to have to explain that."

"You couldn't stop me if you wanted to. While I was waiting for you in the study I arranged the chessmen on your chess computer the way they were after the tenth move in a match between Anderssen and Kieseritzky. It's called 'The Immortal Game' — I expect you've heard of it. Anyway, the one thing I learned about your software is that your program is the only one on the market that could be expected to duplicate Anderssen's next move when placed in the same situation. You told me that Terri McCulloch had taken or destroyed all the copies of the software. Imagine my surprise when the computer in your study also duplicated Anderssen's move exactly."

"So that's what you were up to," said Bishop. "But you're quite mistaken about the chess computer in my study. It's running a chess program I wrote several years ago. That program is good, but it doesn't have anywhere near the capabilities of my new one. Never mind that you've completely lost sight of my reasons for hiring you. Why would I pay to recover something I still had?"

"You wouldn't. But you would pay good money to frame Terri McCulloch for Roland Teller's murder."

Jodie moved away from Bishop. Her eyes flashed back and forth between us. Bishop sat mute, his arms tightly crossed.

I crushed the envelope into a ball and bounced it off his forehead. "What's the matter? Does the Great Oz lack for words?"

Bishop roared and slapped at the envelope where it floated in the water. "You are an insolent cretin. Terri

McCulloch stole that software, sold it to Teller and killed him. There's rock solid evidence to support every one of those assertions. You yourself recovered the software from her purse."

"I don't doubt Terri stole a *copy* of your software. And I'm sure she pitched it to Teller. But even Teller wasn't dippy enough to license software without talking directly to the principal. I think he contacted you after he was approached by McCulloch and told you what he had been offered. The funny thing is, you weren't really hurt by the theft. As her experience with Mephisto proved, it would be very hard for Terri to sell the game. And while she did take a copy of the source code, and maybe even destroyed a backup or two, someone as experienced as you would have backups to your backups.

"But the theft did give you an idea. It gave you the idea of killing Teller and pinning the blame for his murder on McCulloch."

"You should write for the *Inquirer*, Riordan. What possible motive could I have for such a thing."

"Revenge, of course. And I don't mean for the software theft. I mean revenge for something she did to you that hurt you very much more. She gave you AIDS." Bishop blanched at the word.

I turned to Jodie, "And she probably gave it to you too, cupcake — or Eddie here passed it on. In any case, you wanted revenge just as bad. That explains why you tipped me to The Power Station with the concerned friend act at my office."

Jodie squealed and jumped out of the hot tub. She ran back towards the house. I continued pounding on Bishop: "At first I couldn't figure Teller's role in the scheme, but now I think you told him you needed his help to make a better case against McCulloch for the software theft. You probably offered Teller the legitimate rights to your game in return for his cooperation. The risk to him was slight — McCulloch would find it hard to prove he was lying — and the reward for being the publisher of your game was great.

"Or so it would seem to him. What you didn't mention to Teller was that a key component of your plan involved chilling him off with Terri McCulloch's gun. You set him up by sending him a key to the East Palo Alto apartment and asking him to meet you there. Then you shot him. With Teller out of the picture, my role was to bear witness to the whole story and encourage the police to think McCulloch capable of murder. You may not have planned on me being at the apartment house that night, but it actually helped your cause since it forced me to pass on your lies to the cops that much sooner."

Bishop tilted his chin up and stroked his beard like before. He was about to give me the benefit of his superior intellect. "I think the blows you received to your head have scrambled your brains completely, Mr. Riordan. My training as a chess tactician and computer scientist has taught me to analyze problems dispassionately in a thoroughly logical manner. Your theory doesn't hold together; there are too many inconsistencies and unexplained behaviors. How could I have obtained the key to Terri's apartment to send to the unfortunate Mr. Teller? I have not had any contact with Terri since she left my employ. Second, if the chess computer in my study has the significance you claim, then why would I leave you alone to play with it? That would be the last thing on earth I should wish you to see. Finally — and this point is the most damaging of all — why would I give a copy of my chess program to Teller? Him of all people. Why would I risk losing control of the most sophisticated chess software in the world merely to revenge myself on a cheap prostitute?"

I laughed at him. "Your dispassion is slipping a little Bishop. I don't know how you got hold of Terri McCulloch's apartment key, but I'll make a special effort to find out. You weren't concerned about my playing with the chess computer in your study because you didn't expect a cretinous private eye would be able to make anything out of it. As for your last point, your mention of chess tactics is quite appropriate. In the Immortal Game, Anderssen begins his match with Kieseritzky with a gambit. He sacrifices one of his pieces at the start of the game to gain the advantage at the end — just like you risked losing control of your chess program by giving it to Teller. The piece Anderssen sacrifices is a bishop: that opening is known as a bishop's gambit."

The guy behind me wasn't very good. But then, he never really had been. I heard him as soon as he stepped onto the redwood decking. He made a rush for me, swinging at my head with a wicked leather blackjack. I twisted to my left and the sap burned at my ear and cheekbone instead of cracking open my skull. The sudden movement threw me off balance and I ended up on all fours at the edge of the hot tub. As I struggled to stand up, the lad with the blackjack took a long step and dove straight into my kidneys. My hands slipped forward into the water, and the next thing I knew my attacker had a fistful of my hair and was thrusting my head under the bubbling froth.

Fortunately I was too far into the water for him to have much leverage. I reached up and grabbed his wrist and then dug my toe into the decking and pushed for all I was worth. He tried to pull back, but it was too late. We both fell into the tub, a mass of swirling bubbles and tangled clothing under the water. My foot touched bottom and I shot up to the surface for air. I found Bishop cowering in the corner of the hot tub and his goon attempting to wrap me up in a bear hug. I slipped my hand under my suit coat and jacked out the Glock. After days of walking into blackjacks and drawn pistols, Riordan finally pulls out his gun when it will do some good. I swung the butt down square on the brainpan of my dance partner, felt his grip slacken and then watched as he floated on the surface like a dead mackerel. It was Todd Nagel of course. I yanked his head out of the water so he could breathe.

Bishop saw which way the wind was blowing and tried to scramble out of the hot tub. I reached my hand up and grabbed him by the waistband of his swim trunks and pulled him back into the water. I slammed the automatic into his jaw and viciously wedged the barrel into his mouth.

I pushed it down his throat until I heard him start to gag. "Got milk?" I said through clenched teeth.

Chapter 29

endgame

*d*UCKWORTH and I were already sitting down to a lunch of Big Macs and fries at the East Palo Alto McDonald's when Stockwell came up.

"Who the hell is that?" he asked, gesturing at Duckworth.

"He's my partner," I said. "We're starting a new business doing people's colors."

"Sea foam green," said Duckworth. "That's a color that would work for you, Lieutenant. Much better than that tepid, uninspired brown you have on today."

Stockwell elbowed his way onto the plastic bench next to me. "Is that right? Well, I think you two would look great in dog dick pink. What do you have to say about that?"

Duckworth tittered.

"Dicks and the color pink are topics I wouldn't care to broach with Mr. Duckworth, here," I said. "I asked him to join us because of all the help he's given me on the case. I felt I owed him."

Stockwell eyed Duckworth suspiciously, working over-time to process my comment about dicks. "Okay," he said finally. "I expect you'd only blab it to him later."

"Now you're learning. You want to order some lunch? I might even buy."

"No, my wife doesn't let me eat this crap — and I don't want to drag this out any longer than necessary. This isn't exactly a social occasion."

"And all this time I thought you liked me. All right, then. What do you have for us?"

"Well, first of all, you fucking broke two of Bishop's teeth off. Did you know that?"

"I might have noticed a certain gap-toothed aspect to his smile when the San Mateo County Sheriff's deputies helped him into the car."

"Oh, very observant of you. He says you rammed a gun down his throat."

I took a big bite of my hamburger and munched it thoughtfully. "They are right about this sauce. It *is* special."

Stockwell glared at me and then grabbed a couple of fries and popped them into his mouth. He chewed them like they were fighting back.

"Ketchup?" asked Duckworth.

"Shut up."

"Enough about Bishop," I said. "He should be glad I did-n't rip him apart with my bare hands. What did you find out about the people who are dead?"

"That you were right. The autopsy showed that both McCulloch and Hastrup were HIV positive."

"So McCulloch infected Hastrup, and when he found out he was positive he killed himself," said Duckworth.

"Yeah, looks that way. We never did find a note, but it turns out he donated blood a couple days before he died. They routinely screen donations for HIV, and when they got the results back from his, they called and told him he was positive. The administrator at the blood bank said he took it very badly. Said he fell to pieces right on the phone."

"Still," said Duckworth. "That's no reason to kill yourself. They can do a lot more with the virus than they used to."

"For Hastrup, it wouldn't just be the health aspect," I said. "For a macho asshole like him there would also be the stigma of having a disease that only gays and drug ad-dicts are supposed to get. That and the fact that Terri McCulloch had given it to him. He'd see it as a humiliat-ing betrayal."

"You seem to have a keen insight into the macho asshole mentality," said Duckworth. "Wonder why."

I looked over at Stockwell and watched him shovel in a handful of fries. "Don't look at me," he said with his mouth full of masticated potato. "You brought him."

"Everybody makes mistakes. What about Bishop and Jodie? Do they have it?"

"Bishop refuses to take a test, and there's no way we can force him. Nor can we subpoena his medical records. The law guarantees confidentiality. Jodie does admit to being positive, however. It looks like she'll admit to a great deal more, too, in order to save her hide."

"But what about Nagel?" asked Duckworth. "He's the real mystery man. What's his connection to all this?"

Stockwell popped another fry into his mouth and smiled. "Yes, he is the mysterious one, isn't he?" Stockwell gave me a hard elbow to the ribs. "We finally matched up that fingerprint from the picture in McCulloch's apartment. The one you said didn't mean anything. Who do you think it belongs to?"

"Your mom?"

"Fuck you. It belongs to Nagel, of course. He's the one who hit you from behind and he's the one who killed Teller. There's almost no doubt of it."

"Great," said Duckworth. "But that still doesn't explain who he is."

"Did you ever think that Bishop's last name was a little too cute? I mean him being a whiz at chess and having a name like Bishop and all."

"Yeah," I said. "It did seem a little coincidental. It could have worked the other way around, though. He has the name and he decides he's going to try to live up to it."

"Well, that's not the way it worked. The way it worked is his name was originally Nagel. Todd Nagel is his younger brother."

"Ah ha!" said Duckworth. "I knew it all along. I'll be right back." Duckworth got up from the booth.

"Where's he going?" asked Stockwell, and ate still another fry.

"To get the color wheel. But back to Nagel. I guess that explains how he could afford the house in Daly City. Bishop must have been giving him money."

"That's right. We got hold of the bank records and there's a regular stream of checks from Bishop to Nagel. The phone records tie them together too. Bishop had another unlisted number that Nagel regularly called. Not that it matters. The fingerprint and the fact they are brothers is more than enough."

"All right. Let's see if I can walk us through this. McCulloch is working for Bishop. She contracts AIDS — either by sharing needles or through sex. She infects Bishop. Bishop tumbles to it and fires her. Or maybe he doesn't even know about the AIDS at that point and he fires her for drug problems like Jodie told me. Doesn't matter. In order to get back at him, McCulloch steals the chess software and tries to erase all of his copies."

"Probably, but Bishop had an off-site back up service. To protect against earthquakes, etc. Even if she zapped every copy in the house, there's no way she could have got to that."

"What I figured. So she takes the software and goes to Teller with it. He'd love to get his hands on it because he's trying to squeeze every dime he can out of his business, but he doesn't trust McCulloch. Teller contacts Bishop and asks if she's legit. By now Bishop knows about the AIDS if he didn't before. He could just warn Teller off, but instead he cooks up a scheme to revenge himself on McCulloch by framing her for Teller's murder. He co-opts Teller by promising him legitimate rights to his software and then sets him up for the kill at McCulloch's apartment. But how does he—"

Duckworth came back to the table with another Big Mac. "Here you go, Lieutenant. I hate to see a big, strapping man like you go hungry. And I'd like to eat a few of my own fries — thank you very much."

Stockwell looked down at the hamburger. I could tell he was beginning to get an idea about Duckworth, but hunger won out over homophobia. "What the hell," said Stockwell. "My cholesterol is only 205. I've got a good 35 points before my heart seizes up."

"The longest journey begins with the first step," I said. "But here is what I want to know — and I've wanted to know it for a very long time. How did Teller get a key to McCulloch's apartment? And don't give me that nutzo theory about Teller having an affair with McCulloch because that just doesn't wash."

A big glob of special sauce ran down Stockwell's chin. He wiped it with the back of his hand, then licked it off. "The landlady," said Stockwell. "Bishop bribed her to give him a key. Bishop sent a copy on to Teller with an invite to meet him there. Nagel shows up instead and knocks you out and then kills Teller with McCulloch's gun. A gun, by the way, that was a gift from Bishop."

"How'd you get all that?" I asked.

"The landlady told us about the key when we explained to her exactly what conspiracy to commit murder was. Jodie gave us most of the rest of it, although she wasn't there for the kill."

Duckworth pulled the straw out of his soft drink and waved it frantically to get our attention. Droplets of coke splattered Stockwell's shirt and he swore sharply. Duckworth was oblivious. "Time out you two. All this is fine and good, but I'm having trouble with the motives. I can see how Bishop would want to get back at Terri, but would he really kill an innocent man to do it? And would Jodie really go along — even if she was infected?"

"Teller was far from innocent as far as Bishop was concerned," I said. "Bishop felt Teller had ripped off the user interface of one of his earlier games. Killing Teller to en-snare McCulloch would be Bishop's idea of a masterstroke of revenge on both of them."

Stockwell grunted. "And I can explain the Jodie part if you'd quit waving your straw around like a fucking fairy wand."

Duckworth straightened in his chair and set his shoulders. He passed the straw over Stockwell like he was doing an incantation, said, "Turn to shit."

Stockwell sighed. "You guys really belong together, you know that? If you believe Jodie, Bishop blackmailed her into helping. Her dad's a Federal Appellate Court judge. She says Bishop threatened to tell pops that she was HIV positive. The old guy was freaked enough over her life-style and Jodie couldn't bear him knowing the AIDS shit too. By the way, she claims it wasn't only AIDS and the software theft that prompted Bishop to get revenge."

"What else was there?" I asked.

"Get this: she said that Bishop was in love with McCul-loch. She said the final straw for him was when he heard that Terri and Hastrup were seeing each other."

I thought that through while Stockwell finished his hamburger in two bites. "And McCulloch?" I asked. "How did she die?"

"The how of it is pretty straight-forward. It's the why I'm not sure about. The autopsy report says she died from a heroin overdose, complicated by the presence of keta-mine and alcohol in her system. Well and good. What I can't tell you is whether she did it on purpose, by accident, or—"

Duckworth jumped in. "Or whether Bishop and Nagel killed her. I'll bet you anything that's what happened."

Stockwell shrugged and began a mopping up operation

with a wad of napkins. "It's possible. But Jodie says no, and we can't find any evidence to tie Bishop or Nagel to the heroin and the K."

"Did the SFPD interview any of the street people in the Tenderloin?" I asked. "Maybe someone saw McCulloch scoring the stuff."

"You know the high regard in which I hold the San Francisco cops. They say they made the rounds and that no one saw her. But that don't mean squat when it comes right down to it."

"No," I said. "I suppose not. Anyway, my vote is accidental. There's not much point in Bishop engineering a frame for McCulloch if he's going to turn right around and kill her. Might as well have done that in the first place. As far as her doing it on purpose, she wasn't the type. She was much tougher than Hastrup, for instance. As a matter of fact, I think she liked being HIV positive. I think she delighted in the idea of dominating men, humiliating them during sex — and ultimately — killing them."

"Sounds like just the kind of gal you want to take home to meet mom and dad," said Stockwell.

"Yes, but think about it," said Duckworth. "There's not a single person involved in this who you could honestly say was blameless or untainted. Not Teller — he willingly helped Bishop. Not Jodie — she was in it too. Hastrup was McCulloch's pawn. Bishop and Nagel are obviously out. The landlady's out. Even Dale Pace is out. Every one of them is dirty in some way."

I looked out the window at a blonde woman sitting in an idling car in the drive-up line. She was nobody I knew, but the blonde hair got me thinking. "You're wrong about that, Chris," I said. "There's one person who's clean. Margaret Teller."

Chapter 30

lonely knight

i CALLED her that afternoon. I guess I had some idea of asking her out, but when I inquired how she was doing the conversation got away from me.

"I'm fine, Mr. Riordan," she said. "I mean, August, of course. It is very thoughtful of you to call. We buried Roland two days ago, and while I am sure I will go through many more phases of grief, at least I am past the anger. At least I no longer blame everyone in the community for his death."

I said that was good.

"Good? Yes, you could say that. However, the anger was a companion in many ways. It gave me strength to fight off loneliness and this dreadful feeling of an inevitable fate. So, I will miss the companion, but as I said, I value the progress."

The line was silent while I fought for something to say. Margaret Teller let me off the hook. She said:

"Just today I was thinking back to the night of Roland's death. I realized I knew something bad had happened — even before the police had phoned. There was a kind of sign. A harbinger, I guess it's called. I was in the living room reading my book, and all of a sudden, a picture crashed from the wall. No one had touched it for days, or even weeks, I'm sure. Yet it simply fell from the wall. It was not a picture that Roland particularly cared for or admired, nor had I some unexpressed mental association of it to him, but when I thought back to the night I remembered its falling filled me with anxiety." She laughed awkwardly. "I suppose you think that's silly. I suppose you think it was only a coincidence."

When I finally spoke, my voice cracked like a teenager's. "No, I don't think it's a coincidence. I think you went looking for it — after the fact. If it hadn't been the picture, you would have remembered a broken glass or a watch that stopped. Those kinds of things happen every day — even when there are no other events of significance. You went looking for a sign to reassure yourself that there's an underlying order to the world. But there is no fate, Margaret. There is no destiny.

"Einstein said that God does not play dice with the universe. He was right, but not in the way he meant. God doesn't play dice with the universe because the universe doesn't need him. The craps table is set up and running. Whether or not God put it there is besides the point."

To this day I still don't know what possessed me to say that. I knew this was not the way to win Margaret Teller's heart.

There was a long pause. "We are very different, Mr. Riordan," she said finally.

"I thought you liked different. I thought that was why you married Roland Teller."

"Yes, and you see what it got me. I disagree with you about fate. I know what mine is now and I see there is no purpose in fighting it. Brad Willford asked me to marry him yesterday and I consented. I belong with him and people like him." A beat went by. "I don't think you should call me anymore, Mr. Riordan."

Later that afternoon I went to the bank. With everything that had happened in the past week, I had never found time to cash Bishop's retainer check. I was too late. The cashier informed me that Bishop had stopped payment on it.

I was determined that the case not be a total bust so I drove out to the section of King's Mountain Road where I lost my hubcap and got out of the car to hunt for it. After an hour of searching I found it wedged under a thorn bush, half filled with brackish rainwater and drowned crickets. I tossed the crickets over my shoulder for luck, and polished up the hubcap with my handkerchief.

Squinting down at my reflection in the bright metal I said, "You and Kieseritzky."